Christmas Spirit

JULIE CAMERON

ISBN: 978-0-9864179-0-0

ACKNOWLEDGMENTS

My deepest thanks and appreciation to all of my friends and family, who stuck with me through every one of the different iterations of this story. Thank you for at least pretending to be so excited each time I pushed another version in front of you, and asked for one more opinion.

Special thanks to my amazing writing coach, Doug Kurtz, who helped me find my voice and my point of view.

DEDICATION

To my own sisters, Marcia and Lisa.
Like Emma with her sisters, I could not live without them.

Dan,
I am so happy you are a part of our lives. Thank you for taking such good care of my favorite brother!
Love,
Julie Cameron

Table of Contents

CHAPTER ONE

Emma Anderson loved all things Christmas, and one of her many favorite traditions of the season was making gingerbread houses with her older sisters and their kids.

Marlie, the closest in age to her (being only one year older, at thirty-two), always hosted the event at her house with her two children.

Laura, whom they liked to describe as "infinitely older" (but who was actually only two years ahead of Marlie), came with her three kids to join them, so it was usually a mad-house—lots of noise, lots of creative imagination, and lots and lots of sugar.

With Christmas less than two weeks away, and the snow falling gently outside, Emma was elbow-deep in confections in Marlie's warm, ginger- and cinnamon-smelling kitchen. They had baked the walls of the houses, and formed miniature cottages using icing to hold them together, giving them what very closely resembled small Hobbit huts.

Marlie, glowing from pregnancy, sat down at the table to help her two children, Jessica and Spencer, decorate their houses. Laura moved around the table as she instructed her three children, Michelle, Carrie, and Tommy, on their houses, while they not-so-surreptitiously snitched pieces of candy decorations.

"You should have seen the look he gave me when I told him I wanted to decorate the office. He does not like Christmas, in the extreme," Emma said, continuing her story about dragging her boss, George, into the spirit of the season. She was hoping for some sympathy, and even advice, from her older sisters.

Tommy, the oldest cousin who, at the ripe old age of nine, believed he knew everything, overheard Emma and asked, "How can anybody hate Christmas?"

"Does that mean Santa won't bring him any presents?" Jessica asked, with a frown on her tiny five-year-old face.

Emma knew that, even at five, Jessica was unusually sensitive to the plight of others, especially at Christmas, and she was no doubt concerned that someone was going to lose out.

"Don't you worry, Jessica," Marlie reassured her daughter. "Your Aunt Emma would never allow anyone to be left out on Christmas. And considering how much she cares about George, he won't suffer. Much."

"So, how is 'Operation Make George Fall in Love You' going?" Laura asked. "Any updates?"

"I don't know. " Emma sighed, feeling dejected. "I wish he'd finally get around to discovering his duplicitous girlfriend and dump her already. My New Year deadline is looming."

"I think you were absolutely right to give yourself a deadline," Marlie said. "You're thirty-one now, and not getting any younger. You've spent enough time pining over the guy, and now it's time to shi—" she stopped speaking, and glanced around at all the kids, then continued in a more PG-rated version. "Poop or get off the pottie."

Emma chuckled when she heard Marlie say quietly under her breath, "Although that wasn't nearly the impact I was going for."

As they all bustled with various jobs around the kitchen, getting the houses set up for the kids to decorate, Emma switched to more optimistic thoughts and said, "I figure Christmas is a good time to turn up the heat. How can anyone resist falling in love at Christmas? Right?" She turned to Marlie and Laura, looking for answers, or at least some encouragement.

"That's the spirit, Em!" Laura exclaimed, as if sensing that Emma needed some cheerleading on her side. "And you said he liked your sexy girl-pirate costume at Halloween, so it sounds like he's starting to notice you more already."

"True," Emma said, in an effort to keep the positive energy flowing. "Except he seems to have some really major hang-ups about Christmas. Every year it's a bigger fight to even get decorations in the office."

"Honey, I don't think the man's capable of loving anyone. Look who he keeps picking to date," Marlie said.

"Yeah, from what you've told us about his latest, Marlie's got a point," Laura said. "Maybe you should just tell him you're in love with him, and see what happens?"

Emma was horrified at the thought. There was no way George would be receptive to his assistant dropping that kind of bomb on his desk. The man hated romance manuscripts—and as owner of a Denver publishing company, he saw thousands of them cross his desk—so there was no way he was going to be pleased to find himself smack in the middle of one in real life. She could picture the book description: *Young and frivolous (but capable) assistant falls for her hugely successful business-owner boss who's twice her age.*

Oh, yeah, you bet. That would go over real well. She wouldn't have to wait for New Year's to start looking for another job. George would have her out the door the next day.

"I still like my job, you know."

"Yes, but you're planning to leave it anyway if your plan doesn't work," said Laura.

Huh. Apparently they expected her plan to fail? Well, that was a major confidence sucker. What happened to the sacred bonds of sisterhood?

Emma slumped in defeat. "You're right, you're right," she said, "I know, you're right. Logically. But emotionally, there's no way he's ready for that yet. He's getting there, I know he is, but he's not there yet."

Marlie and Laura exchanged glances with each other, then Marlie leaned in and said, "To be honest, Em, we're struggling a bit here."

"No kidding. First you're 'yay, rah, go Emma' and then you're 'it's never going to work' gloom and doom. Pick a side already. Please? The suspense is killing me." She grinned at them so that they knew she wasn't angry. She wasn't. She loved her sisters to pieces, but sometimes she didn't know whether she was coming or going with them.

"We're trying to be supportive, but Laura and I both feel you'd be better off with someone else. We think your plan is a good one, but mostly because it has a deadline. He's too old for you, and he's emotionally…well, let's just say 'unavailable,' and we don't want that for you."

"I get that, believe me," Emma replied, with no small hint of sarcasm to her voice. "You've both been telling me that since I started there two years ago and was stupid enough to tell you that I had a crush on my new boss. But you don't know him like I do. He's a good guy." She sighed, disappointed that she wasn't getting the support she had hoped for from her sisters. "I just need to get his full and undivided attention."

"Good for you, Emma," Laura exclaimed. Finally.

"Well, Christmas is all about miracles after all," Marlie said, in a voice dripping with sarcasm.

Emma saw Laura kick Marlie under the table to interrupt her, and Marlie jumped.

"Ow. What?"

"What Marlie means is," Laura said, "we will support you, in any way we can, however it turns out."

"I have been supportive," Marlie exclaimed, as she rubbed her shin. "Which one of us has been trying to fix her up with other men to help her get over George? Speaking of which, there's this new single dad at the school…"

Both Laura and Emma moaned. Emma loved Marlie very much, but if she didn't stop trying to fix her up, she was going to have to shoot her.

"Hear me out—" Marlie started to say.

"No," Emma said emphatically to interrupt her.

"Why? Why won't you even consider—" Marlie continued, still trying to present her case.

"No," Emma said, interrupting again even more firmly.

Laura, always the peacekeeper, broke into the battle by saying, "Marlie, at least give her until her deadline. You still have a sound plan, Em: get him to love you, or get another job. You can do it," she exclaimed, as she pumped her fist into the air in support. Then, as if she'd suddenly remembered something, she continued, "Hey. You know what? You should bring him over to Marlie's for Christmas Eve dinner. Lots of love, lots of family, lots of food, lots of Christmas spirit."

Marlie looked skeptical, but she also looked as though she was at least trying to be supportive. Emma was worried, but she was nothing if not determined. She might be able to get George to Marlie's house for Christmas Eve dinner. As far as she knew, he never went anywhere on that night. She had almost asked him to come with her last year, but she'd chickened out at the last minute. She would do it this year though. She had nothing left to lose now that she was in the whole "do or die" mode.

"He's more than welcome, Em, if you want to invite him," Marlie responded, then smiled warmly at Emma. "And speaking of Christmas Eve dinner...any word from Jack on if he'll be home in time to celebrate with us this year?" she asked Laura.

Emma knew that it was a deliberate attempt to change the subject, and she was grateful.

"He'd better be," Laura responded, "that's all I can say. This will be the third year in a row he won't be home for Christmas. How can his company keep doing that to him?" Then she moved away from the table so the kids didn't see her trying to keep from crying.

Marlie, with a concerned look at Laura, got the kids organized, and distracted, with putting the candy on the houses.

Emma followed Laura, then hugged her and whispered, "I'm so sorry...I wish I could help."

"I know you do. I wish he could quit and go someplace that appreciates him," Laura said, as she sniffed indignantly. "He's just not ready to make that change, especially in this economy. But Christmas isn't the same for us without him being here."

"I know... We'll think of something," Emma replied, hoping it was true.

"Maybe Santa will bring him a new job," Laura said, and sighed, as she worked hard to compose herself. "Come on, let's decorate some houses. I think I'll go art deco this year."

They returned to the table and joined the chaos of happy kids decorating themselves and their houses.

She and Marlie would work on the Jack situation.

CHAPTER TWO

Emma pulled her red Jeep Wrangler into a space in the parking garage of the Denver Center of Performing Arts and cut the engine. She mentally braced herself for the cold trek that was waiting for her outside her nicely heated Jeep.

Now that she was thirty-one, she figured she should probably start thinking about getting a car that was maybe a little more professional (not to mention better on the gas mileage) but she loved her Jeep, and it had been everywhere with her. And for a car with a soft top, these things could really put out the heat, which she decided was its most valuable feature, especially on days like this morning. She loved living in Colorado, but she wasn't a fan of the cold.

Anyone who lived here knew the saying, "If you don't like the weather, just wait ten minutes and it will change." Of course, that could mean snow on the 4th of July, or shorts and flip-flops on Christmas, but today that meant the sun was out and trying to heat things up, in spite of it being only twelve degrees outside. With a little more than a week until Christmas, the forecasters were already predicting it would be a white one.

Sure. Like they'd know.

Bundled inside her long wool winter coat and her black Ugg boots, she hugged the box with her mini musical Christmas tree to her chest. The mini tree was the latest in her arsenal to blast George with Christmas.

She had wanted to bring her gingerbread house as well, but decided to give it another day to set. Besides, tomorrow it would be easier for her to carry it, since she wouldn't also have her special tree.

For the last few months, she had been fervently waging this war on him, and she felt she was making headway, although slowly. He was a good man, and she liked working for him, but for some reason, he was always so guarded and reserved. The first time she'd made him laugh had been a huge shock to her, because she hadn't ever noticed the lack of it up until that moment—just a vague feeling that something was missing. The man was definitely stingy with his sunny disposition.

There had been moments when she'd worried he might get annoyed by her obvious efforts at flirtation (like finding out his favorite dessert—thank you Marlie for that suggestion—and bringing it into the office for him), but he seemed to be enjoying her attention. Several months ago, he had told her to stop calling him "Mr. Landon" and call him "George" instead, which she took as a definite sign of progress.

She was sure that this was a perfect time to ramp up her campaign. Because, after all, who could resist Christmas? The joy, the sparkle, the love, the traditions, the excitement, the well-wishes—it all played into her master plan of getting him to break down some of his walls and open up to her.

She was nervous about today though, because she was afraid of pushing him too much, too fast, and she didn't want to lose the small steps she had accomplished so far (she was becoming addicted to the thrill of victory whenever she could make him smile). Today was the day the decorating company was coming to do the office, and although George had approved it, he hadn't been happy about it. He had fought her tooth and nail until she had finally worn him down, by threatening to rearrange his files and then go on vacation for two weeks. She'd had no idea a man could hyperventilate so quickly.

She hurried down the parking lot stairs and concentrated on thinking warm, positive thoughts. *Everything would be okay. Everything would be okay.*

The center was decorated for Christmas and advertised performances of *Scrooge* and *The Nutcracker*. She wondered if she would be able to get in a performance before Christmas. It would be fun to take her nieces and nephews to a show before the season got away from her. She'd have to check with her sisters and see if there was still time.

She left the promenade and headed up the street toward the big blue bear statue outside the Convention Center right next door. He looked like he was desperate to get inside out of the cold, too, but then, being that he was a forty-foot-high permanent fixture of the building, and already blue, she figured he was beyond caring about the effects of the elements. It was almost comforting to know that he would be there, still looking desperate to get inside, during the heat of the summer, too.

She smiled at Big Blue, and gave him a mental "good morning" before she headed toward 16th Street, enjoying the sound of her Uggs crunching in the fresh snow that had fallen during the night. She imagined the skiers would be thrilled for the fresh powder, but as she never much cared for the sport herself, she only gave it a passing thought.

Turning right onto the 16th Street Mall, the outside pedestrian mall that ran for one and a quarter miles through downtown, she headed toward her destination. The mall vendors were out shoveling their sidewalks and opening their shops for the day, and she always enjoyed seeing their bustling activity first thing in the morning, no matter the season or the weather.

She waited for one of the free hybrid-electric mall shuttles to pass before she crossed the street. Peeking inside the Appaloosa Grill restaurant window, she waved to a group of servers who were setting up inside. They all recognized Emma, who was a frequent lunch customer, and waved back at her, smiling and miming that it was too cold outside. Laughing, she hurried up the street, realizing she was going to be cutting things close if she wanted to get to the office before George started his day.

But she took a few extra minutes when she reached Marv, a man who was always on the corner selling the paper for the homeless. He was a middle-aged man who looked like he had seen his share of hard times, but he was always here every morning, come rain or come shine. He was more reliable than the US Postal Service, but she guessed that wasn't saying much these days.

"Buy a copy of the *Voice* and help the homeless at Christmas time?" Marv asked, then recognized Emma as she approached him. "Merry Christmas, Emma."

Fumbling with her box, she reached into her coat pocket, where she always remembered to stash a few dollar bills for just this reason, pulled one out, and handed it to Marv.

"Merry Christmas, Marv." She declined taking the paper he always offered, since she'd already taken one from him on Monday.

"God bless you, Emma." He smiled a brilliant smile that lit up his entire face, and also showed several missing teeth.

Continuing up the street, she headed toward Stan's Coffee Shop, which was a vital part of her morning routine in spite of the fact that she didn't drink coffee. She couldn't help herself, because she loved to catch up on the gossip with Stan, the barista and owner of the shop.

Stan and his husband, David, seemed to know everyone in Denver, and, more importantly, everything about each and every one of them. If you needed an update on the word on the street, you popped in to buy a cup of coffee from Stan and stayed for the gossip, which was freely given.

It was like having a living, breathing *People* magazine for local Denver, and she didn't even have to pay for it. She realized it was tacky, but she loved a good gossip session as much as the next person, and sometimes the information came in very handy. It was in this very coffee shop that she had found out George's current girlfriend, Crystal, had been stopping by for her afternoon coffee, and, according to Stan, her "afternoon tryst" with a man who was not George.

That had been the deciding factor for Emma. Crystal so didn't deserve George. What woman in her right mind cheated on George? Sure, the man was a little closed off—sometimes to the point of frustration—but that just made Emma want to open him up, because she had seen glimpses of the gooey center that she knew was inside.

Thus, her current campaign. She was done waiting for him to wake up and stop dating shallow women, while she was sitting just outside his door. Literally.

As she entered the coffee shop, the door chimed and Stan, who stood behind the counter as always, looked up and greeted Emma with enthusiasm.

"Morning, Emma."

"Morning, Stan. Merry Christmas. May I get the usual, please?"

"One decaf mocha latte, and a regular coffee, black, coming right up." He turned to fill the order, then glanced at her box and asked, "Is that a mini Christmas tree?"

She hugged the box to her chest and was reminded of happy memories. Her mom, an even bigger Christmas fanatic than Emma (which was almost scary), had given Emma the music box tree when she'd landed her first desk job as a call-center rep for a moving company, as a way of brightening up her cubicle. She had told Emma that everyone needed a little bit of Christmas to keep them thinking happy thoughts around the holidays, and it had never failed to make her smile.

"Yep. It plays Christmas music. My mom gave it to me many years ago, so now I'm using it to subliminally overwhelm George with Christmas this year to get him out of his grumpy old mood."

Stan carried the coffees to the register and rang up her total. "Honey, you couldn't jump-start that old coot's Christmas heart with a jack-hammer. He's had way too many years to work himself into that curmudgeonly funk."

She chuckled optimistically as she handed Stan her money, and waited for her change. "I'm working on him, though. This is going to be the year he falls in love with Christmas."

"Are you sure it's Christmas you want him to fall in love with?" He eyed her dubiously.

"Of course it is, Stan. It is my goal in life to get George into the Christmas spirit, even if it kills him. I plan to have him beaming from ear to ear by New Year's." She hoped she had successfully squelched Stan's implication that there might be more going on with her feelings toward her boss, because if he knew, the whole world would know—telephone, telegraph, TeleStan— and her plan would be blown to smithereens before she even got close to her self-imposed New Year's deadline.

"Good luck with that then, girlfriend. If anyone can do it, it's you." He smiled cheerily at her, and she was glad at least someone believed in her abilities.

She took her to-go cups, waved goodbye to Stan, then left the shop and continued down the street to her next favorite stop—the street musician who set up his station not far from Stan's Coffee.

Jeff was in his mid-twenties, and always looked grungy but happy. He played his music with more enthusiasm than talent or tone quality, but it always cheered her up to see him. She enjoyed the mornings when he was there, believing them to be just a little brighter as a result of his over-the-top energy, and she set the to-go cup with the coffee down next to him.

"Thanks for the Christmas music, Jeff. Sounds really good today."

Without breaking stride, she dropped the change from the coffee shop into Jeff's money bucket. He interrupted his playing for a moment to take the time to thank her with an enthusiastic sing-song, "Thanks, Emma. Merry Christmas."

She turned in a circle and waved, then headed to the Republic Plaza building, realizing that she was now going to be a few minutes late. It didn't really matter; George wasn't a clock-watcher. As long as she got her work done, he didn't expect her to be restricted by specific hours.

She entered the marble lobby through the revolving door at the entrance to the building. Being careful to stomp the snow from her Uggs on the rubber mats at the door, she took a moment to wave to the bedraggled security guard, then hurried to the bank of elevators that serviced the top floors.

CHAPTER THREE

She stepped out of the elevator and glanced at the *Landon Literary* logo that hung on the wall behind a large wooden reception desk. It never failed to give her a thrill when she saw it, making her feel as though she belonged to something exciting. She smiled at the company's receptionist of three years, who sat behind the desk wearing a headset and handling incoming phone calls with the efficiency of a drill sergeant.

Sandy, who was in her early twenties, was a petite, pretty blond who held down the front office in the same way a ruling queen managed her kingdom. Without missing a beat in her phone conversation, she waved an overnight package at Emma to get her attention, then finished with her call and disconnected.

"Oh, hey, Emma, I have an overnight for George here."

"Great, thanks, Sandy. I've been expecting this from a new author that I wanted him to check out." She took the package, and began removing her coat as she continued through the hall to her own office area.

She rounded the corner of the reception area to the executive wing of Landon Literary, where the most creative (and, in Emma's opinion, the most attractive, even with all of his emotional armor) Landon had his office. She hung her coat on a rack next to her desk, which was just outside of George's office, then dumped everything from her arms onto her desk, being very careful with her musical tree.

First, and with a heartfelt ceremonial wish sent to her mom, she took the small tree out of the box and attached it to the stand so that it would turn while the music was playing. Several little wooden Christmas ornaments of rocking horses, tiny trees, snowmen, and nutcrackers hung on the small flocked branches.

"Emma, what—" George began, before he noticed her tree and frowned at it. "What is that?" He pointed at it with the paper he held in his hand.

She turned around and smiled at him. Even though he was probably at least fourteen…fifteen…okay, sixteen years older than she was, she couldn't stop herself drooling just a little bit every time she saw him. He was an awfully pretty package, but for some reason he wanted everyone to believe there was nothing inside the box. When she had first started working for him, he always gave her the impression of something you would find in a museum—fine art, surrounded by velvet ropes, and a whole lot of expensive security measures set up to keep everyone out.

At forty-seven, he had dark hair only slightly starting to turn gray at the temples to hint at his age, and deep, deep blue eyes the color of the ocean, and usually just as cold.

He wore tailored suit pants and crisply ironed shirts that fit as though they were made for him (because they were, actually), and they always made her wonder if he looked just as sexy in jeans and a T-shirt. Not that he would be caught dead wearing jeans, let alone a T-shirt, but a girl needed to have her fantasies.

But it wasn't just that he was stunningly gorgeous. The longer Emma worked for him, the more he revealed about himself on the inside, and the more she fell in love with him. He was, in reality, a kind and generous man. In addition to all the high-profile charity fundraising events he sponsored and attended, he had a list of charitable contributions a mile long that he never told anyone about (except for her, because she filed his receipts and did his expense accounts).

But what had finally convinced Emma, and had nearly broken her heart at the same time, was the large contribution he made every Christmas to the Big Brothers Big Sisters association, complete with a heartfelt, personalized card. A card that he never signed. Ever.

She had seen the first one the year she started at Landon Literary. He'd asked her to mail it, but he'd forgotten to seal it, and, being the efficient assistant that she was, she'd snooped. That card, to those kids, was the most beautiful thing she had ever read. No one without a heart could possibly have written the words in that card.

That was the day she had started noticing that there was a whole lot more to George Landon than he let on.

And that was the day she'd started falling in love with her enigmatic boss.

"It's a Christmas tree music box, George. What does it look like?" She had been so caught up in her thoughts that she had almost forgotten he'd asked her a question, and that the appropriate thing to do was to respond, not to drool on her knock-off Manolo Blahniks (which had still taken her three months to save up for in spite of them being fake). She wound up the music box and the tree started to turn while it played "Have Yourself a Merry Little Christmas."

She looked hopefully up at George, but he just looked pained.

"It's to help get you into the Christmas spirit." She was hoping he would get the not-so-subtle hint, and at least smile at her.

He obviously chose to ignore her because he waved the paper he was still holding in his hand and changed the subject. "What is this invoice from Holiday Mood?"

Disappointed—although, sadly, not surprised—by his negative reaction to her tree, she took the paper from him and looked at it, even though she knew exactly what was written on it. "Oh, that's for the office Christmas decorations."

Then she handed the paper back to him.

"All this for a few lights and ornaments?" He had an incredulous expression on his incredibly handsome face.

"Yes, George, all that for more than just a few Christmas decorations." She was starting to get exasperated. She decided her best tactic was to continue to put away her things, and all but ignore him, since they'd already been down this argument before—just yesterday, in fact—and she did not want to go through that all over again.

"Did I agree to this?" His voice was escalating into a roar.

Apparently he didn't remember the argument as well as she did. Was he seriously hoping she had forgotten about the decorations? If so, then the rest of her Christmas bombardment treatment was going to be a rude awakening for him.

"George. We talked about this. You said we could finally decorate this year instead of sending out those horrible fruitcakes to everyone. Stop being so grumpy, and get into the spirit of the season."

"I can be grumpy if I'm paying for it," he replied, well...grumpily.

Okay, yes, he had a point about paying for it when he didn't even want it, but she wasn't willing to concede that to him. Especially not out loud.

"You'll feel more excited after Holiday Mood comes and works their magic," she said, trying to cheer him up.

George gaped at her for a moment, as though completely taken aback that she would challenge him on this. How was that a surprise to him? She challenged him on everything. It was her job. Plus, it was for his own good.

"Did that new manuscript you wanted me to read arrive yet?" he asked her, at the very same moment she handed him the overnight package, as if she could read his mind. That shouldn't have surprised him either, after working with her for two years, but she could tell that it still messed with his head whenever she did it, and she got a kick out of her ability to knock him off his game like that.

He almost grinned at her—she could see it, right there on his face, dying to spread—as he opened the package. The look on his face morphed into anger as he took a moment to read the front cover of the manuscript, then he tossed it in Emma's trash can like it was last week's lasagna.

"Print up a rejection letter and leave it on my desk for me to sign later."

"Really?" She was shocked that he would be so callous about a manuscript. "Aren't you even going to read it first?"

"No. I don't have to. We aren't publishing it."

She retrieved the manuscript from her trash can and clutched it to her chest like a mother hen protecting her chick. "But we always—"

"Just do the damn rejection letter and leave it on my desk," he said, interrupting her before she could even get the question out.

This was not like him at all. What was so wrong with this manuscript that he wasn't even willing to give it a second glance? It was written by a new author, but Landon Literary had always been receptive, even nurturing, to new writers. George practically specialized in cultivating new talent. So why wasn't he even considering this one?

"*Fight or Flight*, by Dean Erickson," she said, reading the cover out loud. "I thought you liked suspense thrillers."

"Not by this author, I don't. If I had known this was the author you'd spoken with, I wouldn't have had you waste your time."

That didn't make any sense. And she had enjoyed talking to Dean, and had wanted to give him a shot. His storyline sounded so compelling, even she would have considered reading it.

"I can ask Harry to look at it." She was still hoping she could get him to change his mind.

"Knock yourself out," he responded, and she felt a tremendous sense of relief that she had misinterpreted his angry reaction. "But we still won't publish anything written by Dean Erickson."

She stared at him, completely disbelieving this was the same man she had worked for the last two years. Why was he being so mean?

"I'll be in Legal," he said, then paused to make sure she was paying attention before he continued, "hiding until the 'Holiday Mood' passes."

Oh, ha, ha, ha, very funny. Nice play on words though, she had to give him that.

"They're decorating Legal, too," she reminded him, just in case he thought Legal would protect him in some way.

"Then I'll be leaving for the day from there," he barked back in response.

But she saw him smile as he rounded the corner out of the executive wing, and a thrill of pleasure and triumph ran through her. He wasn't exactly singing Christmas carols, but he had smiled, and that was a good thing. She gave a quick fist pump in the air as she added another tally to her mental "He Grinned" column. She was definitely making progress.

And New Year's was still weeks away.

Now, about this new manuscript… She was going to give it to Harry, no matter what George said.

* * * * * * *

She was still celebrating her small victory from her much-enjoyed bantering with George when the man she was just thinking about—okay, the other man she had just been thinking about—Harry Landon himself, approached her desk.

George's younger brother was a good guy, and she liked him very much, even if he spent far too much of his time flirting with her. He was harmless enough, because Harry Landon flirted with all women, so she never really paid much attention to it. But he was a bit of a freeloader when it came to the business, and sometimes that rankled her a bit. It was almost as if he were allergic to work.

Or at least he thought he was.

In his early forties, Harry was almost (but not quite) as attractive as his brother, dressed in his casual business attire, which for Harry meant dark jeans and a sweater. He never dressed quite as formally as his brother, but there was definitely something about those Landon genes that gave both of the Landon men drool-worthy attributes for filling out their jeans. Both George and Harry definitely had nice asses—er...assets.

"I came by to watch the look on my brother's face when the decorating people show up." Then he propped his aforementioned nice asset comfortably on Emma's desk to chat.

"He said I could decorate." What was with these guys and Christmas anyway?

"Yeah, I heard. I swear, you two are like an old married couple arguing over the monthly bills. You are the only one who can get away with arguing with him like that, you know."

"Because he can't live without me, and he knows it." She waved off his comment with a flick of her wrist. "The filing system alone has him completely stumped. And who else could he get who would willingly put up with all his crazy clients on what he pays me?"

"No argument here,'" he said, and he leaned in closer to her.

She never paid any attention to Harry when he flirted with her. She viewed his passes as a reflex reaction, like a tic or a twitch. She might have fallen for it the first time he tried it on her, but, fortunately, she had TeleStan in her back pocket, and he had set her straight from her very first day of work at Landon Literary.

Stan had been very clear on the Landon brothers: George never attached himself to anyone or anything, so don't go there. And Harry attached himself to everyone and everything, so don't go there.

"I prefer the wholesome-assistant-who-has-no-fear-bossing-me-around type," Harry continued. "When are you going to quit working for my overly starched shirt of a brother, and come organize my office?"

Frustrated with Harry's continuous lack of participation in his own company, she scowled back at him. "When you finally start showing some signs that you even know where your office is, I'll find you an assistant worthy of the task."

He leaned back and appeared shocked at the thought of having his own assistant—probably because that would imply having to actually do regular work.

"Are you threatening me?"

"What's George's thing with Christmas?" She decided it was time to change the subject, since there was no changing Harry.

He shrugged, apparently taking her abrupt shift in the conversation as no big deal. "Beats me. I always thought Christmas was great. Our father would hand George buckets of money on Christmas Eve, and the day after Christmas when all the shops opened back up, George and I would go out and get whatever we wanted. George always turned it into some kind of great adventure."

"'Buckets of money'? That's what Christmas means to your family?" She took a moment to consider his statement before asking her next question, unsure if she might be crossing the "too personal" line. "So how do you celebrate it now?"

Apparently nothing with Harry was "too personal" because he answered her right away without any compunction.

"We don't, really. We still get together the day after Christmas and swap expensive presents, but Christmas is a little like birthdays… They don't seem to have that same spark as when you were a kid."

"I still don't understand why he hates Christmas as much as he does." She sighed with frustration, and even she detected a hint of sadness in her voice. How could he claim to hate Christmas so much, and still write those beautiful cards to those kids each year?

Harry studied her a moment, then grinned. "You kinda got a thing for my big brother, don't you?"

Oh, geez, now Harry was in on the act. What was with everyone? Apparently she wasn't any better at keeping secrets than her sisters were. Although…maybe letting Harry in on her plan would be helpful.

Then again, he wasn't exactly the expert on committed relationships.

So no, then.

"That is the most ridiculous thing I have ever heard you say. Not to mention, incredibly clichéd. Nobody falls for their boss anymore." That came out sounding a little too loud, even to her own ears.

"Oh, come on, what's not to like?" he said, teasing her mercilessly. "He's filthy rich, and according to ninety percent of the women in this company, he's a hottie to boot."

"Superficial much, Harry? Besides, I could never fall in love with someone who only dates psycho swimsuit models. Who can compete with that?" She knew that neither of them liked the incredibly scary woman George was currently seeing. Crystal was a beautiful woman, and Emma could see why George would be interested in her because of that. But she couldn't understand why he didn't noticed how mean-spirited Crystal was in her core. Harry wouldn't go near her, which should have spoken volumes to George about her personality.

"Yeah, I really don't understand what he sees in Crystal. She scares me to death." He shuddered hard enough to almost knock himself off the edge of the desk.

"Ella."

19

Harry and Emma both froze at the sound of the strident voice that came from the direction of the reception area, and sounded as if it was very close—too close for Emma's comfort.

But then, Spain would have been too close for Emma's comfort.

"As if just conjured... Did you say her name three times?" Harry whispered, as if he were afraid of attracting the attention of the Boogie Man. "I gotta go."

"You have absolutely no backbone whatsoever," Emma whispered back in as forceful a tone as she could manage without being overheard.

She wanted to keep him with her so that she wouldn't have to deal with Crystal alone, but all her hopes were crushed when he bolted from the room with a speed that would have made even the Flash eat his dust.

A split second later, Emma saw that George's current evil-swimsuit-model girlfriend had rounded the corner and was descending upon Emma in all her splendid fashion-designerness. The woman was wearing clothes that had to cost more than Emma's apartment and her Jeep put together.

And she was such a bitch.

Oops, did that resonate as the teensy-tiniest bit catty?

Up until meeting Crystal, Emma had never seen herself as the catty type, but apparently she was breaking new ground. Crystal just seemed to inspire that feeling of instant loathing.

At five foot six, Emma considered herself to be fairly normal in height, and although she wasn't remotely close to the swimsuit-model caliber that Crystal was, she thought she held her own in the shapely department (as long as she was careful to avoid the salted-caramel chocolate cupcakes Stan was famous for—one a week, tops, that was her limit, except on special occasions like holidays, or maybe when a new Robert Downey, Jr. movie came out).

She had never considered herself a beauty, but she occasionally got compliments from men on her hazel-gray eyes, which her sisters often told her complemented her dark-brown hair and fair Irish complexion. However, if she was being honest with herself—and she usually tried very hard to be honest with herself—she had to admit that Crystal pushed all of her inferiority buttons, and that tended to make her just a tad bit snarky.

"Ella, I've been calling your name from clear down the hall. Didn't you hear me?" Crystal's voice echoed off the walls in the office.

How George could stand listening to a voice that could break the sound barrier was beyond Emma. So, just to be contrary, she lowered her own decibel level to something closer to just around human hearing range, and replied, "I'm sure Ella, whoever she may be, heard you all the way to Kentucky. But I'm Emma."

"What?"

Crystal was understandably confused, being that Emma was sure the woman never bothered herself with the minor details of mere mortals. Or it might also have been because Emma was speaking at that human decibel level and all. Either way, Emma didn't really care. She just wanted her gone.

"My name. It's Emma, not Ella." She made sure to speak succinctly and slowly, so that Crystal would be able to understand her. Maybe it would help if she spoke in single syllable words, too.

Crystal waved her hand impatiently, and asked, "Whatever. Is George around?"

Emma hated the superiority Crystal always tried to flaunt, so she went into George's office and sat in his chair behind his desk to put the woman in her place.

As she had suspected, Crystal followed her into George's office as if she believed she had the right, but Emma knew that she never would have done it if George had been present. She might currently be George's girlfriend, but she also knew her position wasn't certain. Not yet, at least. George didn't go through women as quickly as Harry did; Crystal certainly had some staying power.

"He's in Legal in a meeting," Emma replied, and she turned on the false charm. George wasn't here, Crystal's cheating days were numbered, so Emma felt she could be magnanimous. Just a little bit though. "Was he expecting you?"

Then, to drive her point home, she pretended she was looking for something inside his desk in order to further emphasize that she, not Crystal, did have the right to be in his office. And even better yet, she had the right go through George's drawers any time she wanted.

She smiled to herself as she thought about the significance of going through George's drawers, and hoped it made Crystal squirm.

"No, I thought I'd just pop in and surprise him." Then she leaned in conspiratorially like they were besties, and asked, "Has he bought my Christmas present yet?"

Emma leaned across George's desk, then looked around to make sure no one else was listening, as if they were both spies for the Allied forces, and said, "No."

Apparently deciding that Emma wasn't giving her the deference she so clearly deserved, Crystal straightened and sighed. Dramatically.

"Huh. Well. I don't suppose you could put a little bug in his ear for me for—"

"No." There was not even the remotest chance in Hades that she would put any bug of Crystal's anywhere near George.

She wouldn't be above giving Crystal an earwig though. Now, see? That was just nasty. How did this woman manage to do that to her every time they had a conversation?

The woman harrumphed, then flicked her long blond hair in order to better flash her diamond earrings. "This year, I think I'll let George give me something to match the earrings I picked out for my birthday. I'm thinking a little bauble for my finger is just the thing."

She waved her wedding ring finger at Emma, then turned and sashayed out of the office in a style that would have made any one of the evil Disney queens proud. But that could have been Emma's imagination getting away from her again.

Slightly sickened by the thought that George was only narrowly missing marrying a blond-haired Maleficent, Emma slumped into his chair. Geez, that woman was exhausting. How could George even stand her?

She heard her phone intercom as it buzzed on her desk outside George's office.

"Oh, 'Ella,'" Sandy's voice said over the intercom speaker in an almost perfect imitation of Crystal, "Holiday Mood is here for you."

That was enough to snap Emma out of her musings, and she snorted a laugh as she rushed out to her desk and pushed her intercom button to respond.

"On my way."

Then she headed off to reception to greet the holiday decorators, and hoped the results wouldn't cause another argument with George.

CHAPTER FOUR

Emma stepped out of the elevator into the reception of Landon Literary, excited about having her gingerbread house with her today, and looking forward to seeing George's reaction to it. It would no doubt prompt another conniption fit on his part, but he had been smiling more at the ends of their arguments than he used to, and she was taking that as a good sign.

She gasped when she saw that the office had been completely transformed. The reception area was tastefully decorated in golds, silvers, and hundreds of tiny white lights. There was a large tree completely decked out in the waiting area, a silver menorah with royal blue candles sat on the coffee table, and a fresh green garland with tiny white lights was strung around the desk and walls.

"Good morning, Sandy." Emma was all but singing to the receptionist with excitement. She was thrilled by the magic Holiday Mood had created with their decorations. She wasn't getting her hopes up that George would like it, too, but she was trying to stay optimistic. The decorations were so beautiful, she hoped they would at least make a crack in his grumpy demeanor.

Sandy turned and Emma saw her eyes light up when she spotted the gingerbread house.

"Hi, Emma. Oh, I love gingerbread houses."

"Me, too. A time-honored tradition." Emma was glad that Sandy shared her enthusiasm.

"Thanks for getting us the decorations this year." She started to sing, "It's beginning to look a lot like Christmas…"

Thrilled with Sandy's holiday cheer, and anxious to see George's reaction, Emma continued on to her own area. The executive offices were decorated in much the same way as the reception area, with a big tree in the corner, and lots of garland and lights in gold and silver.

She noticed that George was already in the office, and was madly searching through the file cabinets. She took a moment to admire the decorations. Then she took a moment to indulge in admiring George, before finally asking, "Morning, George, looking for something?"

He growled in frustration, and absently ran his fingers through his hair, but she could see that his mind was apparently still rummaging around in the file cabinet—she knew this because he was glaring at it, as if he expected it to give up its secrets. And any lesser file cabinet would have, too, but not hers. Hers was made of sterner stuff.

"I can't find—" Then he spotted the gingerbread house, and she thought he looked suddenly worried. Worried? About a gingerbread house?

"What is that?"

Here we go again. She calmly placed the house on top of the loyal-to-her-only file cabinets, practically under George's nose.

"Clearly, it's a gingerbread house." She pulled out a file and handed it to George, who looked surprised that it was the exact file he had been unsuccessfully trying to locate.

"How…?" he started, then apparently thought better of it and gave up.

"Gingerbread houses are a time-honored Christmas tradition," she continued to say, as if reading her boss's mind was nothing out of the ordinary.

She couldn't help herself. She always got an almost giddy pleasure out of freaking him out like that. She couldn't, of course, read his mind (although she certainly wouldn't enlighten him to that minor detail), but she did know him well enough by now that it probably looked pretty spooky from his side of things.

"You and your traditions are a pain in my ass," he mumbled, as he started flipping through the file in his hands.

She adjusted her gingerbread house to be sure it was safe yet well displayed, then began her morning routine of getting herself organized and putting her things away.

"What is that white blob?"

Emma turned to see he was examining the house more closely. That had to be a good sign, right? She returned to stand next to him and looked where he was pointing.

"That's my snow fort. My nephew, Spencer, made one for his house, too, so we could have snowball fights."

He looked at her as if she had finally gone crazy, which was not a look a woman usually appreciated from the man she loved. Then he reached over, broke off a snowball, and ate it.

"Hey. You're eating my ammo," she cried, and swatted at his hand to get him to back away.

"Isn't that what these things are for?" He spoke calmly, as if he hadn't just defiled a creation she had spent the better part of a night creating.

Okay, so it wasn't Picasso, but it was not meant to be eaten. Well, not yet, anyway.

"At least wait until after Christmas."

"It'll be stale by then." He sounded like a sullen child who'd just been told he had to wait until after dinner before he could have his ice cream.

"You are so missing the point." She was glad that he seemed to at least like the taste of the house, but she was disappointed that her efforts of holiday cheer had once again gone straight over his head. She finally turned her back on him in capitulation and sat down at her desk to work.

He hadn't said a word about the office decorations.

And without even turning around she knew he had reached over to steal another snowball.

"If you don't stop eating all my ammo, I will have to hurt you," she warned him. So there. Let him think that, in addition to her mind-reading abilities, she also had eyes in the back of her head.

"Mercenary little Christmas elf." But she heard him chuckling as he went back into his office.

She thumped her head on her desk in frustration. Well, at least she'd made him laugh. Honestly. How could anyone be so resistant to the charms of the holiday season? It was the happiest time of the year.

* * * * * * *

George sat behind his desk in his office—his office which had, unfortunately, not escaped Emma's Christmas invasion. He supposed he should be grateful that it was all done in good taste, and hadn't ended up looking like Santa's elves had come in and thrown a frat party.

He would still have preferred going through the aggravating season by ignoring it as he usually did, but for some reason his overly exuberant assistant was practically throwing it in his face this year. He had no idea why this year was so different for her, but he was willing to go along with it in order to just get through it.

He picked up one of the manuscripts from the stack on his desk, and realized it was another romance. Whenever he came across one of these, he was immeasurably grateful he was the head of the company, because it meant that he could pass them off to someone else to review instead of having to slog through them himself. Christ he hated romances.

He couldn't believe women bought into this drivel. The storylines were so off-the-chart unrealistic, and no one could possibly live up to the standards of the characters. Didn't women know there was no such thing as the heroes they made up in these stories? Apparently not, because these things made up a large chunk of their sales.

He took the manuscript and went out to talk to Emma, who was working on her computer.

"I want Harry to take a crack at this manuscript. He seems to like these things, if his comments on the other ones I've given him are any indication." He handed her the manuscript.

She looked at it, then groaned and rolled her eyes, which seemed odd to him because he had always pegged her as the romance type. Then she suddenly gasped, and covered her mouth as if she was trying to hold back a smile. He followed the direction of her gaze, wondering what could possibly be on the ceiling that was so funny, and saw mistletoe hanging over her desk.

What the hell?

He was even more surprised than she had been, and he stepped back quickly as if it were able to reach out and bite him. No way would he get slapped with a sexual harassment lawsuit. What had she been thinking to include mistletoe in their office decorations? She had gone too far this time with her damned Christmas shit.

He heard Emma cough, and he could see that she was trying hard not to laugh.

"Emma, that isn't funny, not to mention entirely inappropriate for the office."

"I certainly didn't put it there," she cried, and threw up her hands as if to declare her innocence.

He continued standing there, scowling, knowing that she would crack eventually. But she didn't. Maybe she hadn't been the one to put it there. Could the decorations company be that incompetent?

"Get it down immediately." He didn't care who put it there, it had to come down. Now.

She sighed, and he wondered if she was frustrated with him for, once again, not succumbing to her incredibly annoying attempts at getting him to like Christmas. Well, she could just keep sighing. He would never like it. Happy feelings for it had died when he'd turned ten, and no amount of decorations or a chipper assistant would change that.

He watched as she positioned her chair under the mistletoe, and climbed onto it, all the while glancing at the ceiling and trying to judge the distance. He had to admire her persistence, even though he could tell she wasn't going to be able to reach the mistletoe from the chair she was using.

He must have been scowling at her because she said, "I don't know why you're so worried, George. They're only poisonous when ingested."

She stretched and tried to reach the mistletoe, but he could tell she wasn't tall enough. Then he nearly had heart failure when the goddamned chair swiveled suddenly, and she started to fall off of it.

In an instant, his reflexes kicked in and the next thing he knew he had caught her around the waist to steady her. His eyes caught and held hers, and he saw a flash of heat in those hazel-gray eyes just before she lowered her lashes.

Was that coyness? Christ, she was just like every other woman. She probably had been the one who had put the mistletoe there in order to manipulate him into falling for another stupid holiday tradition. He should kiss her, and see how she reacted to that. He'd probably scare the hell out of her.

Then he realized he was being an ass. She didn't have a manipulative bone in her body. She might be over-the-top with her traditions, but he had to admit that she wasn't like every other woman he'd known, who were only after him for his money.

She was Emma, his assistant. He was the one who had to remind her each year when it was time to give her a raise. Besides, he didn't have Harry's panache when it came to women, and he didn't want to scare her.

He did want to kiss her though.

Where the hell had that come from?

He dragged himself out of his own head, and belatedly came to the realization that he was still holding her, tightly.

Definitely not appropriate office protocol. How had that happened? He moved abruptly to put some space between them, and she faltered slightly as the chair moved again.

"Get down. I'll do it." His voice sounded gruff even to his own ears. He had grabbed hold of her again, but it was simply to keep her from falling, and nothing more. Purely a safety precaution. He certainly didn't want her to fall and break her neck, then sue his ass.

He had never been quite this close to her before. He had never noticed how nice she smelled. There was something citrus, and floral... Was that even possible? Could a person smell like fruit and flowers at the same time?

And what the hell did that matter? Jesus, he was losing it.

She looked flushed, and he hoped to God he hadn't made things awkward between them, because he definitely didn't want to lose her as an assistant. He'd lost five assistants in the two years prior to Emma's arrival thanks to his brother, Harry, who kept using them—and then dumping them—for his own personal dating pool.

He certainly did not want to lose Emma from a stupid misunderstanding over inadvertently holding her too close to keep her from falling off a goddamned swivel chair. The thought made him so upset, he almost yanked her off the goddamned swivel chair.

She looked startled when she landed back on the floor, but he ignored it. He carefully climbed onto her chair, then deftly reached up and snatched the mistletoe from the ceiling just as his brother, Harry—speak of the devil—entered the area.

"Well that backfired on me entirely," he drawled, and George could hear the humor in his voice. "George, that wasn't meant for you at all. That's my mistletoe for Emma, so put it back."

Emma laughed, but George thought it sounded strained. He looked at her suspiciously as he jumped off the chair, and wondered if he was about to lose yet another woman from his assistant pool to his brother's hit-and-run dating practices.

He had already sent Harry to the New York office for six months last summer to keep him away from Emma. He'd do it again if necessary.

He started to hand the mistletoe to Emma, but looked at Harry, then back at Emma, and scowled at both of them. He sure as hell wasn't going to help Harry steal away the best assistant he'd ever had.

He worked to ignore the voice in back of his mind that was demanding to know what other reasons he might have for working so hard to keep Emma away from his brother, as he went back into his office, shoved the mistletoe into his desk drawer, and slammed it shut.

George looked up to see that Harry had followed him, and had sat down in one of the chairs in front of his desk. The fact that Harry was still grinning made George feel fairly certain he wasn't going to like this meeting.

His thoughts were confirmed when Harry said, "Hmm…I don't know that I've ever seen you quite so…uh…what's the word? Possessive."

"You go through my assistants like water." George realized he was practically shouting at him, and lowered his voice. "I am not going to let that happen with Emma. She's too valuable to me."

Jesus, Harry was absolutely correct, he was feeling possessive. Very possessive. He was developing feelings for Emma. How was that even possible? She was almost half his age, and she was his assistant, for chrissake. Those were lines that should never be crossed, and Emma would agree with him. She'd probably knee him in the groin if he ever came close to her.

He almost grinned at the thought of his very capable Emma putting him in his place. Then she'd probably feel bad about it, and offer to kiss his boo-boo.

That thought brought his attention back, and made him shift uncomfortably in his chair. He cleared his throat and glared at his younger brother.

"As I said…" Harry continued, as if he hadn't just been read the riot act by his older brother. Were they too old now for him to beat the shit out of Harry, just on principle? He was pretty sure he could still take him. No, he'd never hit Harry in his life. He certainly wasn't going to start now, especially not over a woman.

"Don't go there, Harry. You know I'm dating Crystal."

Harry groaned, then said, "Is that what you call it?"

"What is your big hang-up with Crystal? She's smart, she's beautiful and she fits in well with my life. She's comfortable meeting and talking with all the people at the charity functions I have to attend, and even manages to get companies to donate large sums of money at those events."

"You can get all of those things from a high-priced escort service, and not have to worry about them stabbing you in the back when you aren't looking."

"I don't know where you get that idea, and I would appreciate you not being so antagonistic around her. You only make things difficult when we're all together."

"No problem. I will do my best not to even be visible when she's around."

"Get to the point. Why are you here?" George was fed up with their conversations about Crystal, which never seemed to get anywhere beyond Harry's disapproval.

He firmly believed that Crystal had all the qualities he needed in a partner. When she sometimes got frustrated that their relationship wasn't making more progress, he bought her something expensive, and she let it go. He didn't need, or want, advice from his younger brother, who changed girlfriends more frequently than he changed his sheets.

Crystal was the woman who fit into his life.

"You didn't come here to discuss my love life." He prompted Harry to keep talking, hoping he would get to the real point of his visit.

"No, I didn't. But if you ever need help with that…" He chuckled when he saw the look of disgust George gave him.

"Fine," Harry said. Then he cleared his throat and continued, "I need a transfer of funds into my slush account. I'm picking out your present, and I don't have time to go home and do the transfer myself."

George thought about pointing out that his office was just down the hall, and had a perfectly good, state-of-the-art computer collecting dust on his desk, but he decided it wasn't worth the argument.

Exasperated, and not bothering to hide it, he turned to his computer and began typing furiously. "Really? And just how much is my present going to set me back this year?"

He knew that he sounded ungrateful, but he was still unable to stop it from coming out that way. They went through this routine every year, and frankly, it was getting old. Harry would buy him something he not only didn't need but didn't particularly want, then he would have to turn around and find something equally as ridiculous for Harry.

It was all a singular waste of time. And for what? They each had their own money to buy whatever they wanted.

"Whatever happened to 'It's the thought that counts' when giving gifts?" Harry asked in a voice laced with sarcasm.

"Between you and Emma…" George muttered, not appreciating Harry's attempt at humor in the least.

He was getting really tired of everything about Christmas. It only held painful memories for him, and he was tired of having to go through them each and every year. He'd made up his mind. This would be their last year for this stupid gift exchange. Next year, no more Christmas. At all. Period.

Finished with both his computer and his younger brother, he turned back to Harry. "Done. Now, if you don't mind, some of us actually work for a living."

"I'm telling Santa you said that," Harry retorted, as if that would hold any threat.

George sighed. He loved Harry more than anyone, including himself, but he was suddenly feeling tired and cranky, and just wanted the day to be over already.

He watched as Harry stopped at Emma's desk to flirt with her again, and he continued to watch as Emma laughed at something Harry had said. Jesus. He was going to lose another one. Not just another one this time, he was going to lose Emma. His Emma.

When had he started to think of her as his?

He had to get a grip on himself before he completely lost his mind. Emma was the kind of woman who needed a lovable man. He was not that man. That was why he was with Crystal. She loved his money, and that was all she asked for from him. That was all he deserved.

He noticed the manuscript was still on Emma's desk, and he realized that in all the craziness with the mistletoe, and Harry's transfer request, he had missed the opportunity to dump the thing off onto Harry.

He sighed in frustration, but he decided to leave it where it was, knowing that Emma would eventually pass it off to Harry for him.

Yet one more reason she was such a great assistant.

* * * * * * *

Emma was working on her computer when George came out of his office later in the afternoon, pulling on his coat.

"I'm having lunch with Crystal at the Appaloosa, and then taking her shopping for her present, so I won't be back until around three."

"Be sure to sit in Dennis's section," she reminded him. "He'll take good care of you."

He remembered that this Dennis guy was one of her favorite waiters at the Grill who always gave impeccable service. George appreciated that she constantly thought of the little things like this to make his life easier and more manageable. She really was above and beyond in service to him, and he knew he was lucky in that. He was not going to fuck that up by reaching for something…else.

"Dennis. Got it," he replied absently. He also knew that he could trust her to have already made the necessary arrangements for him as well. She would have called over there and taken care of his bill on the corporate card, so that he wouldn't have to do anything except sit back and enjoy his lunch.

"You should stop by Stan's for coffee after lunch and say hi to Stan before you go shopping." She looked up at him as if expecting him to say something to her.

What the hell was that all about? He looked blankly at her, not understanding at all what had suddenly gotten into her. He didn't do coffee in the afternoon, and she knew that.

"Do you want me to get you something from Stan's?"

"No." She sounded disappointed, as if he'd said exactly the wrong thing.

It didn't matter, he knew she had an addiction to decaf mocha lattes no matter what time of day it was, so he'd pick one up for her on the way back and surprise her.

* * * * * * *

George pushed his way through the revolving door at the entrance to the Republic Plaza building, while he talked on his cell with Harry.

"I don't care what Emma told you, there isn't a chance in hell that Landon Literary will ever publish work by Dean Erickson."

Harry continued to push from his side of the phone, and George was frustrated. "You don't have to understand, Harry, you just have to listen and do what I'm telling you on this one." His tone and his words were more emphatic than he had intended, but he could feel his anger rising to the breaking point. He wasn't mad at Harry, but he'd be damned if he'd ever give a leg up to Erickson.

Across the street, Crystal was waving at him, and he absently waved back at her, as he wrapped up his conversation with Harry. He was running a little behind schedule, which usually pissed Crystal off, but he knew he had to finish this conversation before their lunch because she hated even more not having his complete and undivided attention when they were together.

Sometimes Crystal was more work than he had the energy for, and he knew he would be making this all up to her in some big way—as in dazzling, sparkling, and very, very expensive—but he didn't care. It didn't matter. He could afford it, and she would expect it.

He looked up and down the street, then crossed just at the same moment a bike messenger sped around the corner at top speed and crashed into him.

As if in slow motion, he spun around from the impact of the kid on the bike. Stunned, he watched as his phone flew out of his hand moments before his head crashed, hard, into a light post, and bounced off of it again. Excruciating pain lanced through his head at the same time that he lost his balance and started to fall. The last thing he saw was the pavement as it rose up to meet his head when he collapsed onto the sidewalk.

Then everything went black.

CHAPTER FIVE

rantic with worry, Emma rushed into the Rose Medical Center emergency-room waiting area. She had never heard Harry in such a panic before. It hadn't helped matters that his cell reception in the hospital had been crap, and she had basically heard him in Morse code.

What had happened to George?

The first thing she noticed when she entered the waiting area was that Crystal was fake-crying—yes, definitely fake-crying—as prettily as only Crystal was able to do, in spite of the fact that there wasn't much of an audience to perform for in the massive waiting area. Leave it to Crystal to make everything about herself.

She took this all in as good news though, and figured that whatever had happened to George couldn't have been too bad, otherwise his "fiancée" would most likely be in hysterics. Right? Wouldn't she be more worried that her cash cow was at risk before she could get him down the aisle?

Not that that would ever happen if Emma could help it.

"Harry? What happened?" She noticed Harry nervously pacing around the room. Apparently, he was immune to Crystal's award-winning histrionics, because he didn't even glance her way as he rushed up to Emma.

"Oh, thank God, Emma, you're here. You'll take care of everything now. I'm just going to…I'm just…" Harry stopped his incoherent stammering, and just stared at her blankly.

Okay, maybe it hadn't been his cell service that had him talking in stutters. She reached over to touch Harry on the arm to calm him, but he abruptly stepped away from her and practically ran out of the hospital.

Watching Harry freak out, her own fear escalated. What had happened to George?

"Nice. Harry at his finest. Bolting in the face of a crisis." That was Harry's typical behavior, after all, and she shouldn't have been surprised by it.

Crystal abruptly stopped her fake crying, and glared at Emma. "Well, if he's leaving, I'm sure not staying. I hate hospitals."

Crystal rushed out almost as quickly as Harry, and Emma was left, dumbfounded, staring after both figures as they retreated.

"Seriously?" She was completely unable to comprehend what she was seeing. First Harry, now Crystal. "Well, that's just lovely. How am I supposed to break it to George that his fiancée is vapid and—"

"She's not my fiancée," said a deep voice from directly behind her.

Letting out a startled squeak, she whirled around to see George, dressed in hospital scrubs, standing right behind her.

"My God, George, you nearly gave me a seizure." She clutched her chest and tried to get her heart to calm down again.

George looked at her in surprise, then asked, "Did you hear what I just said?"

She was still frazzled from his abrupt appearance, but she was definitely pleased to see he was not seriously hurt. Although, she wondered what he was doing in hospital scrubs if he was being released. Had his clothes been damaged?

"What?' she asked, but didn't bother to wait for him to answer. "I thought it was something serious, the way people were acting."

"Apparently, I'm in a coma." His voice sounded annoyed. If he were in a coma, he would be a lot more than just annoyed. And he certainly wouldn't be standing there talking to her about it.

"Yeah, you look like it." She snorted a nervous laugh. Was he kidding? This was no time to be kidding. She just wanted to get him checked out of here and back to the office so she could get back to focusing on her plan of getting him to fall in love with her.

The clock was ticking.

But he was crooking his finger at her and gesturing her to follow him inside a room just off the nurse's station. Did he want her to get his stuff for him? Okay, fine.

He gestured for her to go inside the room, and she saw there was someone sleeping in the bed, hooked up to all sorts of beeping monitoring machines. Then she realized who was in the bed.

She felt the bottom fall out of her stomach, and her heart followed close behind. No way...

"Oh. My. God. George?" She gasped as she looked at the George in the bed, then back at the George standing next to her, then back at the George in the bed.

"Yeeeaaah," was all he replied, as if that said it all.

Stunned and frightened, she looked at ghost-George, who was still standing next to her. She very slowly, and very carefully, poked a finger at him. It went right through him, creating an electrical—but definitely not unpleasant—spark between them, causing them both to jump.

Then she turned and carefully walked over to the body in the bed, and looked at the sleeping-George for a moment before turning back to ghost-George. She didn't know what to do. None of this could be real. How could he be in a coma?

"You're in a coma?" As if that hadn't already been made incredibly clear. She knew that sometimes she could be a little slow on the uptake, but seriously, this would challenge anyone's abilities. She wasn't thinking clearly. It wasn't as though people saw ghosts every day, or that there was a protocol to following when trying to cope with that type of thing.

"I did say that already," he replied with definite irritation in his voice.

"Well, what are you doing out here?" She waved her arms frantically around to indicate the room. She was so scared she was starting to shake, and she wasn't making any sense.

"I don't know." He shrugged, as if this were an everyday occurrence for him. But then he ran his hands through his hair, which she recognized as his tell that he was frustrated. Good to know that a person's usual habits didn't change just because you got turned into a ghost.

"I woke up and no one could see or hear me. Then I realized that I was no longer part of my body, and I was wandering around, completely naked, like a crazy person trying to get someone's attention. I came out into the waiting room and tried getting Harry's attention, and even Crystal's—who, by the way, sucks at pretending to cry—but neither of them noticed me. No one noticed me. Christ, I was so surprised when you heard me, I thought I was hallucinating."

She looked at him in concern. If she was so scared she was shaking, what must he be going through? His spirit was no longer attached to his body, which was lying in a bed hooked up to life support.

"You were naked?" She really had registered all of what he had said. She just couldn't seem to get her mind beyond that one very important part—er, detail—in his story.

"Apparently, I can make things materialize or—"

He stopped abruptly, and she thought she could actually see his mind rewinding and finally registering her really, really, stupid question.

"That's what you got out of all of that?' He had an incredulous look on his face. "That I was naked?"

Yep, he had caught her really, really stupid question.

Heat suffused her face. Realizing her mind had just wandered into territory it shouldn't have gone—especially not out loud—she shrugged apologetically.

Probably not a good thing to be thinking about your boss naked, and she shook her head slightly to clear it. She had to get a grip on herself, and start thinking of ways to help him.

"What I'm trying to tell you, Emma, is that I've split from my body somehow, and you're the only person I've found so far who can see or hear me."

He was right, this was bad. And she was starting to freak out. George was a ghost.

Because, holy shit, George was in a coma.

Okay, calm down.

Focus.

Take a deep breath.

Think.

She just needed to wrap her mind around it.

Lowering herself into the chair next to the bed, she closed her eyes for a moment until the room stopped spinning.

Then she opened her eyes, and studied ghost-George intently, as she tried to sort through everything in her mind that she had ever read, or heard, on the subject of ghosts. The problem was that she really only had novels and movies for resources. Not exactly reliable information.

On the other hand, considering the subject matter, how reliable was any resource?

It suddenly occurred to her that she now had a very reliable source standing right in front of her.

"Hmm…so, did you see a bright light?" She infused her voice with as much confidence as she could manage in order to help her look like she knew what she was talking about. Which she didn't.

"No, I see what you see."

"Huh." She nodded her head as if that made perfect sense. "Have you seen any other ghosts walking around?"

"Like…?"

"I don't know…" she replied with a shrug, "like Amelia Earhart? I'd love to find out what really happened to her."

He just stared at her. Okay, then. That was a "no" on Amelia Earhart. Check.

"How about Elvis? Is he really dead?" She decided to change her celebrities to one she hoped he might find more interesting.

George crossed his arms over his chest and glowered at her. Nope, not an Elvis fan either, then.

In the back of her mind, she knew she was being completely ridiculous with these questions, but she was still in panic mode, and she seemed to have no control over what was coming out of her mouth.

"Emma. Aren't you missing the bigger picture here?" He had apparently reached the end of his patience, because he was speaking in a louder volume, and that jolted her back from her wandering thoughts. "How am I supposed to get back into my body?"

"Well, that… Apparently you have some unfinished business or—"

"That'd be if I were actually dead," he said, interrupting her. Rather loudly, in her opinion.

"That's true, but look at on the bright side. At least this way you have escaped a fate worse than death." She was pretty sure being in a coma and a ghost had to be better than being engaged to Crystal.

"What could possibly be worse than death?"

"Oh, trust me, there's worse." She nodded her head emphatically. "I happen to know that today, Crystal was taking you shopping for engagement rings."

"Jesus." That was all he said, but he looked as if she had slapped him, and he gaped at her without another word in response.

"I see you agree with me now." She tried very hard not to grin in satisfaction.

George collapsed into a visitor's chair as though every bone in his body had suddenly melted on him, and she was worried she had said too much. She hadn't realized this would come as such a shock to him, since he had been dating Crystal for almost a full year (which was about six months longer than the last woman he'd dated).

Not that she was upset that he was so surprised. She hadn't meant to freak him out, but this could only mean that he wasn't nearly as far into the relationship as Crystal thought he was, and there was still hope that when he found out she was cheating on him, he wouldn't want to try to work things out with her. Maybe he wasn't in love with the Blond Maleficent, and Emma did still have a chance with him?

"Christ," he muttered, as he ran his fingers through his hair again.

She scooched her chair closer to the bed to look more carefully at George's comatose body. "Have you tried lying down and getting back in?"

"Of course I've tried lying down and getting back in," he snapped back at her. "The damn thing won't take me back."

"Don't call him that, he can hear you."

She was appalled that he could call his own body names, especially considering it was right there in the room with them. She was completely freaked out by seeing George laid out in the bed so lifeless. She had to get him to wake up.

"Of course he can hear me. He's me, and I'm standing right here talking to it…you…him. Wow. That didn't even make sense to me."

"Don't you listen to him," she cooed to the body in the bed in an attempt to soothe him. "We'll figure this out."

Poor George. This all had to be incredibly hard for him, especially finding out that Harry couldn't see or hear him as a ghost. They had to figure something out.

She reached over the bed rail and touched coma-George's arm to comfort him.

"I can feel that…" Ghost-George gasped from over in the direction of the visitor's chair.

"What?" She looked up absently at Ghost-George in the chair, but continued to caress Coma-George's arm soothingly.

"I can feel you holding his—my—arm," Ghost-George responded.

She immediately let go, and hastily moved back from the body.

Oops.

"Sorry." She was embarrassed that she had been caught stroking her boss's arm. The coma boss, not the ghost boss, but still. Not good.

She had liked touching his arm, and it had seemed like a natural thing to do. But she realized that it was a grossly inappropriate thing to do—not gross-gross, because she had enjoyed it and had wanted to touch George for a very long time, but definitely grossly inappropriate. She mentally kicked herself for being so stupid, while she braced for his rejection.

He came around the bed to the side where she was standing, and she resisted the urge to hide under the bed in embarrassment.

He spoke softly to her. "No, I mean, maybe that's a good sign. Huh? That I'm still a part of my body?"

She studied him intently, trying to gauge his reaction, but mostly to understand what he meant. How was she supposed to know the answer to that question? This was way out of her area of expertise. But she felt as though she needed to give him some hope.

"Look, George, I'm not the expert on ghosts here, but it seems to me there's some reason you're wandering around outside your body right now. We just need to figure that out, and then you can wake up."

There. That sounded informative, and it had the added bonus of giving her something to focus on other than the fact that the man she loved was in a coma.

A nurse came into the room, but stopped abruptly and looked around in confusion. "Were you talking to someone?" She went over to check Coma-George's monitors.

"Uh, yeah, uh, well." Emma realized she was stammering as she searched her mind for a rational explanation that didn't include explaining how she was talking to the ghost of the person lying in the bed. "I heard that you're supposed to talk to coma patients because they can probably still hear you," she finally said, grateful that this tidbit of medical theory surfaced in her brain just in time.

"Very smooth," George said to her. Then he smiled and nodded his head as if he approved.

He'd smiled. Well, didn't that just make her feel all warm and fuzzy inside. Even as a ghost—and she was still struggling with that part—he could make her giddy with just a smile.

The nurse, too, smiled at Emma as she continued to check the monitors. "Are you his wife?"

Was it her imagination, or was the woman on a fishing expedition with that question? She narrowed her eyes at the nurse, before she remembered that she herself had just been caught taking unfair advantage of the body in the bed—caught by the owner of said body as a matter of fact—and decided she had no room to judge the nurse if she was attracted to George, too.

"What? No!" Emma exclaimed a bit too enthusiastically, at the same time George bellowed, "Absolutely not."

Okay, that outburst was uncalled for. Even if the nurse couldn't hear it, Emma sure could, and she glared at George for his overly emphatic response.

"Oh, well, it sounded a little like you were arguing with him a minute ago..." she said, "you know, like husbands and wives do...so I thought..."

The nurse eyed Emma suspiciously, then finished with her fussing over the monitors and wrote some notes in George's chart. When she was done writing, she closed the folder and finally looked up at Emma. "Okay. Things look good here," she announced, and promptly left the room.

Emma was humiliated, and her face was once again heating up. On top of still being embarrassed that she had all but molested George's body while he was in a coma and helpless, she was pretty much convinced from the look on the nurse's face that she had been worried about being trapped in the room with a nut-job—that nut-job being herself, of course, since the nurse couldn't see George, who was really the far bigger nut job at the moment—and that was the proverbial straw.

She had to get out of here. This whole thing was beyond her abilities, and she needed to get away to think, or she was never going to be any good trying to help George get back into his body.

She needed some air, so she decided to pull a Harry and make a hasty retreat. She tried not to run down the hallway in case the nurse was nearby and saw her.

She could hear George, as he followed and called after her. "Come on, Emma. You gotta admit, you do argue with me. A lot."

She did, that was true. And that was part of the reason she enjoyed working with him. She liked that he always seemed to respect her opinion, even when it was different from his own.

"I really need some air. Is it hot in here to you?" She looked over at him, and blushed even deeper. The whole ghost thing wasn't sinking in. He looked so normal. "Yeah, no, probably not. Okay, so, can we maybe just…I don't know, continue this outside?"

She went out through the doors at the entrance of the hospital with her head high, and her cheeks feeling like she was running a malaria-induced fever. She needed to get her head back together. She still had work to do on her plan for getting him to fall in love with her. And on top of that she also had to figure out how to get George out of his coma in order for that plan to work. With renewed determination, she headed off toward her Jeep.

"Emma, come on, just stop for a second," George hailed from behind her.

As if her body was somehow conditioned to his commands, she stopped abruptly. She stopped so abruptly that George, who had obviously been much closer than she had expected, kept running. And he ran right through her.

She gasped from the jolt of energy that went through her from the contact. It was absolutely amazing. As if they had blended into a single entity. Every molecule in her body woke up and made itself aware as George passed through her, and it completely took her breath away. She saw George falter for a moment as he came out through the other side of her. Then he turned around to look at her.

"What was that?" She sounded a little breathless, because she was still reeling from the heady sensation.

"I don't know, but it didn't suck." Then he grinned at her, and she wondered if he had enjoyed it, too.

Feeling her cheeks flame up all over again, she picked up her pace once more, and stated as threateningly as she could manage in her current state of bliss, "Don't do it again."

There wasn't much heat behind her threat, she realized, because secretly, she hoped he wouldn't pay any attention to her and try it again. It had been an amazing sensation, and she wouldn't mind repeating it.

"I didn't mean to do it that time, but you stopped too fast." She noticed that he was still grinning at her, which didn't help. He was pretty much irresistible when he grinned at her. "Please, Emma, just stop for a second."

She slowed down and eyed his position, wondering if she could somehow accidentally get him to step through her again. Then she mentally smacked herself in the forehead to get her brain working again. Focus, Emma, focus.

"Look, you're the only one who can see me, which puts me in a very... well, difficult position right now. Maybe you're the only person who can help me." He sounded almost desperate, which had to be a new experience for him. "So I really think we need to stick together."

Well, duh. Of course she was going to help him; she loved him. She just needed to figure out how. But she couldn't seem to focus when he was just so...right there. She really needed to figure this out. She needed to talk to Marlie and Laura about it. They'd help her figure it out.

Wait. No. She couldn't tell them she was seeing George's ghost. They'd lock her up and throw away the key. They already thought she was crazy, being in love with someone so much older. Well, and the fact that he was her boss. And did she mention that he was so much older? Yeah, they loved that part.

"I'm appealing to your natural, and abundant, inclination to help people in need here, Emma," he continued, apparently taking her silence as unwillingness. "And if there is anyone who is more in need at this moment, I don't know who that would be. You and I both know you're going to give in to your good Samaritan instincts eventually, so how about we just cut right to the end where you agree already?"

"Okay, George." She had already come to the conclusion that it was down to the two of them to figure it out together. No one else was going to believe she was spending time with his ghost, so they would have to figure it out on their own.

He looked smug. Yep, he knew she wouldn't abandon him. He could read her like a book. He wasn't an excellent publisher for nothing. He knew his subject matter.

"First thing we need to do is find you a coat. You're going to freeze out here." She tried to ignore his smug look of victory.

"I'm a ghost, Emma. I don't feel the cold." He stood there, still with that smug look, which only got…well, smugger.

"Well, I'll freeze just looking at you walking around in those hospital scrubs." She was going to hold her ground on this because she was unwilling to give in and admit to what even she could see was totally irrational behavior.

"Okay, I'll change into something else." He shrugged, as if it was perfectly natural for his assistant to demand it of him.

"You can't just change your clothes in the middle of the street in broad daylight." She looked around, shocked that he would even suggest such a thing.

"You keep missing the part about me being a ghost. No one can see me," he explained, as if he were suddenly speaking to a three-year-old, which might have been because she was starting to sound like one, even to herself. But she couldn't seem to stop it. This was all new to her, and she was starting to crack under the pressure.

"Well, I can. And I'm not going to watch." She turned around and covered her eyes. She really didn't want to see a naked George on top of everything else. Okay, so, yes she did, but no, she didn't.

"You can turn around now," he said, a second later.

Emma peeked between her fingers to check. "Are you dressed?"

"Yes, completely." She heard him chuckle, apparently amused by her propriety.

She turned around and looked at him, then practically had to physically shove her tongue back into her mouth.

He was wearing jeans and a sweater, and she stared at him in appreciation. She had never seen him in jeans before. She had imagined him in jeans before, but even that didn't compare to the reality. She stopped staring when she realized she was undoubtedly giving herself (and her thoughts) away.

"Okay...that will do." Her voice sounded like she had run a marathon and couldn't catch her breath. She turned and continued down the street toward her car. "Can you do anything else?" she asked, in an attempt to divert the attention from her reaction to him.

"Like what?" He looked at her suspiciously.

"I don't know, like visualize world peace?" She knew she sounded flippant, but what had he thought she would ask for? A new pony?

She had reached her Jeep, and was settling herself into the front seat when George materialized instantly in the passenger seat. She jumped in surprise. Geez-oh-Pete. He had to quit doing that to her. "We are definitely going to need some ground rules if you're going to haunt me constantly." All these surprise attacks by him were having a negative impact on her nervous system.

"Such as?" Again, he looked suspiciously at her.

"Well, for one thing, what are you going to do all day?"

"Since you're the only one who knows I'm"—he cleared his throat, then continued—"like this, I thought I'd stay with you until this gets sorted out."

Was he serious? What did he mean by the "stay with you" part in that sentence? Did he mean stay with her, stay with her? As in, in her apartment with her?

"You want to stay with me at my apartment?"

"Yes."

"In my apartment."

"Yes. Where else would I go?"

"Well, there's your own house." Her stomach did a little flip-flop; she wasn't sure if it was because she was excited about having him all to herself, or if she was nervous about having him constantly following her around.

"It would be better if we stayed together right now. You did promise to help me. You can stay with me at my house, but I think that would take some very clever explaining on your part." He grinned at her and she nearly had a heart attack. As much as she would enjoy playing house with him at his home, she knew he was right. It would look very strange.

Not to mention, Crystal would kill her.

"Okay, I agree, you should stay with me." Had she sounded just a bit too eager to have him move in with her? "We're going to need some boundary rules."

That sounded better. More like she did this kind of thing all the time. She started the car then turned to look at George, and patiently waited for him.

"What?"

"Seat belt," she replied, and just barely managed to bite off the "duh" that was next in line to come out of her mouth. He looked at her as if "duh" was also about to come out of his mouth, and she felt herself blush for the third time in under an hour. "Ah. Right. I keep forgetting."

"What kind of boundary rules?"

"For one, stay out of my bedroom, and my bathroom, especially since I'm guessing you don't need either one of those in your current condition."

It was going to be hard enough having him around her, in her space, without him having the ability to pop in and out whenever he felt like it. Sleeping…showering… Oh, God, why had she agreed to this again? Ghosts didn't need to shower, right?

Oh, great, now she was thinking about him in the shower. She had to pull herself together, or she was never going to live through this. There were definite advantages to having him around more often, especially if she had him all to herself (take that Crystal.). But as a ghost?

She just needed to re-group, and adjust her plans accordingly.

"And you have to get over your Scrooge attitude about Christmas." She had to rein in her wandering thoughts and focus back on the subject. "Because if you're going to be around me constantly, I won't let you ruin my Christmas spirit."

"Oh, give me a break—" he started to say, but she cut him off.

"That's it! Christmas spirit."

"What are you talking about?"

"You're Scrooge."

"Oh, for God's sake, Emma."

She looked at him again, and was completely convinced. "Yep, Scrooge."

Oh my God, she was so brilliant. She couldn't believe she hadn't thought of this before. That was what was wrong with him. That was why he couldn't get back into his body. He was some kind of Ghost of Christmas something-or-other (she'd never really liked Dickens that much—too much gloom-and-doom stuff).

"First of all, Scrooge wasn't a ghost, he was visited by ghosts," George felt the need to clarify.

"Well, either way, I'm sure this is what you need to get back into your body. I think you need to experience a real Christmas and get over whatever it is that has you so against it. It's clearly a *Christmas Carol* thing going on here."

Her mind was reeling from this new revelation, and she started working out the possibilities for solutions. Suddenly, Christmas Day represented not only her own internal ticking clock, but also the key that would unlock his heart. It had to be. It had worked for Scrooge, hadn't it? And George wasn't anywhere near as horrible at Scrooge. He was just…guarded.

So she needed to start planning her next move based on this new insight. She certainly wasn't going to take him anywhere depressing like a cemetery. That was just creepy in the extreme, unless it was Halloween, and then it was all kinds of fun. From now on, everything they did, and everywhere they went, needed to happen so that he could experience the best parts about Christmas. No one could resist falling in love with—or, more hopefully, *at*—Christmas.

"Well, okay...let's see..." she said, thinking out loud. "You've already missed the Parade of Lights, but we can hit Larimer Square and see all the store window displays."

"What is it with women and shopping?" He groaned. "Even as a ghost you want me to take you shopping. You realize I don't have any money, right?"

"I said window displays, George, not shopping." She checked her rearview mirror and changed direction, so that they were headed toward downtown Denver.

"What's the difference?" He didn't appear to be convinced by her distinction.

How sad it was, she thought, that his first inclination toward women was that they only wanted him for his money, when she wanted, oh, so much more from him than that. And by New Year's Day she would have it, or she would end up having to leave him to the Crystals of the world.

But that was simply too unbearable to think about, so she continued to drive in the direction of Larimer Square and kept thinking positive thoughts that this would be a truly merry Christmas for the both of them.

CHAPTER SIX

George reluctantly followed Emma as she glanced back at him every few minutes. Apparently, she was worried he'd disappear on her, but she had nothing to worry about. She was his only lifeline right now, and he wasn't giving that up anytime soon.

So he stuck with her to Larimer Square to shop. He had visited this street numerous times over the years, but this was the first time he'd noticed that it was completely illuminated under a canopy of lights down the middle of the street.

She intended to stop him at the windows of each and every storefront to point out their displays? He was going to go out of his goddamned mind.

Did she seriously believe this was going to get him back into his body? A bunch of displays?

Fine. He didn't have any other ideas, and since she was the only one who knew he even existed, it was better than wandering around the hospital trying to get someone's attention. She was certainly enjoying herself, so what the hell.

She stopped him in front of the window of an art shop. "Oh, look. Look at the tiny glass slipper that's lying in the middle of the castle steps."

As he looked into the widow, he heard her sigh as if this was the most amazing thing she had seen in her life. All he saw was the shoe, and the woman it belonged to dashing into a hideously orange carriage, heedless of the fact that one of her feet was bare.

Why the hell would a woman run off and leave one of her shoes behind? How stupid was that?

"And there goes Cinderella, rushing to get to her coach before the hour strikes midnight, and all the magic disappears." She looked up at him to see if he was paying attention.

It figured that she would only see the magic in the situation. Well, that was Emma in a nutshell. She was always so positive, and she believed in everything.

"Oh, look at that beautiful dress," said a woman who had come up next to Emma to look into the window. "Wouldn't you just love a dress like that?"

"Yes." She didn't sound very convincing about it. "But where in the world would you ever get the chance to wear it?" And she laughed with the woman over the extravagance.

How interesting… She might believe in fairy tales, but she definitely had a practical side as well. That thought made him chuckle, and she glanced at him in surprise.

She might not believe it, but he could see her wearing a dress like that to one of the charity functions he attended.

Before he could dwell too long on that strange thought, she motioned for him to follow her to the next shop window. This window belonged to a bookstore, and had a scene from the *Polar Express* by Chris Van Allsburg (he knew this because the book was prominently displayed next to the scene).

He peered inside and saw a small, ornate train that was puffing smoke. The engine was attached to four passenger cars, next to which stood the conductor, who was boarding several tiny figures of children. Every couple of minutes, the train whistle would blow, and he had to admit that he was impressed by the display.

"Look!" exclaimed a kid who came running up to the window, dragging his haggard-looking mother, who was loaded down with packages. "The kids are all getting on the train to go to the North Pole and see Santa."

"And listen," Emma said, when the train blew its whistle. "Even the train is impatient to get moving and reach the North Pole in time for Christmas."

How did she get that from a train whistle? But the kid sure bought into it, if the rapt attention on his face was any indication.

He stepped back and smiled as he watched her chat with the kid and point out all the details in the display, and he realized that he was enjoying himself, too. He wasn't sure when that had happened, but her excitement and enthusiasm had started to rub off on him, and he was looking forward to the next display. He knew it wasn't the damned windows he looked forward to seeing; it was the anticipation of what she would find so enthralling in each and every one that gave him the kick.

She was so excited, and so full of happy energy, as she chatted with the other people who were also looking at the displays. How could one person get so fired up by silly scenes in windows? It was utterly mesmerizing.

Suddenly, she stopped short in front of a restaurant and gasped.

"Look at that tree, George. Isn't it amazing?" Her whispered voice sounded reverent, as if she were inside a library or a church.

He didn't see anything particularly amazing about it—it had ornaments and lights, and it was green with that white stuff all over it. It looked pretty much like any other tree he'd seen.

"What's the big deal?"

"It's flocked to perfection, and it sparkles like the Hope Diamond." She was staring at it as if hypnotized. He looked around and was relieved to see that no one was watching them—or, more accurately, her. He felt sure that she wouldn't appreciate anyone believing she was talking to herself, and she would no doubt blame him for it. "I've never had a flocked tree. My apartment is too small, for one thing, and flocking can be such a mess. But they sure are beautiful, aren't they? Like a light snowfall had just finished dusting it."

He still didn't get it. You've seen one tree, you've seen them all. But for some reason this one made her happy. He wished he could buy it for her.

* * * * * * *

The outside of Emma's apartment building was decorated with festive lights and garland, which didn't seem to surprise George in the least. She watched him as he took it all in, noticed he was grinning, and hoped that meant that he was starting to get used to the idea of Christmas.

She swung open her front door, and entered her apartment with a happy feeling. She'd had an absolute blast showing George the window displays. She turned back to face him, and saw that he watched her with an amused expression on his face. She was going to take that as a good sign.

"Admit it, George. You had fun. It was a beautiful day, and you enjoyed looking at all the Christmas window displays, didn't you?"

He had been awfully quiet as she metaphorically dragged him from one window display to the next. In the beginning, she had been more than afraid he would disappear on her rather than be put through any more misery. But then he'd changed, and eventually he'd seemed to be enjoying himself.

"Actually, it was more fun watching you look at all the window displays." That was a surprise to her. "I still couldn't care less about Christmas, but you sure get off on it. And I'll admit, today was very entertaining. That, and I didn't have to pull out my credit card once."

He grinned at her, and her knees shook. Holding on to the door to keep from falling over, she closed it carefully, then took off her coat and hung it on a coat rack by the door.

She held her breath and waited as George scanned her apartment.

"Emma, I am shocked and amazed that you, of all people, don't have a tree." That would be the first thing he noticed. And he was never going to let her live it down.

"Oh, well, like I said before, it's a lot of work and mess." She loved her little apartment, but the one flaw with it was that it wasn't big enough for her to have a Christmas tree. "Plus, it seemed like a wasted tree when I'm usually the only one who sees it, so I thought I'd go the environmentally conscious route and try it without this year." But then she looked at George and the expression on his face told her she hadn't fooled him, so she sighed. "Yeah, I miss it…"

She shook off her mood, because that wouldn't help George move forward, or get back into his body. She needed to keep up the momentum, and think of something else they could do together.

This was turning out to be more difficult than she had anticipated. Spreading the Christmas joy eight hours a day all over him at the office was not as tough as having him around 24/7 in her life and in her home. What if she drove him away instead of toward her?

What if she sang off key in the shower? What if she snored in her sleep? Or worse, what if she talked in her sleep?

Okay, now she was just making herself crazy. She would proceed as she always did this time of year, and he could just tag along for the ride. It would be fun. How could it not be? George was here in her apartment—

Holy, shit! George was here in her apartment! What would he think about it?

She started to panic.

This was insane. What had she been thinking?

No, no, this was good.

Calm down.

Proceed as usual.

What would she normally do at this moment, if George weren't standing in the middle of her apartment? She'd watch a holiday movie, that's what she'd do. Great idea. Do that.

"So, for our next Christmas adventure, I thought we could watch *It's A Wonderful Life*. No Christmas therapy treatment should be without it."

George groaned, but she pretended not to hear it, as she continued, "I'm going to make popcorn."

"I can't eat it," he grumbled back at her.

"Well, no, and that's very sad for you. But I can."

Undaunted by his inability to participate in the gastronomical side of Christmas, she went into the kitchen, leaving him to his own devices.

She definitely needed to pull herself together.

* * * * * * *

George looked around the room to see if he could get any idea of who his young assistant was when she wasn't at the office. He stopped in front of her computer, where he saw stacks of papers shoved under her desk. He tried to turn the pages, but couldn't move a single sheet.

"What are all these?" he asked in frustration, feeling the answer to some big mystery lay just beyond his reach. Literally. He finally knew precisely what that expression meant firsthand, and he figured he could have lived his entire life perfectly content without having made that particular discovery.

Emma came back into the room and started kicking the pages further under the desk.

"Those are just my stories. I haven't finished any of them yet." She feigned an attempt at nonchalance that he could see right through. That was interesting.

"You're a writer?" That was a surprise. It was the first he'd heard even a hint of this about her.

"Aspiring," she stated, and he watched as a flush crept over her cheeks. Christ, she was cute when she was nervous. Her hazel-gray eyes turned a deeper shade of green when she was flustered, and he thought he saw a flash of insecurity in them.

He turned back to look at the stacks, which ended up resembling more of a collapsed deck of cards as a result of her trying to shove them further out of his already unattainable grasp. "Why haven't you brought me any to read?" He was more curious than ever to see what she was expending so much effort trying to hide from him.

"As I said, 'aspiring.' Nothing is nearly finished enough to show you. What if you hate them?"

Even more interesting. This was a side to Emma he hadn't seen before. Normally so confident and secure, especially when it came to her job and managing him, she was suddenly throwing off signs of a self-effacing nature he didn't normally see from her.

It wasn't all that surprising, he reflected. Almost every author he'd met had the same doubts about their own work. It was his job to coax them out of their shells and get them to produce award-winning (or, at the very least, money-making) material.

"I won't know until I've read them." He turned on his persuasive charm to get her to open up to him. He grinned at her, and he could have sworn she stumbled just a bit.

"Maybe someday, when they're ready," she squeaked out, as she headed back into the kitchen.

Had she just run away from him? What was in those stories she was writing that had her so flustered?

He obviously wouldn't find out tonight, but he'd see about what he might do with them later. He figured he might as well practice using his newfound power of making things materialize to see if it could extend beyond changing clothes, and came up with the idea of a present for Emma to test it out.

He concentrated, and was pleased with how easily the tree she had admired in Larimer Square materialized in the corner of the room. He had scaled it to fit perfectly, and was very impressed with himself.

This was fun.

He added garland with the same flocking around her ceiling, then added the Polar Express train under the tree. Should he add the Cinderella scene, or would that just be overkill? No, this was enough for now.

Pleased with the result, especially considering this was the first tree he had ever put up, he waited with anticipation while he listened to her in the kitchen getting her popcorn made. He had to admit, he was a little excited, even nervous, about Emma's reaction, and hoped she would be pleased with him and his attempts.

* * * * * * *

In the kitchen, Emma rummaged through her cupboards and located a microwave popcorn packet. She was in a frenzy over George's attention to her manuscripts, and she was eternally grateful he hadn't been able to read them. He was a highly successful publisher of Pulitzers. He read Hawthorne and Faulkner for palate cleansers, for crying out loud! He passed off romance novels—like the ones she wrote that were shoved under her desk—to Harry to read, because he didn't like them and didn't have the time for them. Of course, Harry never read them either, but that was beside the point.

She was never going to give him any of her stories, even if she did someday finish one of them. Way too much fraught-with-disaster and evisceration-of-her-heart potential there. Nope. Never going to happen.

Normally she preferred to use her Whirley-Pop to make popcorn from "scratch," but she was worried about leaving him alone too long to snoop more, so microwave would have to do for now.

It wasn't as if she left half-composed sonnets of love to him hanging around (not that he could pick them up, luckily, if she did), but there could still be something she didn't remember that might be equally as embarrassing. Like dirty underwear or her vib—

Oh, crap!

"So, I was thinking—" she started to say as she came dashing back into the living room, trying to figure out how she would be able to bolt into her bedroom without it appearing as if she was, in fact, bolting to her bedroom.

But she stopped dead when she saw the Christmas tree and gasped in pleasure. "You did that for me?" She was so awed by it that she forgot all about trying to get to the bedroom.

"Apparently I can imagine just about anything."

He'd given her a Christmas tree. George Landon, who hated Christmas above all things, had given her a tree. And not just any tree, but the one she had loved in the window. But this one seemed even more beautiful, and even more brilliant than anything she had ever seen in the entire world. Ever.

This was not a man without a heart.

"Oh, George, thank you," she whispered, and her eyes started to fill up.

She rushed over to him and tried to hug him, but passed right though him instead, and they both felt that pleasant electrical sensation they had experienced the first time. She was instantly embarrassed by the interaction, and her face felt like it was on fire. "Sorry…" She felt as if she had done something morally illegal instead of merely spontaneous.

"It won't last," he said, and cleared his throat. "The tree. I'm sure it will disappear when I get back into my body."

"I don't care if it only lasts the night. It's beautiful, and was very, very thoughtful." She couldn't help herself, even if she was acting like a high school math nerd who'd just been asked out by the captain of the football team.

She went over to touch the ornaments on the tree, and her hand passed right through the image.

"Well, it will certainly make cleaning up a lot easier," he told her, flippantly, as if he were just as nervous or something.

She laughed and, tried to wipe her eyes surreptitiously when they started to tear up again. The bell on the microwave dinged, rescuing her from yet another awkward situation.

She went into the kitchen to get the popcorn, and to once again collect herself. What had just happened? Was he giving her gifts now? What did this mean?

She had the attention of the most amazing, yet frustratingly complicated, man she had ever known, and she was scared out of her wits because she had no idea what to do next. God, she wished she could talk to her sisters right now.

She might have considered throwing herself at him to see how he would react, but that was far more complicated when dealing with vapor, as opposed to actual flesh and blood.

So now what?

Keep on with the plan, and wait for him to tell you what he wants. That's what.

She returned to the living room with the popcorn, and gave him a tentative smile as she turned on the TV, put in the movie and settled into the couch. Deciding to pretend they were best friends, Emma patted the couch next to her and coaxed him to sit next to her. "Come on, part of your immersion therapy."

He looked confused, but then he sat next to her and sniffed the popcorn. "We're going to have to do this when I'm corporeal again and can actually eat some of that."

Her heart flipped over at the implication that they would continue at least some sort of relationship after he got back into his body, but she casually smiled at him in what she hoped was her best "no pressure" look. "Anytime."

"I get to pick the movie though," he claimed, like a kid calling "shotgun!" on a long car trip.

She continued to smile her casual smile. "Not a chance." She pressed the "play" button, and the movie began. Then, knowing it would throw him, she added as casually as possible, "And tomorrow night, immersion therapy continues with Zoo Lights with the kids."

Yep, that did it.

Two words that could strike fear into the hearts of the bravest of all men. "Kids" and "zoo" in the same sentence. He looked panicked, and she started eating the popcorn, feeling only slightly guilty.

But he was still with her.

CHAPTER SEVEN

Emma, Marlie, Laura, and their whole gaggle of kids piled out of a minivan in the parking lot of the Denver Zoo. She absolutely loved the Zoo Lights. They crossed the parking lot, then stood in the line to go through the entrance gates with a mass of parents and kids of all ages waiting to get inside to see the animals and lights.

She smiled to herself as she watched a shell-shocked George, trying to take it all in, as he passed through on his own, and she giggled over the thought that no one was going to stop him and ask for his ticket.

She enjoyed the tradition of coming to the zoo every year with her sisters and the kids. It always looked like a Christmas fantasy wonderland. Every habitat was lit up with millions of colored lights, and various holiday-themed displays blinked through the trees, paths, and walk-ways. The zoo carousel was flashing and turning, while playing holiday music. Most of the zoo animals were awake and active, as if they were as excited to see all the children as the children were to see them. Crowds of winter-dressed people were wandering around admiring the displays, and trying to keep track of their charges.

"That's just awful about George," Laura said to Emma, who had told them earlier about George's accident.

She was so tempted to tell them that he was a ghost, and that he was standing right behind them, looking completely out of his element, but knew that would be a dumb idea.

"What's really awful is that bit—" Marlie started to say, then looked at all the kids and continued, "bad, bad woman he's dating just leaving him in a coma in the hospital by himself like that. That's some true love for you right there, I can tell."

"She's not very good with hospitals," George grumbled. But she noticed that he didn't appear to be any happier about Crystal's defection than Marlie was.

That was a good thing. Right?

"Well, Harry wasn't much better," Emma whispered.

"Oh, come on, give him a break."

"I think I'd take Jack in a coma right now over being a billion miles away again," Laura said with a frustrated edge to her voice. They all looked at her as if she'd lost her mind. "Okay, not a coma, but at least he'd be home."

George leaned in to whisper to Emma, in spite of the fact that no one else could hear him, and said, "He's having an affair on her. You know that, right?"

She glared back at him, because he didn't know Laura or Jack, and had no right making hasty judgments. She loved him, but that didn't mean he could make snarky comments about her sisters.

The group started wandering around among the different displays of lights, but she hung back with George in order to talk more freely.

"You could tell her that being in a coma isn't all it's cracked up to be. Especially at this time of year," he stated, grumpily.

Did that mean he was getting into the holiday mood?

"Really?" she asked.

"Of course! This is our busiest time of the year. Demand for books increases, while we're trying to get this year's accounts closed, and at the same time we're planning for next year—"

"Not to mention, it's Christmas, Mr. Scrooge," she interrupted, equally as grumpily. Just when she thought he was finally coming around, too. Why had he given her such a beautiful tree if he wasn't starting to warm up to the holiday?

"Will you let up on the Scrooge bit. I keep telling you, Scrooge wasn't the ghost. And I'm not living his story, because Scrooge was a tightfisted miser. I have never been tightfisted with my money," he said, sounding defensive.

"You're right, my bad, Mr. Ghost of Christmas Present. But money doesn't fix everything. It certainly isn't doing you any good at the moment," she replied, and then wanted to bite off her own tongue.

She was afraid she had been too hard on him because he turned abruptly and stomped off toward the giraffe habitat.

"Here's a question for you," he said. "If you're so against money, how is it you get into all this Christmas commercialism right here?" He waved his arms around to indicate the activity surrounding them.

"'Christmas commercialism,' George, is you believing you need to pull out your credit card whenever anyone wishes you a merry Christmas," she said.

He shrugged. "Not disagreeing with you there."

She wanted to tell him that his tree was the best gift she could have received from him, and it hadn't cost him anything. But then she remembered that he'd had to go into a coma in order to give it to her, and she thought it would be best not to use that as an example.

"This?" she said instead. "This is families, enjoying their time together, celebrating Christmas, building happy memories and family traditions. It's seeing Christmas through the eyes of their children, and the people they love, as they get excited about everything they see and do together. This is what Christmas is all about."

She hadn't realized that her voice had grown louder until a small boy, holding hands with a woman who wasn't paying any attention to him, pointed at her and asked, "Mommy, why is that lady yelling at the animals?"

His mother, who appeared to be distracted by all the lights (or more likely the nice-looking man standing next to her), finally looked down at her son before gently tugging him along after her. "I don't know, baby," she responded, "maybe she doesn't like giraffes."

The little boy looked back several times at her as he and his mom walked away. She flinched at having been caught, yet again, yelling at a George no one else could see, and spoke more quietly to him. "What is it with you and Christmas, George? Tell me about your Christmases growing up, and the memories you have?"

"Christ, Emma, will you give it a rest already?" he said, nearly snapping her head off. "I'm not getting into my Christmas past with you." And once again, he walked away from her as if that was the end of the discussion.

But she was determined to get the truth out of him, and she followed him, asking, "But why? What were Christmases like for you? To hear Harry talk about them, they were an adventure."

"Yeah, right, they were an adventure," he said, turning back to her and growling. "For Harry. Because Harry didn't know anything. I protected Harry from everything. Christmas sucked, okay? Leave it at that."

For a moment, she was stunned. She simply stood there, imagining all sorts of terrible scenarios while she stared at him, until he groaned and ran his fingers through his hair. There was his tell, suggesting he was in a position he didn't know how to deal with.

What did "adventure" mean? And what "everything" had he protected Harry from when they were kids?

Just as she was about to push him again into telling her about his life, her nephew, Tommy, ran up to her and asked, "Aunt Emma? You coming?"

She turned to see the whole group had turned back and was waiting for her. Only just remembering they were there, as well, she hurried to catch up with them. She had no idea what to say to George in order to get him to open up to her. She could see now that there was more behind his hatred for Christmas than she had ever noticed, and it broke her heart that he could have so much pain over it.

She was convinced that this was the root of his problem. And she had to find the cure to get him back into his body and out of his coma.

* * * * * * *

Later in the evening, the group was watching and listening to Dickens Carolers performing Christmas music. Emma was enjoying herself, especially now that she believed she had the solution to George's problem—get him to spill his guts, detoxify, so that he could get back into his body. But George himself was being a real pissant, and getting on her last nerve. If she didn't know better, she would think he was doing it on purpose just to spoil her mood.

"You're right," he said. "I'm starting to agree with your Scrooge theory, and me being a ghost of Christmas Present."

"You know what, George?" she asked. "Why don't you give me a Christmas present right now, and stop being such a Grinch."

"You're mixing your homonyms, Emma, not to mention your holiday movies," he chuckled.

She turned to him to avoid being overheard by her family and hissed, "Why don't you just stop being so grumpy and start enjoying yourself? Seriously. What's not to like here? Look at how much fun everyone is having. For once, just try enjoying the beautiful lights, and soaking in all the festive atmosphere. Look at how much fun the kids are having." She gestured with her arms, and he looked around.

All the kids around them were enjoying themselves, except for one little boy in another group who was screaming and kicking at his parents in the temper tantrum of an obviously over-indulged two-year old. George lifted one eyebrow in a questioning look back at her.

"Well, okay, not that kid so much," she replied. "But look at our group."

They both watched as Jessica pointed out lights to Spencer, who was commenting back to her. Tommy held his little sister, Michelle's, hand and patiently listened to her as she talked non-stop about nothing in particular, to no one in particular. And Carrie was walking quietly and peacefully with Laura and Marlie, who had their heads together and were no doubt plotting Christmas secrets.

"You have a nice family, Emma," George said, quietly.

"It's what Christmas means to me. Family and tradition," she responded. "We need to find out what Christmas means to you, George, so we can get you back to your body."

"You're so sure of that," he said. "And if that isn't the answer?"

Emma saw the emotions of hope and then despair pass over his face. She was worried, but she refused to let it show. She didn't have any other answers. "Then we figure out what it is. We have time to figure it out, we'll get it."

"Emma, look, about that," he started to say. He ran his fingers through his hair, and she knew, because there was that telling habit again, that she wasn't going to like whatever it was he was going to tell her.

But they were interrupted when a voice behind her asked, "Aunt Emma? Who are you talking to?"

She jumped and let out a yelp as she whirled around and saw her nephew, Spencer, standing behind her.

"Oh, Spencer," she gasped and clutched her chest, as if her heart would come flying out of it at any second. "You scared me to death."

"You keep yelling at some guy named George," Spencer stated, as if it were perfectly normal for his aunt to be talking to thin air, and calling it *George*.

Said thin air called *George* started laughing, and she glared at him. "Yeah, well, that…" she said, stammering as she tried to think of an explanation for Spencer. "See, I'm practicing my speech for when I tell my boss, George, that I need—no, I deserve—a raise."

Spencer looked at her thoughtfully, as if that explained everything, bless him, then said, "I'm sure he'll give it to you then."

She gave George a dirty look because he not only continued to laugh, he had the nerve to snort. Well, that was uncharacteristic, not to mention uncalled for.

She put her arm around Spencer's shoulder and led him away. "Oh, yeah, you better believe it," she said. "And a big fat Christmas bonus to boot."

She didn't think it was possible, but George laughed even harder, and she was sure that, if he hadn't already been a ghost, he would have died of a stroke from lack of oxygen.

Jessica ran up to Emma and exclaimed, "Hey Aunt Emma, it's time for chestnuts!" She excitedly took Emma's hand and tugged on her to follow.

Marlie began singing, "Chestnuts roasting on an open fire," and Laura joined in with, "Jack Frost nipping at your nose." Together they started a sing-along with the kids as they all ran off toward the chestnut vendor.

Still being tugged along, she turned to George and said quietly so that Jessica couldn't overhear, "Come on, George! It's tradition!"

George, noticeably calmer after his laughing seizure, but apparently still in a good mood, threw his hands up in mock frustration and said, "I can't eat them!"

"I know. But I can!" she said, and winked teasingly at him as she ran off to join her sisters. She was even going to have extra, just to make him suffer.

Their group had started an impromptu sing-along around the chestnut vendor, and she looked back to see that George was still standing there, but he was looking like he had the flu.

CHAPTER EIGHT

George waited for Emma as she climbed out of her Jeep, which she had parked in the DCPA parking garage. He was looking forward to following her and getting a glimpse of *A Day in the Life of Emma Anderson.*

What with the three inches of snow on the ground, he was almost glad he was a ghost so that he wouldn't have to deal with walking in it. He didn't like that she had to park so far away from the office, and he decided he was going to make sure to assign her one of the Landon Literary spots in the garage of their building as soon as he got back into his body. How had personnel overlooked this detail? As his assistant, she should have already had her own spot.

He watched in amusement as she blew a quick kiss to the Blue Bear at the front of the convention center, before she headed up toward 16th Street. He followed her as she turned right onto the 16th Street Mall and waved to each individual in the waitstaff group at the Appaloosa Grill.

He had no idea how anyone could be so cheerful first thing in the morning, and was even more amazed that she received such a positive response from everyone in return.

Then she crossed the street to Stan's coffee shop. Okay, the coffee shop. That could explain why she was always so energetic. But she only knocked on the window and made a ridiculous face to Stan, who was in the middle of serving a customer. Stan motioned for her to come inside, but she seemed reluctant.

"We can go inside if you want to get some coffee. You don't have to worry that your boss is going to yell at you for being late."

"No, that's okay, I'm good." She smiled at him, but he could tell from the look on her face that she was in some kind of debate with herself over going inside or not.

He chuckled when Stan imitated her face and waved back at her. He liked Stan, and his husband David, in spite of—or maybe because of—them both being notorious gossips. He had gotten the impression the last time he was in the shop that Stan had been trying to tell him something (something to do with Crystal?), but they were interrupted, and he hadn't had the time to stand around and wait for Stan to get to the point.

"Do you know everyone?" He had never much considered that his assistant had a life outside of his office, and he was starting to feel…what? Jealous? Did he resent all the attention everyone else was getting from her? Maybe Harry had been right about the "possessive" thing he had thrown in George's face to piss him off.

"Pretty much." She shrugged, as if it was perfectly normal that she would have friends everywhere. "That's Jeff over there. He knows that I love Christmas music, so he always plays it for me when I'm around."

She waved at Jeff, who stopped his music to tip his hat to her in a dramatic bow. George stopped himself just before he growled.

Was he really jealous of a street musician? He'd never had these issues with Crystal. When they were together, she hung on him, and never gave anyone else a backward glance.

Emma pushed herself through the revolving door at Republic Plaza, as he passed through it. Literally. He was getting the hang of this misting thing he could do. He waited while she stomped the snow and street sand off her boots on the mats at the entrance, then continued with her into the lobby, where she waved to the security guard. She really did know everyone. They went over to the section of elevators that access the top floors, and she pushed the button.

A haggard-looking Harry approached Emma as they waited for the elevator to arrive. "Any news on George?"

Emma rounded on Harry, and she looked pissed. This was going to be fun to watch.

"Harry, you're an ass."

Harry looked startled by her outburst and George couldn't help but laugh. He had never seen her so riled up. He was just glad that it was directed at Harry instead of himself for a change.

"How could you run out of the hospital like your ass was on fire without any concern for George?" She seemed oblivious to the fact that she was now yelling. Well, good for her.

"Wow, two 'asses' in a row," George said, because he couldn't help himself. "You must be really mad."

"And why would you be asking me about news on George?" she continued, as if she hadn't heard George's comment. "You're his brother. Have you been back to the hospital to check on him yourself?"

"Well, no, that's what you—" Harry started to say.

But the question must have been rhetorical, because she continued without taking a breath. "See? You're an ass. How could you not check on him?"

Harry started to speak again, but the elevator arrived and Emma marched inside. Harry looked like he might not follow, so George reached out and gave him a poke in the back to see if it would have any effect. Harry shot forward and into the elevator, then rubbed at the spot where he'd been touched.

Emma gave George a look that told him he was misusing his super power, but he still couldn't help but laugh. It had been funny to see Harry jump like that.

As they ascended to the top floor, Emma turned her glower back to Harry, who once again tried to speak. But he must have been at a loss as to what to say that wouldn't set her off again, because he finally clamped his mouth shut.

Christ, this was getting fun. He liked having Emma on his side, sticking up for him, even if it was at Harry's expense. What the hell, Harry probably deserved it.

"You tell him, Emma." He knew he probably shouldn't encourage her to beat on his little brother, but he was enjoying himself way too much to try to stop her.

"Oh, shut up," she said, which was probably because he couldn't stop laughing.

But Harry, who looked like he was just about to say something in his defense, shut his mouth abruptly for the second time.

He watched his brother flounder with a female for probably the first time in his life, and could not have been happier. She had spunk. He loved that about her.

"Seriously, Harry. Man up for once, and go find out for yourself about George's condition."

Then, without breaking stride, she stepped out of the elevator, and headed to the reception desk to check in.

"Got anything for me, Sandy?"

"Nope. How's George doing?" She had to have heard at least some of Emma's verbal set-down to Harry, because she was grinning, and wasn't even trying to hide it. From the look on her face, George figured she had once been a victim of Harry's hit-and-run tendencies.

Emma glanced over at George, then returned her attention to Sandy. "Well, he's still in a coma."

"I am so sorry to hear that," Sandy responded, and George could see genuine concern in her expression.

Concern for him? How strange. He wouldn't have expected anyone on his payroll to care. Was she worried about job security if he never regained consciousness?

"Keep me posted if you hear anything new. Let me know if there is anything I can do."

Emma gave Sandy a reassuring smile before heading to the executive wing. She set her things on her desk before she continued into his office, and he waited for what she would say next.

Harry looked like he didn't know what end was up. But George had to give him major points for bravery, because he followed Emma into the office as well.

71

"Emma, I'm really sorry about the hospital. I just freaked out."

George watched as she went to his desk, picked up the stack of manuscripts and gestured for Harry to come closer to her.

"These are the manuscripts George has been working on. You need to finish them."

Harry threw up his hands and started backing out of the room. "I don't do manuscripts. You know that. I'm the sales guy, the people person."

"Well, now you're the manuscript person, too, at least until George gets back." She was speaking so quietly, that George had almost missed what she'd said. Almost, but not quite. He watched in confusion as she again tried to hand Harry the stack, and again he held up his hands to avoid taking it.

"Can't you just do them like usual?" Harry asked in a pleading voice.

"What did he say?" What the hell was going on with the two of them?

He saw Emma glance nervously at him, before she bent closer to Harry and whispered, "No, Harry, I can't. It's time for you to start doing your job."

But he had moved closer, and had heard everything she had said. "Run that by me again?" He made sure he spoke in as calm a voice as he could manage, considering he was about to blow a fuse.

She jumped and let out a squeak, which seemed to startle Harry, because he backed out of George's office as if she was possessed.

In a way, she was.

"It's not my thing, Emma, you know that," Harry said from the doorway. Then he turned and left without another word.

"Someone needs to have a nice long chat with 'not my thing' Harry. This has gone too far." She crossed her arms over her chest, and tapped her foot as if expecting him to do something about it.

He glared back at her. Then he went behind his desk and sat down, feeling like he had just been told the Earth was really a triangle. He knew he was being ridiculous, but he couldn't seem to stop himself from barking at her. "You wanna tell me about this thing you have going on with my brother?"

She came to stand in front of his desk, and he could see that she was feeling defensive because her back went rigid, and she snapped her words out succinctly as if English wasn't his first language. "It is not a *thing*, George.

It's just that Harry has never liked reading the manuscripts you send him, and his reports were God-awful. Plus you were already so buried, I just started taking them over."

He sat there quietly staring at her, waiting for her to finish explaining. But apparently she was done, because she only stared right back at him.

She was in a staring contest. With him, for chrissake. What the hell had gotten into her? Better yet, what the hell had gotten into him? He was in a staring contest with Emma because he didn't like her giving her attention to his younger brother? Unless it was to yell at him on George's behalf, and then it was pretty damned entertaining.

And what had gotten into him? He should be upset that he had been making decisions on manuscripts based on the input of an unqualified company assistant. Except that he wasn't upset, because apparently, she wasn't an unqualified assistant. Apparently, she had some damn good instincts.

He sighed, and looked away first. He had a strange feeling in the pit of his stomach, because he realized that he had wanted her to win more than he had wanted the control over her.

"Exactly what has my brother been doing to contribute to this company?" Had she been picking up all of Harry's work? "If you've been the one doing the manuscripts I keep passing off to him, what has he been doing?"

"Well, um…I'm not too sure, but he's right, he is a good people person." She was such a bleeding heart. It didn't escape George's attention that not fifteen minutes ago she had been ripping his brother a new one, and now she was sticking up for him.

"This puts me in a difficult position, Emma."

"Before you make any hasty decisions," she said quickly, and raised her hands in a defensive gesture. Did she think he was planning to fire her? "Remember that business has been going through the roof, and you needed help, so what does it matter who did—"

"I don't know whether to be incredibly disappointed in Harry, or very impressed by you."

That stopped her short. She blinked, then sat down in a chair as if her legs could no longer hold her up.

"Oh. I thought you were going to be mad."

"Well, I'm not exactly thrilled that you felt the need to deceive me."

He didn't like that they had been doing this behind his back, but her work was not in question. And he wasn't angry with her. Quite the opposite. Her reports were good. They were well thought out, detailed, and insightful.

"I'm sorry, George, really, but you are always so overly protective of Harry."

He had no idea what she was talking about. Especially since earlier in the week, he had contemplated transferring Harry's ass to the New York office. How was that overly protective? So he sat there, and waited for her to elaborate. Because she would.

"Well, you are," she continued, when he didn't respond. "And besides, I really enjoy reading and reviewing the manuscripts."

That wasn't much in the way of an elaboration, because he was still confused.

"You're good at it." What else could he say? All this time he'd thought his brother really had a talent for the editing side of things, and it had actually been Emma. He wasn't sure yet what to do about it, but he'd figure something out.

"So, can I do those while you're...uh...wandering aimlessly?" She looked hopefully at the stack of manuscripts on his desk.

Problem solved. Or half of the problem anyway. He was still disappointed that Harry wasn't more involved with the company, but he'd have to see what he could do about that later. Maybe there was something else he could get his brother involved in that would play to his strengths. Harry had been right when he'd said he was the people person.

"Be my guest." He stood up and gestured for her to sit in his chair.

Her face lit up. She jumped up, ran around the desk, and sat in his chair so fast that, had he been corporeal, she would have knocked him over. She pulled the first manuscript from the stack and started reading it like she belonged there. Maybe she did. She certainly bossed him around enough.

He smiled at the thought of how she always took such control. She'd certainly taken the bull by the horns and given Harry the verbal thrashing he had deserved this morning. He liked that she wasn't afraid to speak her mind, that she was brave enough to go after whatever she wanted.

He was discovering that there were so many things he liked about his young assistant. Spending more time with her was turning into a real eye-opening experience.

"I think I'll go see what Harry's really up to." He might as well take advantage of being invisible, and see what came out of following Harry around.

She looked up as he was leaving the office and shouted after him. "Be nice!"

What was with her? She had just raked Harry over the coals, and now she was making sure his older brother didn't do the same? Besides, what could he possibly do? He was a goddamned ghost—a fact she seemed to keep forgetting. His assistant was nuts, that was all there was to it.

But apparently he liked nuts, because he realized he was smiling.

"Who, me? I'm overly protective, remember?"

"Well, you are," he heard her say, as he left the office. And then he heard the rustle of paper, which meant she had probably gone back to reading the manuscripts.

Yeah, he was discovering that he had a fondness for nuts.

CHAPTER NINE

Emma glanced outside the floor-to-ceiling window behind George's desk and noticed that the sun was setting on downtown Denver. Sunset was always one of her favorite times of the day, because the purple and orange colors in the sky, spreading out across the tops of the snow-capped mountains, were so amazing to watch as the sun faded away.

"Emma," he said in her ear, "you need to learn to read faster. You can't take this long with each manuscript, or you'll drown in them."

She had been so engrossed in one of the manuscripts that she hadn't known he'd come back into the room. She squeaked out a yelp and jumped slightly in the chair.

"You scared the crap out of me! Don't sneak up on me like that. I'm reading a pschyo-thriller, and you nearly gave me heart failure."

"I don't remember getting in a psycho-thriller." He leaned over her to read the title at the top of the page, and she wished she could smell ghosts—she missed being able to secretly breathe in the scent of his cologne whenever he got close, which wasn't very often.

She cleared her throat, then cleared her mind and settled back into the chair to continue reading. She remembered his reaction to the manuscript when it had arrived, and didn't want to get into an argument about it again, so she tried to play it off as if it didn't matter. "Well, it was in here with the rest of them. And I have to say it's really good."

Then, to distract him from it, she added, "But I really like this one." She picked up a different manuscript and waved it around in front of his face. "I don't care how much you bark at me to read faster, I'm definitely taking my time, because it has completely captivated my attention." Historical fiction fascinated her—the hours the author must have put into the research always amazed her—especially if it included a romantic side, as this one did.

"Then if you really like it, we'll publish it, and you'll be able to read it even more because you'll have to do the editing, too, until I get back. But you should be able to decide within the first chapter if they're worth our time."

She knew how much he hated romance manuscripts, and the almost imperceptible grimace that crossed his face gave her a pretty clear indication that he wanted to move on to the next one, which was part of a horror series from an author who had always been highly successful for them. She knew he was anxious to see if this one would be as well received.

She could tell that he was getting impatient—and probably frustrated that he wasn't the one in control—so she reluctantly put down the historical fiction manuscript, and picked up the horror one. She scowled at it, because she had already read through most of this one when George had tried giving it to Harry last week. "Well, I'll tell you one thing," she said. "This one is a huge let-down."

"But he's one of our most famous authors."

He looked like she had just stabbed him in the eye with a fork.

"Famous or not, I think it's pure junk," she replied, as she tossed it back on the desk. She didn't care if the guy was famous or not; he had completely betrayed his loyal fan base with this pile of crap.

"But it's his conclusion to the series," he said, as if that would get her to change her mind.

"I know. That's what's so disappointing. The first five of the series were fantastic. The sixth was on the edge of iffy, but this one's a complete cop-out. Who writes himself into his storyline when he doesn't belong there? That's just narcissistic in the extreme. Either that, or he's suffering from a huge inferiority complex."

She had met the author herself when he'd come to Landon Literary to meet with George, and she knew the inferiority complex theory was definitely not it.

"Either way, we still have to publish it to complete the series," he said. "We'll make Harry do this one."

"Oh, Harry…" she sighed. She knew they probably needed to talk about Harry's general lack of motivation when it came to all things work-related, but she didn't know how to broach the subject.

"You rang?"

Startled, she looked up to see that Harry was leaning against the doorjamb, watching her.

"Burning the midnight oil?" he asked, with a leer in his voice that she couldn't miss. "And in the boss's office, too, how naughty of you."

Harry stumbled into the office and made his way toward her.

She eyed him suspiciously and asked, "Harry, have you been drinking?" Great, this was all she needed. What was she going to do with a drunk Harry on her hands?

"I took your advice—or whatever it was you were giving me this morning—and went to see George in the hospital." He stopped for a moment and swayed dangerously on his feet. "Then I went out and got drunk. Seemed appropriate at the time."

"Just great," George muttered.

Harry tripped over an end table, but righted himself at the last second.

She shot out of George's chair and ran over to help him. If he hurt himself, she'd really have her hands full. She didn't need another Landon in a coma.

"Are you okay?" she asked, grabbing his arm to steady him.

Harry took the opportunity to latch on to her, and he wrapped his arms around her. His words were slurred, and he smelled like a brewery. "George is such an idiot, not recognizing the gorgeous and incredible woman he has right outside his door."

He was even more blitzed than she had originally thought. Made extremely uncomfortable by his words, and even more by his advances, she struggled to get free. "Harry, let go."

George, who looked like he had pretty much reached his boiling point, bellowed out at the same time, "Harry, let her go right now!"

Harry, of course, couldn't hear George, and he obviously chose to ignore Emma, because he said, "I'm not an idiot, Emma. I could really fall for someone like you."

She could see that George was about to have a conniption fit, and wanted to calm him down, but she already had her hands full.

"Stop it, Harry. Let me go," she said, more forcefully this time. But nothing was working, and she was starting to get angry.

Then Harry kissed her.

Holy crap!

Harry Landon was kissing her, and she was uncertain how she felt about that. On the one hand, he was really good at it, and she could see why so many women were hung up on him. On the other hand, he wasn't George. And besides…yuck!

A loud roar came from behind her.

She pushed hard against Harry's chest to get him to stop, but he didn't release her, and she knew she would have to resort to desperate measures. Just as she got her knee up and slammed it into his groin, she saw George swing his fist through Harry's face. She was pretty sure it would have broken the poor guy's nose if it hadn't gone straight through him instead.

Harry grunted in pain and doubled over on the couch, cradling his crotch in one hand and his head in the other.

"What was that?" Harry said through a wheeze. "First I get an electric jolt in my nuts, just before getting it through my brain. What did you do?"

She went from embarrassed to angry in a nano-second. She glared at Harry and asked her own question. "What were you doing?"

"Kick him again," George demanded, looking like a raging bull who was about to charge.

Harry groaned and sat back into the couch as he held his head in his hands. "I'm sorry, Emma, I don't know what happened. I'm a wreck. I miss George."

And just like that, her anger deflated. She felt so sorry for him, because she understood some of what he was going through. George was his older brother, his best friend, his family, and poor Harry had no idea what was going to happen.

She sighed and sat down next to him on the couch. "Look, Harry..." she started, even though she wasn't sure what to say to him. Should she tell him that George was a ghost who'd been with her this whole time, and that they had a plan to get him back into his body? Would he believe her, or would he think she was a lunatic and avoid her in the future?

"What am I going to do when they pull the plug?" Harry asked.

"They're not going to pull the plug," she said, patting his knee like he was a small child who had just lost his first little league game. She still didn't know what she was going to do with him.

He looked at her in desperation, and said, "Seven days, Emma, that's all he gave us. And four of them are already gone!"

"What are you talking about?"

"George's living will, his advanced directive with the hospital," he replied, as if she should already know about this, but was being deliberately dense.

She looked at George in confusion, then back at Harry before asking, "What living will?"

"Aw, shit..." George muttered.

And then he started running his hands through his hair. So, not a good sign.

"George made a living will that states specifically that should he ever end up incapacitated, they could only take seven days to snap him out of it, otherwise he wants them to pull the plug. The clock started ticking when he went into the coma, and now we only have three days left."

She gasped in shock, and her heart stuttered for a beat. She didn't know anything about a living will, and she had thought she knew everything about George. Everything.

She knew about his secret letters to Big Brothers Big Sisters. She knew that he hated romance novels. She knew that he ran his fingers through his hair when he was frustrated or working out a problem. She even knew that he would never be happy with a woman like Crystal.

But she hadn't known about a living will.

"Why didn't you tell me?" she asked quietly.

"Would it have mattered?" George responded. But there was a defensive note to his tone.

"I'm telling you now," Harry responded at the same time.

"Three more days," she said, ignoring them both as she counted on her hand. Then her heart sank as she realized the day they would be pulling the plug on George. "But that's on Christmas Day!"

Harry took her hands and asked, "What am I going to do without him, Emma? And what will happen to this company? I can't run this company, and everybody knows it. I can't even run my life without George."

She'd had enough. She straightened with determination, then stood up, looked down at Harry and said frankly, "First, you're going to start acting like a responsible adult for a change, and take an interest in this company."

She went over to George's desk to retrieve the stack of manuscripts. She was done with whiny Harry, even if he was adorable. It was time for him to start pulling his weight around here. She needed him. The company needed him. And most important of all, George needed him.

"What am I supposed to do with this?" Harry asked, gaping at the stack when she tried to hand it to him.

Yep, adorable. But dumb as a post.

"You're going to read these, and do a report on them—a useful report," she responded in her best teacher speaking with authority voice. And she could have sworn she heard a chuckle coming from George's direction.

"Emma—" Harry started to argue.

"No whining, Harry. Suck it up," she said, interrupting him because she wasn't putting up with his bull crap this time.

She must have finally gotten through to him because he took the manuscripts from her and stood up.

"Come on, I'll drive you home," she said, when she noticed he still swayed slightly.

"What about George?" Harry asked uncertainly.

She looked at George, then back at Harry, and finally said, "You leave George to me. Nobody's pulling any plug on Christmas Day—"

"Emma—" George interrupted with a warning tone.

"Nobody," she stated emphatically. "I don't care what any stupid living will says."

"What do you think you can possibly do in three days that the doctors haven't already done?" George asked her.

All she knew was that she wasn't going to lose George because of some lame-ass living will that he wrote. Nope. She wasn't sure yet what she was going to do, but she was definitely going to do something.

"I'm really sorry about...before," Harry said with a sheepish expression on his charming face.

"It's okay, Harry," she said, patting him on the arm. The poor guy had no idea which way was up or down, and she could certainly understand that. "We'll just chalk it up to the alcohol and forget it ever happened."

"Although, if you ever want to try that kiss again when I'm sober," Harry began.

"Harry..." she chided him. But she grinned in spite of herself, knowing that she couldn't stay mad at him, especially with all that he was going through right now.

"Harry!" George shouted at the same time.

"You're an amazing woman, Emma," Harry said, and this time he patted her on the arm.

She steadied him as he swayed again, and led him out of the office to take him home. She knew the poor guy was going to regret all of this in the morning. He was going to have one doozy of a headache tomorrow, what with the alcohol and George's electric punch, and that was punishment enough.

She noticed that George was still in his office, pacing and back to running his fingers through his hair. He looked like he was taking a cooling-off period, which was just fine with her, since she wasn't sure how she was going to be able to yell at him in front of Harry.

"Do you remember that manuscript you forced on me last week?" Harry asked as they reached the elevator, sans a still-fuming George. "The suspense thriller by a kid named Dean Erickson? It was really good, Em."

"The one George tossed into my garbage and swore we'd never publish?" She wondered again why George would do such a crazy thing.

"Yes, but he obviously hadn't read it yet, because he would never have passed on it. It's brilliant, Em, absolutely brilliant. A bestseller for sure.

We can make a fortune with this author, especially if we can sign him for a series." The adrenaline must have kicked in, because Harry seemed more sober than before, and he was genuinely excited. "This is what I can do to pull my weight while George is…out. I can work this deal, and prove myself with it. And when George wakes up, he'll be proud of me instead of always so disappointed in me."

"George isn't disappointed in you. You're his brother, and he loves you," she said, and hoped that he believed it, because she knew it was true.

"Although he's not too happy with him right at the moment," George said from right beside her, causing her to jump slightly. Luckily, Harry wasn't paying any attention, obviously still lost in his thoughts about the Erickson manuscript.

It looked like George had worked through his fuming stage, although his hair was a disheveled—albeit sexy—mess, and had successfully downgraded himself to somewhere closer to smoldering.

"We just need to find your strengths, and play to those," she continued, speaking to Harry, as if George hadn't just shown up and scared the bejeezus out of her once again. "If you think this manuscript is worth it, I'll help you with it."

"Thanks, Emma. I can always count on you. I'm going to set up an appointment with him first thing tomorrow," Harry said, and he smiled his trademark panty-igniting smile at her.

Good thing it didn't have quite the same effect on her as it did on ninety-nine percent of the other women he used it with.

"That's good," George said. "Get him working on our award-winning author. It's pretty much a given. Even he can't screw that one up." Apparently George wasn't quite finished being angry with Harry.

That was just fine with her, because she wasn't even remotely finished being angry with George.

CHAPTER TEN

Emma unlocked her apartment, went inside, then slammed the door behind her, forcing George to pass through it in order to follow her. She had wanted to slam it right in his face, but that wasn't easy to do while he was an incorporeal being. Kind of diminished the effect.

"Emma, are we going to talk about this?" he asked, for about the trillionth time since they had left the office.

"I'm not sure what there is to say." She was pissed. Royally pissed. How could he not have told her about the living will directive? She could understand that he wouldn't have told her in the two years that she had been working for him—it wasn't like that subject came up often between a boss and his assistant. But now that he was in a coma, and the clock was ticking, and he'd asked for her help? He should have told her.

She hung up her coat and headed to her bedroom. He followed, but she turned at the door and held up a warning finger.

"Boundaries. Got it," he said. He stepped back out of her bedroom, but stayed just outside the doorway in order to continue to talk to her. "You aren't exactly being fair here."

"Fair? Fair? I'm the one not being fair?" Was he kidding? More confused and angry than she could deal with, she paced her bedroom, not even pretending she had a purpose to distract her.

"Emma—" he started.

"You know what?" she interrupted. "You need to go be somewhere else, because I'm so upset with you right now I can't even see straight."

"Come on, Emma, what are you going to do, shoot me?" He grinned at her.

Humor? At a time like this? Was he serious? He thought humor—stupid, dumb, jerk-humor at that—would help? She took a moment to glare at him while determining her options, and saw a flash of concern in his eyes.

"You're right."

"There, you see?" he said, looking relieved. "I knew we could—"

"I'll go somewhere else. You stay here. Don't follow me."

She needed to get away and clear her head. She needed to talk to someone about this who could help her sort through the emotions that were threatening to spill over.

She stormed out of the apartment in search of that person.

* * * * * * *

She desperately needed to see George, which was ironic because she couldn't stand being in the same room with him at the moment.

Lord, she was a walking contradiction. She felt betrayed, and hurt, and a whole lot of other raw emotions she didn't want to name in case it brought them to the surface. And every last one of them completely overwhelmed her.

So she'd decided to visit George's body in the hospital, hoping to sort things out in her head, if not her heart. The room was too warm, and it had caused the windows to fog up, but she could see the blur of twinkling holiday lights just outside in the courtyard, and it felt mystical.

She loved him. If anything, her feelings for him had deepened during their time spent together. She'd always felt those jittery, butterflies in her stomach every time she'd seen him before, but now, she knew she really loved him. She drew a heart in the steam on the window, as if trying to make a statement—something that was tangible, and permanent, at least until it seeped into a blurry mess.

But she was angry with him, too. How could he not have told her? He had practically demanded that she help him get back into his body, and he never once mentioned that there was a ticking time bomb if she failed. Had he thought it would be too much pressure on her, and she'd refuse to help him?

What an ass. He should have told her. She didn't care what his reasoning was, she had a right to know. Whether he admitted it or not, they were now way past the formal relationship of boss and assistant—she didn't exactly know what that relationship was, but it was more than that—and she shouldn't have had to hear it from his brother.

She sat on the bed next to George's body and was scared to see all the wires and needles hooked to machines that kept him alive. The breathing tube in his mouth made her heart jolt in panic. She couldn't look at it. So she stared at his closed eyes instead, willing them to open.

They didn't.

"Why, George? Why didn't you tell me? And why did you put such a stupid condition on your life?"

She still couldn't understand the drastic measures he had taken to be sure he didn't survive. She understood that people didn't want to be left on life support indefinitely. But seven days? Seven days wasn't enough time for anything. How could anyone figure anything out in only seven days? Did he have a God complex or something?

No. He was a good man, who didn't have a narcissistic bone in his body. She couldn't love someone who only thought of himself. And she did love him.

"What am I supposed to do now?" she asked the body in the bed, hoping he'd give her a response. "There isn't enough time. What do I do? Tell me what to do. I can't lose you, George. You big, dumb, stupid idiot. What were you thinking? What am I going to do?"

She slowly laid her head down on his chest and cried.

* * * * * * *

He paced Emma's apartment, unsure about what to do to fix the rift with her. Should he try to find her? Or would that make matters worse, since she had been very clear that she did not want him to follow her? Or was this one of those times when women secretly really did want you to follow them?

He was going out of his mind. He was worried, and he needed to know she was okay. He wasn't used to feeling like this.

He rubbed his chest, feeling an ache, but also a small pressure. Not a painful pressure, but a slight weight in the middle of his chest.

Suddenly, he understood, and he was filled with remorse. Then, just as suddenly, the emotion changed to hope. She hadn't left him. And she was safe.

Because he knew, exactly, where she was.

CHAPTER ELEVEN

Standing outside the door to her apartment, Emma felt emotionally drained, but she was gathering up the nerve to go inside and talk to George. She had no idea how she was going to face him. She felt guilty for being so angry with him—he was only her boss and he didn't owe her any explanations, let alone have to keep her posted on his personal decisions—but she still couldn't help feeling that she had been betrayed.

Steeling herself for whatever he might have to say to her, she went inside.

He was pacing the living room, and if the mess of his hair was any indication, he had been running his fingers through it. A lot. That couldn't be a good sign.

"Emma." He whispered her name with what sounded like relief. He stopped pacing and stared at her.

She gave him an attempt at a smile as she walked past him and headed to her bedroom, stalling for more time. She started going through the motions of getting herself ready for bed, but in her periphery she saw a very concerned George leaning against the doorjamb, waiting.

Had he really been concerned about her? Or was he just worried that the only person who knew he was a ghost had left him alone for so long? Her heart went out to him, and he was obviously still trying to respect her boundary rules. He had also respected her wishes (more like her demand) that he not follow her when she left earlier. Maybe that was all a good sign?

"True, I didn't tell you about the living will deadline," he said, breaking the silence between them. "But then again, you didn't tell me about your little thing on the side with Harry either."

"Stop making it sound like we were having an affair. It was strictly business, and you know it." There wasn't much heat in her words. She was too tired to argue with him over it. Besides, he knew darn well there was nothing going on with Harry, and she wished he would stop implying otherwise. Was he trying to push her toward Harry?

"Yes, but you weren't exactly forthcoming with me either, were you." It was a statement, not a question.

She sighed and slumped down onto her bed, too tired to try to make sense of any of it. Besides, he was right. She hadn't told him about taking on Harry's share of the manuscripts.

"Okay. Point taken. But what now? How am I supposed to help you figure out what it all means to you if they're…you know…on Christmas Day? Kinda defeats the purpose of a merry Christmas, doesn't it?"

Apparently deciding to give up on the boundary rules, he came into her room and sat next to her on the bed. That was fine, she needed him to be closer anyway. Even as a ghost, she still wanted his company.

"It doesn't really matter, Emma. You know I hate Christmas anyway," he said, bluntly.

"But you're going to love Christmas Eve dinner with my family. We—"

"Hang on," he interrupted. "I never agreed to go to your family's for Christmas Eve dinner."

"Of course you're going with me." Hadn't they already decided this?

"No, I'm not. I absolutely do not do Christmas Eve dinner. I haven't since I was ten so I'm not about to do it now." Then he left the room.

Ten? He hadn't celebrated Christmas since he was ten?

"Yes you are!" She got up and followed him, not about to let him cave on her. "That's the whole point to this. To get you into the Christmas spirit so you can stop being a…spirit!"

But he was apparently just as determined in his decision, because he sat down on the couch and said nothing.

Geez, he was a stubborn man.

She didn't want to fight. But she knew, deep down, to the very core of her being, that he had to go to Christmas Eve dinner with her. She knew this had

89

to be what they needed to do to get him back into his body. He needed to work through whatever his hang-up was, and seeing her family and all their traditions would be exactly what he needed to reconnect.

But it looked like arguing with him was not going to be the way to get him to change his mind, so she needed to find a different form of attack.

"What does Christmas mean to you?"

"It doesn't mean anything to me. That's my whole point."

"But we need to figure that out, before they—" she choked off, unable to finish the sentence. She couldn't say it out loud, out of fear that it would make it true.

He stood up and faced her. "You aren't listening to me. It. Doesn't. Matter." He spat each word out in frustration. "Even if you hound me into figuring out the 'meaning of Christmas' and I return to my body, I'm still in a coma."

"No, the reason you're in a coma is—" she started to say, but he cut her off.

"There's no guarantee I'll snap out of the coma. The directive still stands, and they will pull the plug."

She gasped as if he had slapped her across the face. Horrified, she finally realized what he was saying to her.

"You don't care," she said in a whisper. Because saying it any louder might somehow give it more power.

"This is what I've been trying—"

Frightened by his attitude, she stood to meet him face to face, and said, "You don't care if you never wake up. It isn't just Christmas that doesn't mean anything to you."

"It isn't like that. Christ, you make me sound suicidal."

"Not suicidal." She took a good, long, look at him. "Just...empty inside. No wonder Christmas has no meaning for you."

He ran his fingers through his hair, and she knew he was struggling, but she couldn't let him simply give up. Just like Harry, she wasn't sure how she would be able to get along without him.

"For God's sake, Emma, I'm just being practical." He looked at her as if that explained everything. But she could see that he was still struggling with balancing what he felt against what she was saying to him.

"You have to come with me for Christmas Eve dinner." She was desperate to make him change his mind. "I don't know what happened to you that you are this way, but you need to come with me so I can show you—"

"No," he said with finality. "I'm not going with you."

"Yes. You. Are."

She was done coddling, and she was done arguing, and she was done pleading. He would go with her if she had to drag him there. Even though she didn't know how she would accomplish that if she couldn't touch him.

"And just how do you think you're going to make me?"

Damn it. Stubborn and smart.

Fine. If he was going to act like a petulant child, she was going to treat him like a petulant child. He was getting a time out. They always worked on Marlie's kids. She gave him a sad look, then slowly, but deliberately, turned away from him. She went into her bedroom and closed the door on him.

* * * * * * *

She hadn't thought there were any tears left after her trip to the hospital, but apparently they were endless, because she couldn't stop herself from crying into her pillow. She was going to indulge in one last good, cathartic cry for one more minute, and then she was going to go to sleep.

And tomorrow, she was going to give him the silent treatment to end all silent treatments. She wasn't going to crack until he gave in and came with her to Christmas Eve dinner.

She hated to do it, but this was too important, and she didn't know what else to do. She'd never had to deal with this particular problem before—it wasn't as though anyone had written a DIY manual for how to deal with pigheaded ghosts—but she couldn't just give up. She had to keep trying, because he had apparently already given up.

"Emma?" George's tentative voice came through the closed door.

She caught her breath, and then held perfectly still, hoping he would give up and go away. If she responded, or let him come in, she would capitulate, and he would never get back to his body in time.

"Emma? Are you okay?" His voice sounded like he was genuinely concerned, and she almost caved.

"Em?"

He was silent for a few moments (which felt more like hours), and she imagined that he must be standing close, and listening through her door.

"I'm sorry about the deadline, and especially that it's on Christmas Day. And I'm sorry I didn't tell you about it before."

She bit her lip to keep from calling out. Tears started flooding her eyes again, and she wasn't sure she could remain resolute in her time out. Was it this hard for Marlie, too?

"Emma?"

She heard the fear in his voice, but she pulled a pillow over her head to muffle the sound and cried herself to sleep.

CHAPTER TWELVE

Emma glided up to the reception area at Landon Literary as if she hadn't a care in the world. At least, she hoped that was how she looked. She was doing her best to block out the grumpy ghost who followed her, but it wasn't easy.

"Morning, Sandy." She spoke in her sweetest voice, and smiled brightly for emphasis.

"So, you're being nice to everyone but me now, is that it?"

"Morning, Emma. Heard anything on George yet?"

"No, I haven't heard anything. But I'll keep you posted as we get updates." She continued on to her area to start her morning routine, which now included blocking out her boss.

She was even more convinced this morning that she needed to get tough with him, and this was the only solution she had been able to come up with to accomplish that. She knew that it was also a huge risk, considering all the time that would be wasted if it didn't work, but she was out of options. She only hoped he came to his senses before too much time passed, because she knew she'd probably crack after about one day of this. She missed talking to him already.

"I know what you're trying to do, and it isn't going to work," he said, as if he could read her mind. He materialized directly in her path, and grinned at her.

She worked very hard at not melting into a puddle at his feet—he was just so handsome when he grinned at her like that. Resolutely not looking at him, she turned and went to her desk to turn on her computer.

"Fine. I can wait you out."

She sincerely hoped that wouldn't be the case.

He leaned against her desk and stared at her. Flustered, but careful not to show it, she picked up her tablet and went into his office to get away from him, but he followed closely behind. "You can't just ignore me completely. I know you, Emma Anderson. You'll crack eventually. You are far too social a being to ignore someone for very long."

He was right, of course; she would crack. But not yet.

Determined more than ever to prove him wrong, and because there was too much at stake, she sat at his desk and started reading the stack of manuscripts. She watched out of the corner of her eye as he sat down on the couch, stretching his long legs out to get comfortable. He acted as if he had all the time in the world.

And he watched her.

Not too nerve-wracking.

* * * * * * *

After a couple of stressful hours of pretending to ignore George—who was she kidding, no one could ignore George—she came to the conclusion that the silent treatment with a ghost wasn't as easy as it sounded, and she was starting to feel the strain of having him constantly watching her.

Her other problem was that she was going to have to go meet Harry and the new author he was wooing, and she didn't want George coming along and distracting her. But she couldn't tell him to get lost if she wasn't talking to him.

"Damn it, Emma!" George bellowed, causing her to jump slightly in her chair. "Two can play at this game, you know. I can damn well just leave you to stew in your own juices all by yourself."

Well, that would certainly solve her dilemma easily enough. If he left on his own, she wouldn't have to try to get rid of him. For some reason, she was sure he would cause trouble for her in Harry's meeting. Call her silly, but what with him being a ghost and all, it was bound to become an issue in some way.

"Fine. If you're going to be in a snit, you can just do it alone." Then he left the room.

He didn't use the door, he just vanished into thin air, and that was very disturbing to see. She had no idea where he was planning to go, but she wouldn't worry about it. Much.

She decided to head down to Harry's office a little early so that he could fill her in on his game plan, and she could make sure there was coffee, and maybe a few snacks available for the visiting author.

She knocked on Harry's office door, then opened it and went inside.

"I thought I'd come by early to go over—" She stopped dead in her tracks and gaped.

Crystal was straddling Harry's chair—while Harry was sitting in it!

"Emma! Come in. Please, come in." Harry sounded as if he was strangling, and he definitely didn't look like he was enjoying Crystal's advances.

The Evil Queen turned her head and gave Emma a look that could have single-handedly reversed the melting of the polar ice cap, but Emma was made of sterner stuff. Wasn't this woman supposed to be in love with George? Just what in God's name was she doing attacking poor, innocent Harry?

"Crystal," she said, calmly, as she advanced on the woman, ready to pull her by the hair if she had to in order to get her off of Harry's lap. "Did I somehow miss that you had an appointment here at Landon Literary? Or did you somehow miss that you are in the wrong Landon's literary office?" She waited for a beat to let it sink in that the EQ's reign was about to end, before she continued. "You have two seconds to remove your person from this office, and then this building, before I call security and have them remove it for you."

"How dare you talk to me like that, you little nothing of a—" Crystal began, but Harry finally grew a backbone and stood up, effectively dropping Crystal where she stood—literally.

"Don't even think about speaking to Emma like that. Get out."

"You don't have the authority." With the grace of a pageant contestant, Crystal adjusted herself to regain her footing. It was not an easy thing to do in five-inch stilettos, and Emma had to admit a begrudging respect for—hang on, no she didn't. She didn't respect the woman at all. She reached out and casually knocked the bitch back over just as she was starting to stand.

"Funny," Harry said, although he looked anything but amused. "You didn't seem to believe that a minute ago when you were talking about the two of us and what we could accomplish here together in George's absence." His hands were clenched into fists at his sides, as if he were restraining himself from throwing Crystal out the window. Instead, he took her by the elbow, hauled her to her feet, and unceremoniously escorted her out his door. "Don't come back."

But as he started to slam the door on her, she blocked it and glared at Emma. "Don't even think about mentioning any of this to George. Who do you think he's going to believe? The girl who does his filing? Or the woman who shares his bed?"

Then she looked Emma up and down as if she resembled something she'd just scraped off her shoe, and slammed the door closed when she left.

Eewww. Emma wanted to bleach her brain to clear the image of George in bed with that woman. She decided to turn her mind to happier thoughts. Like George finally getting rid of Crystal once and for all.

"Nice job, Harry, I am enormously proud of you. That has to be the first woman in the history of the world who has been dumped by Harry Landon."

"Oh, come on, I've dumped lots of women."

"True. But literally, as well as figuratively? And at the same time? Not when I was there to see it. Thank you for that."

She couldn't help herself; she laughed until tears were rolling down her cheeks. She was so happy that horrible woman was finally put in her place. Ding-dong, the witch was dead. There was no way George would marry her now.

"We can never tell George about this." And just like that, Harry completely burst her happiness bubble.

"Why the hell not?" She finally had the goods on Crystal—even better, someone other than herself who could tell George about it—and he was going to hoard his secret? No. No way.

"He honestly believes that Crystal is a good match for him." Harry slumped back into his chair and looked like his whole world had been turned upside down. "She's a conniving lunatic bitch, but I can't be the one to tell George about her. Do you know, she actually told me that I was the one she really wanted all along, and now that George is in a coma, we could finally be together? Who says shit like that? To a grieving brother? Did she think I wouldn't tell him that? I can't tell him that."

"You realize you aren't making any sense, right?"

"There is no way I'm going to be the one to tell him about this. You have to tell him."

"Are you out of your mind? You heard what she said. It has to be you." How was she going to convince Harry that he was the one who had to spill the beans? She would look like the jealous competition if she tried to tell George, and he wouldn't buy it. It had to come from his brother. He was the only one George would listen to about it.

"He already knows that I hate his girlfriend, we've discussed it. He told me to suck it up and stop ragging on her, because basically she's the one for him. I can't tell him she's a duplicitous, manipulative, two-timing, conniving—"

"You've used conniving already," she cut in to stop him, because they wouldn't get anywhere with him ranting. "Look, I get that you don't want him to be mad at you, but you still have to tell him. Suppose he marries her. How are you going to like having her for a sister-in-law?"

"Sweet Jesus. You're right."

She tapped her foot impatiently, but let him sit there for a few minutes while he tried to wrap his head around a world that involved seeing Crystal on a regular basis.

"Okay. Okay, I'll tell him after he's out of the coma, and back on his feet again."

"It has to be right when he wakes up."

"Not when he wakes up. We don't want a relapse. Right?"

"Fine. But the minute she starts maneuvering herself back into his life, you have to set him straight. We can't give her time to—"

Sandy's voice spoke through Harry's desk phone, "Harry, you have a Dean and Anna Erickson here to see you. Should I send them back to you?"

"Yes, please, Sandy. Thank you." Harry looked flustered—no, not flustered, he looked excited—as he stood up from his chair and pulled on his suit jacket, which had been hanging on the back of it. "Erickson brought his sister with him. And she's also his agent. Have you seen his sister? This should be fun."

He wagged his eyebrows and grinned at Emma, and she knew the poor woman was going to be Harry Toast in a matter of about ten minutes. Harry had obviously found his next hot pursuit.

"Okay, so, there's nothing to be nervous about." She wasn't sure who she was giving the pep-talk to, herself or Harry, but she felt she needed to say something before the author arrived.

"Nervous? Why do you say that? I'm not nervous, I've got this." He certainly looked confident enough, and he winked at her for good measure. Oh, yeah, she could see that he was on top of his game. This was going to be a piece of cake.

She turned at the sound of the door opening, and she found herself face to face with Dean Erickson. He was dressed in black jeans and a sweater, and he held himself as if he owned the air he breathed. He was younger than she had expected him to be—maybe in his early thirties. He had rich, chocolate-brown hair, and a pair of deep, dark-blue eyes. She couldn't place him, but for some reason, he looked vaguely familiar, and she wondered where she had seen him before. Maybe in Stan's coffee shop?

"You must be Dean. Hi, I'm Emma. I'm George Landon's assistant, but I'm helping Harry out today." She shook Dean's hand then stepped back from the door and gestured both the Ericksons inside Harry's office. "You're Anna, right? I'm Emma."

She shook Anna's hand as she came in behind Dean, and Emma found herself looking into an amber-colored pair of the coldest eyes that she had ever seen. They looked like they could drill lasers into a person's mind, and filter through all of your dirtiest secrets.

Harry shook hands with Dean, and exchanged a moment of guy-camaraderie before he turned his attention to Anna.

"Anna. Nice to see you again," he said, and Emma could practically see him licking his chops.

To say that Anna was beautiful was equivalent to calling the Grand Canyon a minor pothole—the woman was drop-dead gorgeous. But something was missing in the way that she held herself. She stood ramrod straight, and looked like she would break if she tried to sit down. There was no welcoming warmth in her expression, as there had been in her brother's.

But Emma could also see the interest that sparked in Anna's eyes as they gave Harry a brief once-over. It was that "Holy cow!" look of interest that Emma had seen on so many women's faces whenever they met him for the first time. It was probably the same look she'd had on her own face when she'd met George for the first time, too.

"Mr. Landon." Anna's voice sounded cold and unfriendly. She had covered her initial reaction well, and was making it clear that she was strictly business moving forward.

Oh, yeah, Anna was going to be a challenge for Harry, and Emma was looking forward to the show. But if she knew Harry—and she did know Harry—Anna might as well have posted a "Welcome" sign on her forehead, because he was going to want to pick up her gauntlet, and melt that iceberg.

She just hoped he didn't end up as the Titanic instead, because she could see that he might have finally met his match. Anna didn't strike her as someone who would fall for Harry's standard smooth-talking charm.

"So, Anna," Harry said, deliberately ignoring Anna's cool demeanor. "Big plans for Christmas at the Erickson house?" Harry gestured for all of them to have a seat around the sectional couch that took up a large corner of his office.

The glass coffee table in front of the couch had been set up with coffee, fresh fruit and juices, and a variety of danishes and pastries. He began piling a plate for himself with food, and Emma knew it was a gesture to help make his guests feel relaxed, and to follow his lead, so she helped him by pouring coffee into mugs embossed with the Landon Literary logo.

"No, we usually just have a quiet dinner with my mom on Christmas Eve," Dean responded after a brief hesitation when it was clear that Anna wasn't participating in the conversation. "We don't really celebrate much now that our dad is gone. Christmas was really his holiday."

"Well, we appreciate you coming in to meet with us so close to the holidays." Emma had to give Harry big kudos for not being intimidated by the cold shoulder treatment he was getting from Anna.

"Let's not waste everyone's time, and just cut to the chase then, shall we?" Anna asked, apparently done with the banter portion of the show. "As you already mentioned, it's close to the holidays, and there's no need to prolong this whole thing with small talk."

"Okay, sure." Harry was no pushover, and he knew what he was doing, so Emma wasn't surprised when, as if from nowhere, he produced a folder and handed it to Dean. "I've worked up a contract for you already. Why don't you take a look at it, and let us know what you think. Take your time with it, and we can set up another time to meet again to hash out the details."

Emma was glad to see that he wasn't going to let Anna's bully tactic dictate how his meeting was going to go. She had not yet seen this side of Harry before, and she was impressed that he could be a businessman as well as a sweet talker.

"As his agent, I'm—" Anna started to say, but was interrupted when Dean put his hand on her arm and stopped her.

"That would be great, thank you. Anna and I will take a look at it, and we can get back to you."

Then Dean, apparently oblivious to the flash of anger directed toward him from his sister—what was that all about?—turned to Emma and smiled.

"You mentioned that you work with George. What must that be like? I hear he's a tough man to get to know."

"Yes, I work with George, and I'm very happy with him—er, working with him. He's a great boss." It wasn't unusual for people to ask her about George, but she was surprised by his abrupt change in subject. And why was he looking at her like that? Was that interest she saw in those deep-blue eyes?

"Maybe we could get together later for a drink and dinner to celebrate our new partnership with Landon Literary?"

What? Had he just asked her out?

"That's a great idea, Dean," Harry said, brilliantly hijacking the invitation, and saving Emma from having to answer. "Why don't we meet up tonight for dinner, and we can go over the contract then. Anna, are you free?"

Dean looked nonplussed, and a scowl crossed his handsome face in such a quick flash that Emma almost missed it when she turned to look at Anna's reaction. Anna blushed, and was obviously surprised by Harry's attention. Score one point for Harry for momentarily knocking her off her game.

"I don't believe that would be—" Anna started to say, but was again interrupted by her brother.

"Yes. That sounds fine." Although Emma could see that he was anything but fine about it. Why was he so angry? He was the one who'd started this date thing in the first place.

"Anna, what's your favorite food?" Harry was pulling out all the stops in order to get her on his good side.

"Pizza." Anna smirked, and Emma was sure she had picked it specifically to throw Harry off. Business dinners were normally more formal than pizza, even in Denver where everything was much more casual.

"Great. I love pizza, too, we have that in common." He smiled at Anna, and she blinked back at him as if she thought he might be joking. "And I know just the place. They have the best Chicago-style pizza you can possibly get outside of Chicago itself."

He looked around the room, and received general nods from everyone, even though they all seemed confused by the abrupt turn of events. "I'll have a car sent around to your hotel at seven. Now that all the logistics are settled, at least for the time being, how about we have some of that idle chit-chat we skipped earlier, and finish our coffee together."

Harry sat back in his chair, grinned his panty-igniting smile at Anna, and sipped his coffee as if he had all the time in the world to sit around and gossip.

Anna looked back at him with a suspicious scowl on her face, and Emma had to hold back a laugh. Until she looked over at Dean, who was glaring so intently at Harry that her laugh died in her throat.

* * * * * * *

She closed the manuscript she was reading, stretched in George's chair, and glanced at her watch to see how much time she had before she needed to leave to meet her sisters. She hadn't wanted to go out for pizza with Harry and the Ericksons, but Harry had practically gotten on his knees to beg her. There was no reason that he couldn't go without her, but he had told her that she needed to keep Dean occupied while he worked on Anna to get the best deal for Landon Literary.

Emma wanted to call bullcrap on that, because she knew he just wanted to work on Anna, period, but in the end, she had agreed. Because, let's face it, who could say no to either of the Landon brothers when they were determined?

Overall, meeting with the Ericksons had gone very well, and she was convinced that Harry had been right about Dean as a new author. The guy had charisma, and a fluid writing style that would appeal to a wide audience of both men and women. His first book was going to be a huge success, and Harry had handled himself like an expert with him.

He had handled Anna very well, too. If Emma didn't know better, Harry looked like he had finally met someone who wouldn't let him get away with anything. She was beautiful, clever, and intelligent, and, from the looks of it, she wasn't falling for any of his patented moves. He had looked stunned by her.

She wished that George could have seen how well Harry had done. He would have been proud of his younger brother.

As if conjured by her thoughts, the ghost himself materialized in his office, and looked around briefly, trying to locate her. She had missed having him around, and almost forgot that she was giving him the silent treatment.

"Are you done pouting?" She knew that he was trying for a sneer in his tone, but his face looked too hopeful, and his words came out sounding more desperate than he had probably been going for. She almost laughed, but caught herself just in time, and began putting on her winter boots and coat as if she hadn't heard him.

He followed her to the elevator and scowled at her. She was getting to him, she was sure of it, and that was a good thing. It was only a matter of time before one of them cracked.

"Calling it a day?" Sandy asked.

"Yep. I'm going to go meet my family at the mall to visit Santa." She hoped she sounded more enthusiastic than she felt.

"Oh, that sounds fun!" Sandy gushed, at the same time George grumbled, "Oh, that sounds like a nightmare!"

Truth be told, she wasn't all that fond of visiting Santa, but it was a family tradition with the kids, and she didn't want to miss it, so she kept up the pretense every year. "Yep, don't want to miss the kids getting to see Santa!"

The elevator dinged its arrival, and she smiled and waved goodbye to Sandy before getting into it.

CHAPTER THIRTEEN

Emma was standing with Marlie, Laura, Spencer, Jessica, Tommy, Carrie, and Michelle at the front of a very long line of parents and kids waiting to see Santa at an elaborate Santa's Village. Although her body was shuffling along with the rest of group, her head wasn't with them—she was wracking her brain trying to come up with a way to ditch George tonight so that he wouldn't follow her on her "date" with Harry and the Ericksons.

How was she going to tell him to get lost if she wasn't speaking to him? Then again, if she wasn't speaking to him, maybe he would just get pissy like he had this afternoon and disappear again, which would solve her problem. She sighed. This ghost stuff was getting on her nerves.

If this didn't mean so much to Harry, she wouldn't be doing it, but she knew how much he needed to prove himself, not only to George and the company, but to himself as well. He was going to owe her big for this one, though. Plus, he was getting the extra bonus of wooing Anna in the process. What was she getting out of this? Nothing but a headache.

She pulled out of her own thoughts, and looked around to try to be more engaged in the moment with the kids. The village stood in the center of the mall, and looked almost as if a piece of the North Pole had been scooped up, then plopped down into this very affluent section of Denver.

The section of the North Pole that had arrived in Cherry Creek this year came complete with its own miniature ice rink where children and their parents were sliding around, laughing and falling, after having already had their pictures taken with Santa.

Santa sat under a structure made to look so much like an ice castle that she'd felt compelled to touch it as they had gotten closer, just to be sure. She wasn't sure what material it was made out of, but she assumed it had to have cost a small fortune to construct. Santa was surrounded by friendly, helpful elves who assisted the kids in taking turns to sit on his lap and tell him their every desire.

The two kids of the couple in front of Emma were getting their pictures taken with Santa and the elves. It was going to make a lovely family Christmas card, she thought absently. Out of the corner of her eye, she saw that George stood to the side of the village watching everything with a horrified expression on his face, and she almost felt sorry for him.

Poor George. This was most likely the first experience he'd ever had with visiting Santa, as she imagined he had been born without the genetic predisposition toward the belief in Santa's existence.

As their group got closer to Santa, Jessica started to squirm. Emma looked down at her in concern, and asked, "Jessica? You okay, sweetie?"

Jessica nodded her head, but there was clearly something she was upset about, and her squirming became more frantic. They went through this same routine together every year—just as Jessica got close enough to Santa to really see him, she would completely shut down in fear.

"Jessica? You said you wanted to see Santa this year," Marlie said, with a hint of impatience in her voice.

Jessica nodded unconvincingly again, and Emma took her hand to pull her out of the line.

"It's okay, Marlie, I'll stay with her. We'll just be over there."

She led Jessica out of the line and off to the side to sit on a bench. Jessica was fighting the urge to cry, and Emma's heart went out to her. She was so intent on the need to help Jessica that she didn't notice George had followed behind.

"Not a big Santa fan?" Emma asked Jessica.

Jessica shook her head in response, then said, "I'm really sorry, Aunt Emma."

She put her arm around her niece and hugged her. Sometimes it bothered her that there was so much pressure on kids to love Santa.

"Oh, honey, don't worry. Wanna hear a secret?" Jessica nodded enthusiastically, probably hoping to deflect the attention away from herself and her panic attack. Emma leaned closer, and whispered into her ear. "Santa scares me, too."

"Really?" Jessica looked up at her with something close to hero worship.

"Well, not the real Santa. Just these helpers who dress up like him to help him out because he can't be everywhere at the same time."

"But won't the real Santa be mad that we don't like his helpers?" Jessica asked, still apparently concerned about being in trouble with someone.

She gave Jessica another hug and reassured her. "No, honey, the real Santa is warm and kind, and understanding."

"I'm glad, because I don't want to hurt his feelings."

Her niece had a kind and sweet heart, and Emma loved that about her. Her own heart warmed in empathy as she smiled reassuringly and gave her one more hug. Jessica crawled into her lap, and she wondered if she should ask her what she wanted for Christmas, but she didn't want to possibly ruin such a nice moment with her niece. So they sat there quietly together, just enjoying each other's company, and their mutual secret, and waited for the rest of the group to join them.

* * * * * * *

George watched as Emma hugged—several times—and comforted her niece, and he felt a pang of remorse. Where had someone like Emma been for him when he was Jessica's age—that nurturing someone who would understand what he was going through, give him a hug, and make sense of everything for him?

His thoughts were interrupted as Marlie, Laura, and the rest of the group joined Emma and Jessica after they were through getting their turns in with Santa.

Jessica appeared much happier now that she was over the trauma, and he watched with what felt a bit like jealousy. He wasn't proud of it, but he was jealous of Jessica being able to physically interact with Emma. Or maybe it was because he still felt the deep-seated loss of such genuine affection in his own life; he wasn't sure.

"Thanks for waiting with me, Aunt Emma," Jessica said.

And his heart beat a little faster when he saw Emma smile warmly back at her niece before joining the group as they started leaving.

"Anytime, sweetie, anytime," Emma said.

Marlie gave Emma a look that he could clearly read in the unvoiced *everything okay?* expression on her face. Emma gave her a reassuring *we'll talk about it later* wink, and the group headed away from the village.

He watched the scene with genuine affection, and wondered if he and Harry could speak volumes to each other with a single look, as Emma could with her sisters.

CHAPTER FOURTEEN

Her ploy to stay in her room to get ready—and thus annoy George enough to make him want to disappear for something to do somewhere else—had apparently been more successful than she had imagined, because when she emerged minutes before it was time to leave, she found her apartment empty of any supernatural beings.

She paid the cab driver twenty dollars as she got out, and made a mental note to expense this back to Landon Literary. She had initially thought she would drive, but parking in Cherry Creek North was far more trouble than the expense of a cab ride. Besides, if she was going to have to help Harry with business (never mind his dating practices), the company was certainly going to reimburse her for it. Harry had offered to send a limo for her, too, but she was worried about having to explain it showing up at her apartment building to George if her plan to get rid of him didn't work.

All in all, it looked like things were going her way, and she was starting to relax for the first time in days.

"Got a hot date you forgot to mention?"

Holy-Mary-Mother-of-Sweet-Jesus-on-a-Christmas-cracker! She nearly jumped out of her skin.

George was leaning against the trunk of the cab, and he didn't look happy to see her. He stood up as the car pulled away from the curb onto the slushy streets in search of its next fare. His arms were crossed, and he was glaring at her. She felt like she had just been caught sneaking into the house after curfew.

What was she supposed to tell him? *Yes, Harry has forced me into going on a hot date with the really good-looking guy whose manuscript you don't want to publish?*

Wait a second. She wasn't speaking to him. She didn't have to say anything to him.

She turned away from his glare that had cut down many a lesser human being, and marched herself into Patxi's Pizza as if she hadn't heard him.

The smell of fresh-baked garlic bread, tomato sauce, and basil made her stomach rumble and her mouth salivate. She loved this restaurant for their Chicago-style pizza—all the extra sauce and cheese made it a knife-and-fork extravaganza worthy of the Windy City itself. She had been happy—make that "less grumpy"—when Harry suggested Patxi's, because it meant it would be a casual dinner, and she had been able to wear her most comfortable pair of black jeans and her favorite red angora sweater.

Although she wasn't late, she was the last to arrive, and as she approached the table, Dean stood up to pull out her chair for her. Okay, nice guy. She still had no idea how to take this whole "date" thing, but at least he was acting like a gentleman.

"I'm glad you were able to make it, Emma. It would have been very boring for me with Anna and Harry talking about the contract together all night."

"Oh, I'm sure we would have found other things to talk about," Harry said cheerfully, as he waved off Dean's comment, then winked at a cranky-looking Anna. It would appear that Emma wasn't the only one who had been talked into participating. Anna was already three-quarters of the way through her glass of red wine, and was clutching it like a lifeline. She really needed to loosen up.

Emma sat in the chair Dean held out for her, and smiled up at him.

"Who the hell is this guy?" George had followed her inside, and she jumped a mile when she heard his voice. He had to stop doing that to her, or she was going to develop a twitch. As it was, she bumped her knee into the table, and all the water and wine glasses rocked precariously against each other before settling.

"Emma? Are you okay?" Harry asked, as he poured her a glass of wine from the bottle they had already ordered.

"Yep, fine."

She took a healthy swig of her wine, and steadied herself not to react when George asked in a lower, more menacing voice "Emma. I asked you a question. Who the hell is that guy?"

Why was he even asking her? It wasn't like she was going to turn around and start talking to him, even if she was speaking to him.

Then it hit her. She finally knew how to get George to run screaming.

"So," she said, as she leaned in closer to Dean. "Tell me about your Christmas traditions. Do you have kids?"

"No, no kids," he started to say, but she could barely hear him over the roar that came from George.

"Goddammit, Emma. First you stop talking to me. Then you think it's amusing to torture me with this shit when you know I can't tell him to shut up." George ran his fingers through his hair, and she almost felt guilty for the stress she was putting him under.

"How does your family celebrate the holiday season? I want to hear every single minute detail." She smiled at Dean, and pretended that she couldn't hear the increasing rumbling from the spirit behind her.

"Fine. But I don't have to stay here and listen to it, or watch you flirt with this jackass. When you get home, young lady, we're going to have a serious discussion. I'm through with your silent treatment."

Then he exploded.

Like a firecracker.

She was amazed to see tiny flakes of gold dust floating as if a giant sparkler had been lit in the middle of the restaurant. It was one of the most beautiful things she had ever seen, and she sat there in silence watching the dust settle on and around her. It tingled where it landed on her skin—her neck, face, and hands—as if it truly had been tiny pieces of fire, and she closed her eyes and sighed. She must have let out an audible sound, because when she opened her eyes again, all three of them, Anna, Harry and Dean, had stopped their conversations, and were staring at her.

"Uh, Emma?" Harry looked like he was about to laugh, probably not in a good way.

Dean looked like he was second-guessing his original decision to ask her out. And Anna was gaping at her as if she had just ordered cockroaches for an appetizer.

"Excuse me." She cleared her throat, which had suddenly gone dry. "I'm just going to go...um...I should...I think...I forgot that I was supposed to...I just have to go and make a quick call. Be right back." She wanted to bolt, but she also didn't want to disturb the sparkling dust on her clothes. Could anyone else see it? She calmly left the table and headed toward the sign marked "Restrooms."

She pushed open the door to the ladies room, and was relieved to see that it was completely empty. She wondered if it would be possible to hang onto this amazing glitter that clung to her. Would she be able to keep it? Or would it just vanish in a matter of minutes? How had he even done it? He must have been really angry.

"Well, well, well, look who's here." Crystal pushed her way through the door, and sneered at her. "Having a little date night with the boss's brother? Now who's stepping out on George?"

"There's nothing going on between Harry and me and you know it."

"I don't know it, actually. What I do know is that you interrupted a very important business meeting I was having with Harry. And you seemed very possessive—even jealous—of his attraction to me."

"That is complete bull, Crystal. You're delusional as well as demented. You scare Harry to death, so there's no way you can start anything up with him."

"My, my, aren't those big words for someone who could find herself in the unemployment line, if I felt like putting her there." Crystal held up her hand and examined her perfectly manicured nails for flaws. "How long do you think you'll last when I tell George about your little fling with his brother—all the time the two of you have been spending alone together?"

"Harry and I have a working relationship, and that is all."

"Not from what I've seen. He flirts with you all the time, and you love it."

"He flirts with all women all the time, and they all love it," she shouted in exasperation. "I'm not anyone special to him, and he certainly knows he's not anyone special to me." She didn't like Crystal believing she might have feelings for Harry, but she was relieved the woman hadn't guessed her feelings for George. Emma could only imagine how horribly that would turn out.

"All I need to do is say a few words in George's ear," Crystal continued, "and you would be gone in a heartbeat. Perhaps you don't realize what happened to the assistant you replaced."

"You have no idea what you're talking about. The woman I replaced left to get married."

"That's the story, according to HR. But I just happened to let it slip that his assistant was having Harry's baby, and George blew a gasket over it. Harry spent a significant—and confused—amount of time in the New York office, and the assistant was never seen again."

"I don't believe you. Harry may fool around, but he has never left a woman pregnant before. It couldn't have been his."

"Oh, it wasn't. For all I know, she wasn't even pregnant." She pulled a bright red lipstick out of her purse, and began dabbing it onto her already perfectly applied lips. "But see how much influence I have over George? One tiny slip from you, and the minute he wakes up from his coma, I'll tell him all kinds of things that went on between you and Harry. He'll be looking for another new assistant before you can get the words 'Merry Christmas' out of your mouth. And poor Harry will wind up back in New York, so he won't be talking either."

She puckered her lips in the mirror, fluffed her hair, then walked to the door and reached for the handle. But she turned back around to face Emma again. "And if all that doesn't convince him, I'll simply let it slip that Harry was responsible for these." She pulled down the turtleneck on her sweater and revealed several black and blue marks on her neck. They looked like fingerprints, and Emma gasped in spite of herself. "And I've taken oodles and oodles of digital pictures, just waiting to be splashed all over the Internet."

"Harry didn't give you those marks. I was there, and I know for a fact that he didn't even touch you." Emma was so furious she thought her head might explode. Had Crystal done that to herself, just to get blackmail pictures? Or worse, had she paid someone to do it for her? The woman was beyond deceitful. She truly was evil.

"Oh, honey, how naïve are you? It doesn't matter if he did it or not. If I say he did it, George will believe me. Didn't my little story about his previous assistant prove that already? And if I go to the police with my pictures, crying rape, who do you think they are going to believe? The victim? Or some lowly assistant who has a crush on the boss's brother, and will say anything to protect him?"

She stopped and smirked at Emma, as if letting her "lowly assistant" comment sink in for full effect. And it did. Emma wanted to strangle Crystal herself, because at this point, who would notice, and it wasn't like she could get more pictures. But they both knew she didn't have it in her to hurt another person, no matter how horrible that other person was.

"I need to be realistic here. George is never going to wake up from that coma. I know all about his orders to the hospital, and he is going to die. So, it only makes sense that I turn my attention to Harry, who will be the one taking over Landon Literary. I am not going to let all that lovely old family money go to someone else."

Emma wanted to point out that she was starting to sound like a hooker, but she decided not to poke the cranky bear at this point. She knew it wouldn't turn out in her favor. So, instead she asked, "What lovely old family money?"

"You really are dumb, aren't you? Did you think the Landon brothers made all their money from a publishing company?"

"Well, yes?"

"They each have a sizeable inheritance that they got from their mommy dearest. And I'm certainly not going to let you stand in my way of living happily ever after with Harry."

"Do you honestly believe Harry could ever love someone who's blackmailing him with a fake rape accusation?"

"Love? Who said anything about love? This is a business arrangement. And if, by some miracle, George does end up snapping out of his coma, I will be right there for him, nursing him back to health as if I had never left his side."

"No one is ever going to believe you just showing back up in his life to nurse him."

"But I have pictures that help me say otherwise, don't I. I don't care which brother I end up with, so long as I end up with the one with all the money. So you need to stay out of my way, if you know what's good for you. And if you don't want Harry going to prison, too, of course." She glared one last time at Emma, as if for emphasis, then sashayed out the door.

Emma was so angry, she thought she might actually pass out. She couldn't form a coherent thought. She had to pull herself together, go back out there, finish dinner with the Ericksons, and then talk to Harry. What had George ever seen in Crystal? How could he have been so completely blind to her? He couldn't possibly have known what she was really like, or he would never have gotten involved with her.

They couldn't risk telling George anything now. She would just have to find another way of getting rid of Crystal. It was even more important now that she knew how horrible the woman really was.

She couldn't tell George, but should she tell Harry?

Hell yes, she should tell Harry.

Crystal was counting on Emma being too afraid of her to say anything to anyone.

Well, that bitch had counted incorrectly.

* * * * * * *

Dinner was exhausting. The encounter with Crystal had thrown everything off balance for her, and she had a hard time focusing on the conversation. Dean had been very attentive. In fact, he had been too attentive, which put her on edge. It was almost as if he forced himself to enjoy her company, and it ended up making her feel nervous and awkward.

She was relieved when Harry offered to give her a ride back to her apartment because it gave her the opportunity she needed to talk to him about the whole Crystal thing. They waved goodbye to Anna and Dean, and she stayed close to Harry in order to avoid any potentially uncomfortable interactions with Dean.

When she and Harry were in the backseat of his limo and heading to her apartment, she asked him to close the privacy screen between them and his driver. He looked amused, until she started telling him about her altercation with Crystal.

"Is that what happened to Kelly?" Then, as if the rest of it finally started filtering through his brain in layers, he said, "That bitch! That manipulative, crazy, lunatic bitch! She had someone strangle her in order to get pictures? She must really be desperate. Why doesn't George see this about her?" He looked so angry she thought he would make the driver pull the car over and go hunt Crystal down to shoot her.

"Yes, she's a lunatic, and she's a horrible person. I hope karma bites her in the ass big time. But our immediate problem right now is what to do about this whole situation." She, like Harry, wanted to rip Crystal's hair out at her perfectly salon-bleached roots. But she had to get control of this and think about it logically so that Crystal didn't feel threatened enough to release her pictures. If she really did have them. And Emma had no reason to believe she didn't. Why would she go to all that trouble and pain without getting her blackmail proof?

"Well, we definitely can't tell George now." He shivered, then poured himself a splash of bourbon from the mini bar, which had been fully stocked.

"As much as it pains me to say this, I agree." She reached across him, and poured herself a splash of bourbon as well. A much larger splash than his.

"Don't worry, Emma, it will be okay. I have people who can take care of this for us."

"Harry! You can't have her killed!"

"No." He laughed. He actually laughed, as if this whole thing was just some silly fraternity prank. "As much as I would like to truly get my hands around her neck, I'm not talking about having her killed. I'm talking about taking a more legal approach." He looked thoughtful, then continued, "At least, mostly legal. I think. We have a good friend who's a private investigator. He can take care of the pictures, no problem. I don't know how long it will take him, but he can take care of it. I never would have thought there was a bright side to George being in a coma, but this way, by the time he wakes up and is completely recovered, this whole thing will have blown over, and we can tell him everything."

She was dog tired. Her head was pounding, and it wasn't from the shot of bourbon she'd drunk. Should she break her silence, and tell George what had happened? Maybe now that he was a ghost, she would have time to convince him before he woke up, and then he could deal with Crystal before she came to him.

No, she couldn't risk it. It was Harry who would pay the price if she turned out to be wrong, and she wouldn't gamble with Harry's life. She would let him handle it with the detective, and hope for the best.

CHAPTER FIFTEEN

George was standing in the entryway to Emma's apartment complex, watching the street and waiting for her when she finally came home. He was still fuming about her spending the night with some young kid. And she was still giving him the silent treatment, because she walked right past him, as if she truly hadn't seen him—not like before, when she'd seen him and pretended she hadn't.

That was worrying. He never would have believed her capable of it, but she had managed to make it much longer than he'd thought.

He followed her to her door, and watched as she fumbled for her keys.

"Come on, Emma," he said, and sighed. He was tired of this whole thing, and wanted to be able to talk with her again. "How long are you going to keep this up? Why is it so important that I go with you to spend Christmas with your family?"

When she jumped slightly and dropped her keys, he realized that she really hadn't seen him, and that bothered him. Was the date so great that she had somehow forgotten she had a ghost following her around? A ghost she'd promised to help get back into his body.

When she continued to ignore him, he decided it was time to take drastic measures. He wasn't going to stand for the silent treatment any longer. He watched her walk away into her bedroom, where she kicked off her shoes and dropped her keys and bag on her dresser.

He grinned at her as she returned to the living room and stopped abruptly in front of him. There was no way she could ignore him standing in the middle of her living room dressed as Santa.

She screamed in terror, ran back into her bedroom, and slammed the door.

Ice filled his veins, as he realized that he had made a terrible mistake. He had gotten her to notice him, but he had scared the proverbial shit out of her in the process. He rushed to her door, fist raised to pound on it, when he realized it wouldn't do him any good. He called after her instead.

"Shit, Emma, I'm sorry. I didn't mean—"

He broke off, upset with himself, and started pacing the room. How could he have been such a heartless bastard? She had told Jessica in confidence that she didn't like Santa, and he'd used that secret against her.

"Emma, God, I'm really sorry. I thought if I could get your attention, you would finally talk to me. I didn't mean to scare you like that." He was so worn down from her ignoring him that he had just wanted her back, and he hadn't been thinking clearly.

He listened at the door. Christ, he would never forgive himself if he had messed this up completely. What made him think scaring the shit out of her would get her to talk to him again? He was such an ass.

"Emma? Please, Emma…"

He immediately changed back into jeans and a sweater, and listened again at the door. But there was only more silence. He was perfectly willing to beg if it came to that. He was so worried, he was willing to do anything to get her back.

"Okay, Emma, I'll do it. I'll go to your family's for Christmas. I can't take this anymore. I miss you. You're a royal pain in the ass about Christmas, but I miss even that."

He looked at the door that separated him from Emma. He wouldn't risk betraying her trust in him over the boundaries by passing through her door to get to her—not after the Santa stunt he'd just pulled—but he was reaching his limit, and he shouted in frustration. "Emma? Did you hear me? I'll go."

She quietly opened the door, and peeked through the crack, apparently steeling herself for another visit from Santa.

"Santa's gone," he said to assure her, hoping that she would come out all the way and talk to him. He was so relieved to see even half of her face finally looking at him—actually looking at him—that his knees almost buckled under him.

She opened the door completely and joined him in the living room, but she was cautious. Was she worried about Santa making another surprise visit? Or about what he'd said, and whether he'd meant it?

"Do you mean it?" she asked, tentatively.

Well, that answered that question.

"Which part?" he asked hesitantly, afraid she would change her mind and shut him out again, both literally and figuratively. "That I'll go, or that I've missed you?"

"Both."

"Yes. Both." He emphasized both words so that she would understand that he had meant it.

She smiled and he felt like the sun had come out after a long, hard, cold, and very lonely winter. Then she threw her arms around—and of course right through—him, and they both laughed awkwardly.

He enjoyed it when they had these…moments…encounters…whatever it was called when they passed through each other. There was something sensual in them, and no one in his right mind would turn that down.

Was it the same for her?

"I keep forgetting that part," she said, and blushed.

Maybe it was.

He liked seeing her blush. He didn't often catch his young assistant in situations where she wasn't completely capable, and he liked seeing her slightly off her game. She'd had the same reaction when he walked through her outside the hospital as well.

"That's the second time I should have gotten a hug from you," he replied flirtatiously. God, she had felt so good in that brief moment of touch. "You hug a lot," he continued, clearing his throat as if it could clear the deeper emotions he felt toward her.

Jesus, he had missed her so much. He hadn't expected to, but he had.

"What can I say? We're a very demonstrative family." She shrugged, as if to say, *doesn't everyone?*

Feeling euphoric over having her back with him again, he grinned and moved closer to her. "When I get back among the living, you owe me two hugs," he said, and he meant it. He really wished he could hug her.

"Okay," she responded, but she seemed self-conscious.

"You really hate Santa, don't you?" He still felt guilty for scaring her. He wasn't sorry that the trick had worked, because it shocked her out of her torturous silent treatment, but he did regret that he had upset her.

"It isn't the concept of Santa, it's the costume. I hate clowns. They completely wig me out, and the Santa costume is just a variation on the theme." She gave a slight shudder, and he felt protective, wishing he could wrap his arms around her and hold her.

"What about all the happy costumed characters at Disney World?" he asked instead, trying to get that image of intimacy out of his head. He should not be thinking like that about his assistant.

"I don't know. I've never been to Disney World."

"You've never been to Disney World?" Didn't every parent take their kid to Disney World?

She shrugged as if it didn't really matter, even though she also seemed a little disappointed. "No."

"Well, I'll take you. As soon as the holidays are over." The words were out of his mouth before he could stop them. But he would do it. He would take her to Disney World, and make sure she felt safe, with him, around all those ridiculous costumed characters.

She looked at him sadly. "George, what if they pull the plug on you before—"

"First," he said, interrupting her, because he had no desire to start that conversation again. "I have to live through your family and Christmas. Let's just take it one step at a time." He waited a moment, then added, "I have one condition on going to your family Christmas thing."

She looked ready to argue with him, and he could see she was working up a good head of steam, so he put his hands up to stop her.

"No, I'm not backing out. But you need to promise not to think about whatever is going to happen on Christmas Day. No talk about pulling the plug."

"But—"

"No. You made me promise not to bring down your Christmas, and I'm asking you to help me keep that promise, by making you promise not to talk about what might, or might not, happen the day after tomorrow."

He looked at her for her agreement, and she took a deep breath, then let it go on a sigh. "Okay."

He clapped his hands together and rubbed them maniacally. He was happy he had at least won this round. "Now, what is our immersion therapy for tonight? I'm so glad you're talking to me again, I'll do whatever you want."

She eyed him carefully, and he chuckled. She had such a suspicious mind.

"Have you seen the movie *White Christmas* with Bing Crosby and George Clooney's aunt, Rosemary?"

"George Clooney has an Aunt Rosemary?" He was completely befuddled. How did she even know this stuff?

"He does," she stated, with a chuckle, as if this was a fact well known by women throughout the continental U.S. "And she sings and dances, too."

"This is a musical you want me to watch?" There was not a chance in hell he was going to put up with watching a musical.

But she merely laughed, damn her eyes, as she put the movie into her DVD player. "What? The Bing Crosby part didn't give that away already?"

Resigned to a night of torture, he settled back into the couch and sighed. "No, I haven't seen that movie."

"You're about to." She was utterly oblivious to the horror going on inside his head. Either that or she didn't care, which was more likely the case.

She settled into the couch as close to him as possible without actually sitting through him, and he realized he didn't care what the movie was, as long as she was there. And she was speaking to him again. He could, and would, put up with anything from her, as long as she was speaking to him again.

But just to be sure she didn't realize the immense power she actually held over him, he said, "Maybe it was better when you weren't speaking to me."

She chuckled, and started the movie. While she watched her movie, he watched her, soaking her in, and making up for the time he had lost. God, he was so glad to have her back. It has been so damn lonely without her.

"So are you going to tell me who that guy was tonight?"

"Oh, didn't I already tell you that?"

"No, you didn't. You haven't been speaking to me, remember?"

"Right. Well, he's an author who Harry's been working on at the office. You should be very proud of Harry getting this author on board."

"But who the hell is he? What's the name of—"

"Shh…the movie's starting, and I don't want to miss it. We'll talk about it later."

She was really into this movie, which meant he was probably going to hate it. And since he still had a lot of points to make up where she was concerned, he decided to let it go instead of risking upsetting her again.

* * * * * * *

The next morning, Emma shuffled into the living room in her bathrobe and over-sized slippers—her favorite slippers, with the sheep faces, that she had picked up on a lark several years ago on her backpacking trip through Scotland.

"Morning. Merry Christmas Eve." George appeared to be in a good mood. "What have you got planned for this morning?"

Still shaking sleep from her cloudy mind, she smiled warmly at him, noticing that he looked happy and relaxed, and she was very glad. Perhaps this meant she was finally making progress with him. Well, not *with him* with him, but with him-getting-back-into-his-body with him. Lord, she was muddle-headed this morning.

Then it finally registered where he was. He was sitting at her desk, and that had her worried. "What are you doing?" She hoped she sounded normal instead of worried, like she felt.

"I'm reading your stories."

"Oh, no! Those aren't finished. They're just—" She stopped abruptly, horrified that he was reading her unfinished (and in her opinion, very unpolished) stories. She rushed to take them away from him, but her hand went right through them.

"How did you…?" She couldn't take the pages away from him.

He grinned at her as if he'd solved the secrets of the universe and waved the papers in his hands.

"Apparently I can do a lot with my imagination." He wagged his eyebrows at her suggestively.

"Then get started on world peace, and leave my stories alone," she snapped, more defensively than she had intended, but he'd thrown her off with his comment. Exactly how was she supposed to take that? What had gotten into him?

He chuckled at her indignation, which made her feel even more awkward. "These are good, Emma. You need to finish them, and then we can talk about publishing."

She was stunned. He liked her stories? He didn't like romantic novels. She had never considered taking them to George. Never.

"Right now, I need to make the fruit compote for tonight's Christmas Eve feast." She shuffled into the kitchen, feeling confused. She was also nervous, and cranky that she hadn't been able to keep him from getting a peek at her stories before she was ready.

In the kitchen, she set out a cutting board, knife, and fruit on the counter for chopping. Then she reached into a cupboard and pulled out a bottle of Grand Marnier.

"This is how you start your Christmas Eve?" he asked with amusement, indicating the liquor bottle. "Maybe I have been missing something here."

"Ha. Ha. Ha." She realized she sounded grumpy, but she couldn't seem to help herself. She had never expected him to get access to her stories, and she was so unprepared for that. She was glad he liked them, but she had no idea how to deal with that. Was he just being nice? Or did he really like them?

"Isn't that supposed to be 'ho ho ho'?" he asked teasingly, leaning in to whisper in her ear.

"Very funny." She tried to hang onto her grumpy, but then she chuckled and ruined the effect entirely. "It's for the compote, it goes into the orange juice. Why are you so chipper all of the sudden?"

He shrugged, then settled onto a kitchen stool. "I'm enjoying myself. Apparently, haunting you is good for me."

That snapped her out of what remained of her morning funk, and she stared at him in amazement.

"You're easy to be with," he continued. "I'm more relaxed around you. There are no surprises."

"Yeah, that's me. Good-old no-surprises, boring Emma," she responded sarcastically as she felt a blush spread across her cheeks. Had he just complimented her? Or had he really meant that she was boring?

He chuckled at her sarcasm. "No, I just mean that I don't have to worry about a hidden agenda from you, and, ultimately, how much it's going to cost me."

They sat comfortably together in the small but cozy kitchen for a moment, simply enjoying each other's company, until he broke the silence.

"Do you know...you are the first woman I've been around for longer than five minutes who hasn't asked me to buy her something. Why is that?"

"Well, as you pointed out earlier, you don't have any money." She cut into a pineapple to begin sectioning it for the compote.

He leaned over and smelled the fruit, then shrugged. "The downside, though, is that you haven't told me what you want for Christmas. What do you want for Christmas, Emma?"

"I already told you, world peace," she answered automatically.

"Seriously, Em." His voice had taken on a warm and soothing tone.

She was overwhelmed by the sincerity she heard in his voice, and her heart beat so fast and so loudly that she was sure it would come flying right out of her chest. She carefully set down her knife, faced him.

"You're still missing this whole Christmas thing. If I tell you what I want you to get me, where's the spirit in that?"

He moved closer to her, looked deeply into her eyes, and said softly, "What can I get you for Christmas?"

"I want you to go back into your body and be alive again." She wanted that more than anything he could ever buy her in a store.

They stared at each other for a moment, and she could see the kindness— was there also affection?—in his eyes. But he suddenly broke the spell by responding a little too loudly, "Wow, you don't ask for much, do you?"

No, then, that wasn't affection she had seen. Heartbroken, she returned to cutting fruit and mixing her compote.

CHAPTER SIXTEEN

George stood with Emma outside her sister's house—Marlie, that was her name—psyching himself up to go inside.

The house was a modest two-story in a middle-class neighborhood that had used to be the site of the Denver airport before it had been relocated to way the hell out somewhere closer to Kansas. There was a large front porch that wrapped around to the side of the house, and he could see four adult-sized and four child-sized Adirondack chairs scattered haphazardly as if they had just been used for some kind of family gathering.

As they walked up the sidewalk, he noticed that the house was outlined in colored lights, and a movable snowman stood next to a glowing automated train that circled continuously around a large evergreen tree in the front yard. The large spruce tree in the middle of the yard was trimmed in miniature colored blinking lights, and several mechanical presents sparkled underneath it.

The whole scene spoke of a happy family, with happy children, and it all made him want to turn and run. His own childhood had not been the loving environment he could see from this house, and he had no idea how he was going to deal with whatever he'd find on the other side of the door.

But he had promised Emma he would make the effort, and he refused to let her down. He would not break his promise to her, and he owed it to her to at least try to get through the night.

What scared him was that he had come to care about her over the past several days. He'd discovered that what she thought about him mattered, and so he would get through this night if it was the last thing he did. Literally. He just had to keep remembering that this was Emma's family, not his own, and he would be just fine. How bad could it be?

He was surprised to realize that he wanted her to have a happy Christmas. After all his resisting, and the growling he had always given her about it, he wanted her to be happy.

She looked absolutely beautiful in her black cocktail dress, with her hair piled up on top of her head. He had decided to materialize a suite and tie for himself in order to feel like he was at least worthy of the stunning woman with him.

She was holding a large bowl containing the finished product of her infamous fruit compote, and several bags hung from her arms. He felt ridiculous that he couldn't help her carry anything, and it was making him feel extremely out of place. He was so nervous, he'd started some deep breathing exercises, and that made her laugh.

"Why are you doing that when it can't possibly make any difference to you?"

"I don't know," he shrugged, feeling stupid. "Habit I guess. Why do you keep asking me to buckle my seat belt?"

She chuckled, and that helped lessen his tension a bit—if she was able laugh at herself, he could at least do the same. And he really liked hearing her laugh.

"You look very nice, George. Thank you for that, since I'm the only one who can see you all dressed up."

"It seemed only right to try to look at least as nice as you." He was very glad he'd made the effort, because it had made her happy. He was warmed by the deep emotions he felt as he continued in a soft voice, "You look beautiful, Emma."

"Thank you!" She seemed to glow from his compliment.

He had never told her she was beautiful before, and now he wished that he had. He wished he'd told her every day since she'd started working for him. They made a strikingly handsome couple, even if they were the only two people who could see it.

She moved to ring the doorbell, but he stopped her. He had to tell her. At least tell her something. He needed her to know.

"Look, Emma… Christmas for me was never… I…" He struggled a moment, trying to find the right words, then finally blurted out, "Look, my father never did the Christmas thing with us, and my mom drank herself through the entire holiday just to get by."

He breathed a sigh of relief. "There. I said it." Not all of it, but that was enough for now. She didn't need to know the rest. It was bad enough that now she knew his father was never there.

She looked at him with a confused expression that quickly turned sad, and he could tell she struggled to know what to do with the information he'd just given her. He didn't like seeing that sad look on her face, and he felt awkward now that the truth was out.

"You really want to hug me right now, don't you?" He grinned at her when he noticed her fidgeting as she shifted her bowl of fruit and the bags in her arms. He could see that what he'd told her had upset her, and she was struggling with the need to comfort him. She was a nurturer, and it was instinctive for her.

"Yes, I do, I really do," she replied, sounding frustrated.

Taking full advantage of her loaded arms, he leaned in, touched her cheek gently with his finger, and sent little sparks of tingling energy down the side of her face and neck. He saw her shiver from the sensation, and felt a visceral thrill that he had given it to her.

He gave her a flirtatious grin, and whispered, "That's three you owe me then."

She laughed, and it sounded nervous. Then she turned and rang the doorbell, pushed open the door, and walked inside the house.

George was surprised to see that Marlie's house was warm and inviting, full of what Emma would undoubtedly call *Christmas mood*. It was entirely decorated with garlands and lights, and a huge tree sat next to the fireplace in the comfortable living room. He could see why Emma was such a Christmas fanatic—apparently it ran in the Anderson family.

The minute they stepped inside the house, Emma was bombarded by a very excited group of kids, the same kids from the zoo. Christ, what were their names again? He watched with what felt like something very close to envy as she kissed each one of them and wished them merry Christmas. She finally handed her fruit bowl to the oldest kid—Spencer, that was his name.

He followed Emma as she and Spencer headed down a hallway to the kitchen, and he watched in amusement as the rest of their group went in about five different directions. Spencer raced ahead and didn't waste any time dumping the bowl of fruit on a kitchen counter, before he ran back out to join the others, wherever they had gone.

"Thanks, Spencer," Emma called after him.

Yep, he'd been right, the kid's name was Spencer. He was getting the hang of this.

He followed Emma as she entered the kitchen and stopped short.

The activity in the kitchen was almost deafening, and the energy level was frantic. It was an assault on the senses. This was nothing like the Christmases in his experience. What the hell had she gotten him into? There were so many people. He would never be able to keep up with her.

"Who are all these people?" He was seriously contemplating pulling a Harry, and bolting for the nearest exit. No. He would do this.

He remembered Marlie, and the other sister—Laura, was it?—from the night at the zoo. They were at the stove cooking and were talking with their heads together and speaking in low voices.

"Those three guys over there?" she whispered to him, apparently so that they wouldn't be overheard, although how anyone could hear anything in this cacophony was beyond him.

"That's Marlie's husband, Bill, the one in the red tie," she continued, "and his brothers Doug, on the left, and Dave, on the right."

Marlie's husband, Bill, was a tall, good-looking man in his early thirties who looked like a young Jimmy Stewart. George thought he would probably like him, under different circumstances.

The one on the left—Doug, she'd said—looked to be about in his late twenties, and the one on the right—Dave—looked like he was about thirty. He could see a slight family resemblance between the three of them. They stood talking and laughing as if they hadn't seen each other since last

Christmas, and were all trying to catch up at once. They looked like they were enjoying themselves together, like three brothers who truly cared about each other.

It made him wonder if he and Harry had that kind of relationship with each other. If someone watched his interactions with his brother, would they see the same thing? He and Harry had always been close, but life had given them a different path.

Emma then gestured with a nod to the group of women, standing around the island in the middle of the kitchen putting together various platters of food. She pointed to the oldest woman in the group and said, "That is our matriarch, Nana, Bill's mom. She's the one who started this whole Ukrainian Christmas Eve theme."

"You're Ukrainian?" His head was starting to spin, and he wasn't sure he'd even heard her correctly.

"Well, no," she said with a chuckle. "But Bill's family is a quarter of one eighth of a sixteenth or something. It's mostly just a really fun tradition for us. You'll see."

She smiled at him, and raised her eyebrow in a questioning look, which probably meant that she was trying to gauge if he was still hanging in there with her. He wasn't going to leave her. He would never betray his promise to her.

"Anyway..." she continued, "the other two women are Bill's sisters, Mary and Katie. Mary's the one arranging the cheese and crackers on the plate next to Nana."

George felt shell-shocked by all the family members, and was very glad he was a ghost and didn't have to meet them all for real. He couldn't explain it, because he'd never been nervous in these kinds of situations before. He'd had years of practice meeting people and remembering their names from all the functions he'd attended.

But this was different. He was nervous about making a good impression.

Christ, he wanted to make a good impression on Emma's family. It was extremely important to him. But he was a ghost. So how warped was that?

"Who's the guy pouring champagne? God, I wish I could drink right now." Was there no end to the members in her family?

Julie Cameron

"That's Don, Katie's husband," Emma continued, completely oblivious to the fear brewing inside him. "Come on, I'll introduce you to everyone. Sort of."

She went further into the kitchen and put her bags down on the nearest counter, then called out, "Merry Christmas everyone!"

Everyone—and there were a ton of "everyones"—responded all at once, and Emma moved around the room greeting each person individually. He followed her and desperately tried to keep up. Again, he was glad he was a ghost.

He watched as she gave Laura a hug and a kiss, then said, "Merry Christmas, Laura. Any word from Jack?"

Jack? Jesus! Now, who the hell was Jack? He didn't remember hearing her name someone "Jack."

He turned to Laura, who looked like she could burst into tears at any minute and was putting forth a concerted effort not to. "He's not going to be here."

Oh, that Jack. Jack the-husband-who-is-never-home-for-Christmas Jack.

"Because he's having an affair," George stated, absolutely convinced that a man never missed Christmas with his family unless he didn't want to be there.

Emma gave Laura another hug and glared at George over Laura's shoulder. He merely shrugged. She could live in a state of denial all she wanted, but in the end it wouldn't do her any good.

Emma then moved to Marlie, gave her a hug and a kiss, then rubbed her belly and said, "Merry Christmas, Marlie. How's little Bill Jr.?"

"Just like his father," Marlie responded happily. "Calm, cool, and collected through everything." She put down her spoon, turned to Emma and took her by the arm to lead her away from Laura. George followed, wanting to hear whatever conspiracy was being hatched between the two women.

Marlie whispered, "Did you bring it?"

"Yep, I've got it," Emma whispered back. "Meet you in your bedroom as soon as I finish making the rounds."

Marlie rubbed her hands together in mischievous glee and hurried out of the kitchen. He decided that whatever was going on, he'd make Emma include him in it, because he definitely didn't want to miss out on whatever put that look on Marlie's face. Nothing like a good conspiracy to help a person get over his nerves.

He continued to follow Emma as she moved on to the group of women and exchanged hugs and kisses with each of them.

"Merry Christmas, Nana!" Hug. Kiss.

"Merry Christmas, Mary!" Hug. Kiss.

"Merry Christmas, Katie!" Hug. Kiss.

Then she looked over at George, apparently to see if he was paying attention, and he gave her a thumbs up. This was getting a little bit easier, and he was starting to get into the swing of it. He was only sorry that he wasn't getting a hug and a kiss from Emma as well.

She then crossed the room to greet the guy who was playing bartender—one of the sisters' husbands, he remembered. The husband handed Emma a glass of champagne as they exchanged hugs and kisses.

"Merry Christmas, Don. How'd the borscht turn out this year?" she asked him.

"Borscht?" he shouted, completely taken by surprise. They served borscht at Christmas Eve dinner?

Emma covered a chuckle with a fake cough, obviously hoping Don wouldn't notice her laughing at nothing. But what the hell? Who served borscht at Christmas?

"I gotta say, this is our best year yet," Don replied proudly, apparently having not noticed anything out of the ordinary in Emma's coughing fit. Maybe he'd been hitting the champagne early.

Emma clinked glasses with Don, and sipped her champagne, then she moved to give hugs and kisses to Marlie's husband, Bill, and his brothers.

"Merry Christmas, Bill!" Hug. Kiss.

"Merry Christmas, Doug!" Hug. Kiss.

"Merry Christmas, Dave!" Hug. Kiss. "Where's Hillary?"

George changed his mind about being glad that he was a ghost tonight. Jesus. Everyone was getting a hug and a kiss from Emma except him. And it was starting to piss him off.

"Oh, she's in the other room with the kids," the brother, Dave, responded. "They're getting Nana's story time set up. You know Hillary, she has everything under control."

"What they're really doing," the other brother, Doug, replied, "is shaking presents and guessing the contents."

Emma went over to her bags, and George followed to see who else—who wasn't him—was going to get hugged and kissed. She pulled a package out of one of them, then spoke quietly to him. "Mill around and check things out. I need to go do some secret stuff with Marlie."

She took her package, left the kitchen, and George was on his own. Well, shit. Now what was he supposed to do? Should he follow her and see what they were up to?

"Hello again," came a quiet voice from behind him.

He turned around and was surprised to see the little girl from Santa's Village—Jessica—the one who was scared of Santa, just like her aunt Emma.

She was standing right behind him, and she was looking up at him. She couldn't possibly see him; no one except Emma could see him. He looked around to see whom she had spoken to, but there was no one else with them paying any attention to her.

Holy shit! She was actually seeing him.

"Uh, hello?" he asked as calmly as possible, trying not to scare her away. "Do you know who I am?"

"You were with Aunt Emma at the zoo, and then when we went to see Santa," she replied. Apparently, ghosts didn't scare her. Only Santa did.

"You knew I was there?" he asked, incredulously. "You could see me?"

She nodded her head, then asked, "Are you Aunt Emma's George?"

He squatted down so that he was on the same level with her, and nodded, unsure what else to say to her. He was completely dumbfounded. All this time, Emma had been the only one who knew he was a ghost, but apparently whatever the hell that gene was ran in the family.

"How come no one else knows you're here?" she asked him, almost as if she had just read his thoughts. Another thing, apparently, that she and her Aunt Emma had in common.

"I don't know, honey." He decided to answer truthfully. No kid appreciated being lied to, and they always seemed to know it when they were. "I think it's because you and your aunt Emma are pretty special." He was absolutely sure of that. Very, very special. "I know in your Aunt Emma's case, it's because she has a really good heart."

"Come on, Jessica, hurry up!" Spencer yelled from the hallway.

Jessica hurried to steal crackers off a nearby platter, then ran back out of the room, leaving George completely mystified.

He followed Jessica into the next room to find all the kids huddled around the Christmas tree counting presents, and shaking them to try to guess what was inside.

Then his world tipped…

* * * * * * *

He was eight, and he was sitting quietly across a formal dining room table from Harry, who was six. The room and the table were elegantly set with festive decorations and a full formal dinner.

He watched in anticipation as his father, Martin Landon, stood at the head of the table and carved the turkey. His father was a handsome man, in his late thirties, and George had always wanted to grow up to be just like him. He was always in charge, and always knew what to do in every situation.

George tentatively looked down at the opposite end of the table from his father at his mother, Caroline Landon. She was beautiful. All that blond hair that always smelled like the sunshine to him. He knew that she had started drinking her wine before they had even sat down, and he could see that she was already unhappy, because she kept glaring daggers at his father.

"James, please tell the cook the turkey looks especially delicious this year," his father said, as he sliced large portions onto a waiting platter.

James, their waiter, bowed slightly and replied, "Thank you, Mr. Landon, I will let her know."

James passed the platter of turkey to each diner. He first served his mother, but she waved him away. When he served Harry, George was worried there wouldn't be anything left by the time it was his turn, because he just kept piling more onto his plate, and it took forever. He could smell the meat, and his stomach growled in anticipation.

Other servers brought side dishes, and served from those in the same manner, but the turkey and the gravy were the best parts to George.

His mother gestured with her wine glass to James. "More wine, please, James."

"Don't you think you've had enough, Caroline?" his father accused, and glared at her from across the table. George flinched at the anger he heard in his father's voice.

"No, Martin, I don't think I've had nearly enough yet," she responded with enough ice in her tone to chill her own wine.

George looked at Harry and he knew that they were each feeling a sense of dread, as they both pretended not to notice the argument. He continued to eat with his head down in the hopes that his father's anger with his mother would go away if he couldn't see it.

George glanced up to see Martin patting down his pockets before he reached into his coat pocket and pulled out a stuffed envelope. He watched in dread as his father placed the envelope on the table next to his plate.

"Before I forget," he announced, then patted the envelope as if it contained George's future happiness.

George looked at the envelope, then looked up at his father with desperate hope and asked, "Aren't you staying in this year, Father?"

"No, I'm going out as usual," he clipped, as if that should have been evident because of the envelope next to George's plate, which he tapped once again.

All of George's hopes were crushed. He set down his fork, picked up the envelope and opened it to see it was full of money.

It was always full of money, just like last year, and the year before, and every previous year for as far back as George could remember. Yet each year he opened it and expected...what? The key to his father's heart?

"I'm sure you and Harry will have lots of fun with that," his father continued, oblivious to the heartbreak in his son's eyes.

"Yes, Father," George replied quietly, and obediently. He set the money down, and choked back his tears as he picked up his fork again to finish eating.

He wouldn't cry. His father hated criers. And he so desperately wanted his father to love him, and Harry. He had made sure that he and Harry had been on their best behavior this year. They had worked so hard, that he was sure his father would stay and help them celebrate Christmas together, or at least take them on their adventure himself tomorrow.

"James! My glass is empty," his mother demanded shrilly from the end of the table.

George glanced at Harry, who was always so excited about the money. He at least had happy experiences, thanks to the "adventures" George was able to make for him. George would take Harry out the day after tomorrow when the shops opened up, and make sure that he, at least, had a merry Christmas.

And he would never let his father know how hurt he was inside.

* * * * * * *

George gasped as he shakily returned to the present. Christ, what had made him remember that? How had he remembered that? Did being a ghost make a person more susceptible to vivid, horrible childhood memories?

Where was Emma? He looked around the room, and had a moment of panic when he didn't see her. Where was he? Where the hell was Emma?

As he slowly came back to himself, he remembered that he was at Emma's sister's house. She had gone off to do something secretive with Marlie, and he had somehow flashed to a memory of the past.

He looked around the dining room, which was so different from his childhood. The table was elegantly set with Christmas decorations and a formal dinner, but it was much warmer than the table he remembered from his childhood. Everyone was seated around it, shoulder to shoulder, and happily chatting with each other, which was also entirely different from the memory he had just left.

He was relieved to see Emma, as she and Marlie came in from the other room. They were wheeling in a chair that was covered with a sheet, and they pushed it toward Laura, who looked confused. Everyone shifted their chairs slightly to accommodate another setting, and the covered chair was scooted in next to Laura.

Marlie cleared her throat, which got everyone's attention, and began the explanation by saying, "Emma and I decided that we couldn't have Christmas again without Jack."

With that announcement, she and Emma whipped the sheet off the chair with a flourish to reveal a mannequin, wearing a man's suit. Then George saw that the mannequin in the chair had an electronic tablet for a face.

"It's wearing Jack's clothes!" Laura exclaimed with an excited laugh, and everyone around the table clapped. "That is so sweet, you guys."

He saw Laura's three kids—he was pretty sure he remembered their names from the night at the zoo as Tommy, Carrie, and Michelle—all ran up to join Laura, who told them, "Look, you guys, it's your dad!"

George chuckled as Emma turned into the voice of a shopping-channel host and exclaimed, "But wait! There's more!" Then she pushed the power button on the tablet, and a man's face came into view.

Ah, this had to be the infamous missing Jack. The rat bastard, Jack, who was cheating on his super-nice wife and really great kids. George wanted to punch the tablet.

"Hi, honey. Hi, kids!" Jack waved enthusiastically from inside the tablet screen, and pandemonium ensued.

George was stunned as he watched as everyone broke out into joyous laughter and applause.

He heard Laura gasp, and then she burst into tears.

He watched as the kids all moved in closer to the tablet, and talked at the same time to get their dad's attention.

Emma and Marlie hugged each other.

But what finally did him in was watching Laura reach out and touch the tablet with so much love on her face that it almost hurt him to see it. She stroked the tablet as if it really were Jack's face.

Sweet Jesus. She deserved better.

"He's having an affair," George growled to Emma. But she swatted him away like he was an annoying fly, so he continued to make his point, "You wait. Nobody's gone for Christmas every year unless they choose to be."

"Would everyone please excuse me for just a quick second? I'll be right back." She glared at him and jerked her head to the side in a gesture for him to come with her.

He followed her into a powder room off the main dining room. It was a tight squeeze for the two of them, and, given her boundary issues at her apartment, he was surprised she was getting this close with him. Apparently, boundary issues weren't top in her mind though, because she looked like she wanted to choke him.

"What the hell is wrong with you?" she demanded.

"You might want to keep your voice down, or everyone will wonder why you're yelling at yourself in the bathroom."

"There's enough noise out there to break the sound barrier, no one's going to hear me yelling at you."

It was loud in the dining room—there was never that kind of noise in the dining room where he grew up—but she wasn't trying very hard to keep from being overheard, and he knew there was one kid out there who had watched them go into the bathroom together. What must she be thinking at this moment?

"Emma—"

"How dare you accuse him of having an affair. What gives you the right? You don't know anything about him."

"It just stands to reason, if he's always gone over the holidays—"

"And that gives you the right to jump to conclusions? Erroneous conclusions?"

"I'm speaking from experience."

She stopped yelling and stared at him, and he could practically see the pieces that were forming in her mind. He'd said too much. She wasn't a stupid woman, and she would eventually put it all together and know the truth. Then she would leave him. Everyone did.

"You're holding up dinner with your family. You need to go back in there."

"We will be talking about this later, " she threatened. "You don't know him. I do. And I know that he is not having an affair."

On that statement, she swung the bathroom door open and stormed into the dining room.

The very quiet dining room.

Shit. Everyone was staring at them. Well, staring at Emma.

"Emma…what's going on? Who's having an affair?" Laura asked. She looked more confused than angry, and George hoped that meant that she hadn't heard everything they'd said. He thought back over their conversation, and was fairly certain that no names had been mentioned. At least, he hoped not. Emma would never forgive him if her family ended up mad at her because of something he'd said. Even if they had only heard her side of the conversation.

"I was…" Emma stammered, trying to come up with a plausible explanation for yelling at herself in the bathroom. "A quick phone call… from a friend…in the bathroom. Not a friend in the bathroom, I took the phone call in the bathroom, to…uh…"

"George," Jessica shouted, and waved at him, happy to see him. All heads turned to look at her, and he waved back and winked.

"George?" Marlie asked. "George is having an affair? I thought he was still in a coma."

"No, Mar," Laura said. "George isn't having the affair, his girlfriend is. What's her name, Em? Christine?"

"Crystal," Emma said, at the same time that George asked, "Crystal?"

But apparently his love life was enough to distract them because they all started talking at once again, and it was as if nothing unusual had happened. Weird family. But he was starting to like them.

Emma looked at him with concern. She was probably worried about his reaction to discovering his girlfriend was cheating on him. He didn't care. It was expected. They didn't love each other. Why shouldn't she have a lover on the side?

Who was he kidding? He was pissed.

True, he never loved Crystal, but that didn't mean he wasn't angry about it. She had obviously found him lacking in some way, and had decided to fill that void with another man.

But it was far worse that Emma knew about it. That was unacceptable.

"It's better if she has a lover. This way, there are no unnecessary attachments on either side. I don't love her. So why should it be a problem?"

But he could see that she was worried about it. Because she was someone who gave her heart in a relationship, and it was unfathomable for her that relationships could be any different. She was a romantic. She read too many of those damned romance manuscripts. Real life was nothing but lies and deceit.

"Guess what, honey?" Jack's voice asked from inside the tablet. "Christmas came early this year. I quit my job yesterday!"

The room went deathly silent. Again.

"Wow. I didn't see that coming." Did the bastard just say he'd quit his job? Could he really be at his job right now? No. No way.

George looked over to Laura for confirmation, and saw that she had started to tear up again. "Oh, Jack, no…"

"No, honey, it's great. They didn't accept my resignation, and we renegotiated my contract. No more holidays away from home. Not even President's Day! Can you believe that?"

The kids jumped up and down, and Laura kissed the tablet.

"Hey, hey, stop that!" Emma exclaimed. "That tablet's borrowed from my office. I have to give it back in perfect condition."

George was stunned. Had he misread the situation entirely? He had been so convinced that Jack was having an affair, and that he didn't love his wife. After all, what man would willingly not spend Christmas with his wife and kids?

But he'd been wrong. So completely wrong. How was that even possible?

"She can keep the tablet, Emma. I'll get you another one for the office," he said quietly. He was amazed by the love he saw between Jack and Laura.

He had no idea such a thing could exist. He had never seen anything like it before. But he could see trust and love between them.

Emma had been right. He looked over at her, and their eyes met. He watched as her eyes teared up, and he saw that same love and trust in her eyes. What did she see in his eyes when she looked at him? Could she see the love he felt for her?

What the hell?

Love? For Emma?

He was suddenly overwhelmed, and he didn't know what to do, so he broke the eye contact and looked away first. He looked back for a brief second and saw the look of sadness that crossed her face before she turned away.

Was he falling in love with Emma?

He looked around the table and noticed that the kids had all started putting their cloth napkins over their heads, and were tying them on in various styles. This family was definitely goofy, but by now he was used to it, and he knew that something interesting was probably going to happen soon. He was grateful for the distraction from his thoughts.

Emma and Marlie returned to their seats, and he watched as they put napkins on their heads as well. He looked around to see that all the adults had napkins on their heads, too. Okay…

"It is time now for the honorable Fulton family Ukrainian tradition of the kutia throwing," Bill announced. "Everyone have on their kutia cap?" He looked around the table to check, as he put his own napkin on his head.

What the hell was a kootcha?

Then Bill looked over at Laura, who was still whispering with Jack and not paying attention. "Laura?"

"Oh, sorry!" She looked around at the group and saw that she was the only one in non-compliance. She put her napkin on her head, then one on Jack's tablet, as George watched and waited with increasing anticipation and amusement.

He glanced over at Emma to get some clue as to what was going on, and she pointed to her head. What? He shrugged at her in confusion. She pointed emphatically to her head, then to him. Was she kidding? Put a napkin on his head? Was this like the seat belt thing?

He decided it didn't matter. If she wanted it, he would do it. But, just to see if he could make her laugh, he materialized a Broncos football helmet on his head instead. He felt immense gratification when he heard Emma cough to cover her laugh. She had to cough several times, and that made him secretly very happy.

"Are you okay, Emma?" Marlie reached over and patted Emma on the back.

"Good. I'm good. Just a tickle." She covered her cough by drinking a sip of water from the glass in front of her. She eyed him over the rim of her glass as she drank, and he could see that her eyes were still laughing at him.

He could get used to making her laugh. It wasn't difficult, since she seemed to be a genuinely happy person to begin with. But he was starting to enjoy her reactions to some of the simplest things that he could do for her.

Christ, it would be so easy to love her. Could she possibly love someone like him? Could she be the one who could—

He was jolted out of his thoughts as Bill's chair scraped across the wood floor, and he stood up with a spoonful of goop in his hand. Bill eyed the children around the table before saying, "Kids, don't try this at home. I am a trained professional."

He paused for dramatic effect, which was certainly working on George, then continued, "If the kutia sticks to the ceiling—"

"The pasta is done!" Don interrupted, and everyone laughed.

Apparently used to this type of interruption, Bill continued undaunted with his performance, "It will be a good harvest this year."

George watched in amazement as Bill threw the goop at the ceiling. It hit the ceiling with an audible "splat," spreading out dark substance for a good twelve inches, spraying several people in its wake. The adults cheered, and the kids squealed, but George watched Emma. She looked up at him and smiled, and he realized he was lost. She loved this shit, and he loved that she loved it.

He loved her.

Somehow, somewhere, he had let himself lose control, and he had fallen in love with her. He had never felt like this before, and he was suddenly scared shitless. She had the power to destroy him. Absolutely.

He wanted to hope that Emma could love him in return. But it wasn't possible. He knew that he was not an easy man to love—his father had taught him that. This was why he only dated women like Crystal. There was no fear of rejection because he already knew they didn't love him in the first place. They only loved him for his money. And he knew that going in.

He and Emma had no future together. He would end up breaking her, just as his father had broken his mother.

He couldn't do that to Emma.

He wouldn't do that to Emma.

CHAPTER SEVENTEEN

He silently watched and waited for the next thrilling event at the Fulton Family Christmas Eve. The table had been cleared from dinner by all the kids, and only the adults remained, scattered around the table, drinking coffee and eating peppermint ice cream with a variety of cookies for dessert. Holy hell but that coffee smelled good, and for the second time that evening, he wished he'd had his body back.

"Laura, please pass the Christmas wreaths over here," Emma requested, and he watched as Laura picked up a plate of the sticky green cookies shaped to resemble wreaths and passed them to Marlie, who in turn passed them to Emma. He had no idea what the hell those things were, but he wanted to try them, too.

Laura's kid, Tommy, came up to his mom and asked, "Is it time for Uncle Bill and Aunt Marlie's presents yet?"

"Yeah, baby, go get everyone together for Nana's story time, and we'll be right in," his mom promised, and everyone got up from the table to move into the living room.

So, apparently something called "Uncle Bill and Aunt Marlie's presents" was the next episode in this madcap adventure. He realized that he was enjoying himself, and he looked forward to whatever was coming up next.

He went over and stood by Emma as he watched Laura push tablet-Jack in the chair, still live and in person, so to speak. They all went into the living room, and he saw that the kids had gathered around the tree.

Emma hung back from the group, apparently to stay with him, and he suddenly wished he could be alone with her. There was so much he wanted—no, needed—to say to her. But he couldn't just pull her aside here and interrupt her time with her family. He needed her full attention. And besides, he wouldn't take this night away from her for anything. It could wait.

She leaned over and whispered to him, "Every year, Marlie and Bill make a present for everyone—something homemade, that everyone always loves—and they're the only presents we open on Christmas Eve because we're all here together for it. Bill always tries to help Marlie with the present each year, so one person gets the present Bill made, which is highly valued."

"Why?" he asked, wondering what Bill did that could possibly be so valuable. Was he an artist or something?

But she merely grinned at him, and replied, "You'll see. But first, Nana reads a traditional Ukrainian story to the kids."

She motioned him to follow her into the living room. She sat on the couch next to Laura as Bill and Marlie handed presents to the kids, who in turn passed them on to their designated recipients.

As he watched Nana settle into a chair and put on a pair of reading glasses, it occurred to him that this family had three generations all under the same roof. He was amazed that all this seemed so normal, so natural, to everyone here, including the kids.

His mother's parents had always stopped by on Christmas Day, but they only stayed long enough to make it clear that the Landon house was just a quick stop before they were off to their next—much more important—destination.

His father's parents never stopped by, but they always sent cards to George and to Harry with checks inside telling them to "pick up whatever it is that's the latest thing for you boys these days."

The room grew silent as Nana opened her storybook and began to read, "One night, on a cold, cold Christmas Eve in a small Ukrainian village, a family gathered around their dinner table…"

* * * * * * *

Once again, George found himself transported back in his mind to a time when he and Harry were young and sitting around their family dining room table eating dinner on Christmas Eve.

Harry was eight, George remembered, and he was scraping the bottom of his dessert dish to get the last bite. George, at ten, was sullenly pushing his dessert around in the dish. He glowered at the thick white envelope sitting next to his dish. He hated those white envelopes.

His mother sat in her usual place, but she looked older and harder than he remembered, from all the drinking she had done over the years. She was already drunk, and gesturing James for more wine.

George heard a very disgusted grunt from his father, and he looked up to see Martin glower at his wife from across the length of the table. His father finished his dessert, tossed his napkin on the table, and stood up.

"Don't wait up," he announced. Then he left the room while George watched and became more and more angry. He was too old to cower any longer, and tonight was the night he would finally find out what his father did on Christmas Eve that was so much more important than his family.

"Go to bed, Harry," George snapped, then tried to rein in his anger. He hadn't meant to take his anger out on Harry, who looked like a puppy waiting for a treat. He would give Harry a happy Christmas, no matter what. "We want to get up early tomorrow for our Christmas adventure."

True to his anxious-to-please nature, Harry jumped up from the table, nearly knocking his chair over, and said, "Okay, George! What are we doing this year?"

"It's a surprise. Now go to bed, and don't let me catch you sneaking up again." His tone sounded so much like his father's that he almost apologized for it. But he didn't want Harry to follow him.

He hated his father for putting him in this position each year. It was a father's job to make sure his children went to bed on time the night before Christmas. It was a father's job to put that kind of excitement on their faces. What was more important to his father than seeing Harry so happy?

"Okay, George, I won't!" Harry exclaimed, as he ran from the room.

George turned to James and asked in a concerned whisper, "Will you make sure my mom gets to bed okay?"

Although he had never heard his father say those words before, George reasoned that he should have. This was yet another responsibility his father never took on in his role as the head of the family.

"Of course, George," James responded, as if this particular task were a given, or part of his job description.

George left the room as quickly, but with as much dignity, as he could manage. He knew he only had a few more minutes before he would hear the sound of the front door closing behind his father as he left for the weekend, and he needed to get himself ready.

Following his father, he bicycled up to a small stone cottage in a quiet suburban neighborhood. He leaned his bike against an old, gnarled tree across the street from the house and watched through a large bay window that faced the street. He could see a mother with her son and daughter sitting around a Christmas tree, laughing and shaking presents.

George's father, Martin, joined the group in the window, and George watched as he hugged and kissed each of the children warmly on the tops of their heads. He continued to watch as his father held the woman in his arms, and they shared a deep and passionate kiss.

He could only stand there in shock as the obviously happy family settled down to open presents together. And he watched them from the yard across the street, as tears streamed down his face.

He had finally discovered where his father went every year on Christmas Eve, and it was not at all what he had expected.

He had long ago come to terms with the fact that his father didn't care about his own sons, let alone the woman he'd married, and as a result had always believed that the man was simply incapable of love. The scene in front of him of the happy family, with the loving, even doting, father told him a different story.

He continued to watch, his heart breaking, and his anger boiling, as his father picked up the young boy and hugged him fiercely. His father had never hugged him. He had never seen his father hug Harry.

He felt an immediate stab of jealousy and anger watching the interaction on the other side of the window. He wiped furiously at the tears to dry his face. He wanted to throw something at the window, and shatter the happiness he saw there.

With a sad and empty realization, he finally came to the conclusion that it wasn't that Martin Gordon Landon was simply incapable of love.

It was that Martin Gordon Landon was simply incapable of loving him.

CHAPTER EIGHTEEN

Georges came back to the present in a rush. He could immediately tell that the Ukrainian story had ended because the excitement level in the room was high, and everyone was sitting around shaking their presents, making guesses as to what was inside.

He glanced over at Emma, who had a strange look on her face as she stared back at him. Had he done something when he'd checked out during the flashback? He smiled what he hoped was a reassuring smile at her, even though he felt like screaming and going on a rampage.

He could still feel the hurt and anger and jealousy from that ten-year-old boy in his mind. He thought he had dealt with it, and moved on, because God knew his father certainly didn't deserve his attention, or even a single ounce of his hard-won energy. But he was not going to allow any of it to interfere with Emma's Christmas.

He reigned in his anger as he heard Marlie instructing the group, "Okay, everyone, on the count of three. One…two…three!"

There was a mad scuffle as everyone ripped open their presents and pulled out knitted hats. He could see that each hat was slightly different from the other, and everyone exclaimed how they liked their own best. Of course.

He glanced over to see that Laura was showing her hat to Jack, who was still connected through the tablet. The guy definitely had staying power, that was for sure. George felt a little guilty that he had so completely misjudged him. He continued to watch as Laura then pulled out a second hat, which must have been for Jack. She showed the hat to Jack as if she were Vanna

White presenting a vowel, and then secured it on his tablet-head. He smiled. He was starting to like Emma's sisters.

He heard Emma laugh and he looked up to see that she had pulled out a very deformed hat. Christ, that was an ugly hat! One side drooped, looking like it was slightly longer than the other side, and it was a mix of brown and gray yarn, which he did not think matched at all.

He was apparently not up on the latest women's fashions because if Emma's reaction was any indication, she had just been presented with the Hope Diamond.

"Oh, I got Bill's! I got Bill's!" she exclaimed, as she adjusted the hat on her head and modeled it for everyone.

George burst into laughter. He honestly couldn't help himself. She was just so goddamned adorable. "Oh, my God, it's defective!"

But Emma was obviously thrilled with her oddly shaped gift, because she got up and gave Bill a huge hug. "I love it, Bill, thank you!"

George's heart was racing, and he was completely caught up in the moment. He looked at Emma, with all the love he felt, and said, "On you, Emma, it's a classic."

She preened in the deformed hat, smiled at him, then sat back down on the couch. She looked so happy. And that made him happy.

"Oh, Emma, I have another Christmas present for you," Marlie sang in a happy voice. "His name is Bob."

Everyone moaned, and Emma slumped on the couch, saying "Way to ruin the mood, Marlie."

"Now, just keep an open mind. There's this new dad at the school—"

"She's fixing you up again," Laura moaned in exasperation, while at the same time, George demanded in a surprised yell, "She's fixing you up?"

He must have been too loud, because Emma jumped, and Jessica had her hands over her ears. Shit. He'd scared the sweet kid who knew about him, which he certainly hadn't meant to do. He looked over at her and smiled, then he mouthed a "Sorry" to her so that she knew he wasn't mad.

She smiled back at him, and his heart melted. Jesus, what a sweet kid.

"What? He's really nice!" Marlie continued pushing her case. She looked like she was trying to calm down the masses. Apparently they'd all been down this road before, if the sounds of moaning and laughing were any indication.

Bill patted Marlie on the arm, but George couldn't tell if it was in sympathy, or was an attempt to get her to let it go before it was too late.

"Honey, give it up. The last time you fixed Emma up, she didn't speak to you for a week." Then he gave her a look that said, *Do you really want that to happen again?*

"But, seriously, Emma, you have to get back out there." Marlie kept trying, blatantly ignoring her husband.

"No, no I don't. Not with the guys you know, at least," Emma replied, firmly, and George hoped that would be the end of it.

She'd said no, thank Christ. He had no idea what he would do if she went out on a date. He'd follow her, that was for damned sure. But he had no idea how he'd keep the guy away from her. What guy could stay away from her?

"So you're just going to sit around and pine for some guy in a coma the rest of your life?" Marlie asked.

Wait. What?

The room went silent, yet again.

"What did she just say?" George asked. Please God, let him be the guy in the coma she was talking about. Did this mean that Emma might have feelings for him? Him? The man even his own father didn't like?

He waited for what seemed an eternity, but apparently he wasn't going to get an answer because Emma only stared at Marlie with an expression of mute horror on her face.

Yes, horror. The expression on her face was absolute fear. That was the expression he inspired in the woman he loved.

He waited longer, but still she said nothing. And he was consumed with such sadness that his knees buckled. He didn't know how he would survive it if she hated him.

"Smooth, Marlie," he heard Laura say. "I think we've had enough excitement for the night. Come on, Jack, I'm taking you and the kids home now," she declared, as she gathered her kids together, and they pushed Jack out of the room.

"I'm sorry, Em." Marlie sighed heavily, and she must have realized she had gone too far. "I didn't mean it to come out like that. It's just that you talk about him all the time—"

"Marlie," Emma interrupted.

But George had heard it. She talked about him all the time? That had to be a good thing, right? Unless it was to say how big a pain in the ass he was.

George's heart constricted as he saw her cover her face with her hands. Was she embarrassed? Embarrassed wasn't a bad thing, was it? A person didn't get embarrassed like that if they didn't care. Right?

He was grasping at straws, and he knew it, but he couldn't help but hope. He was suddenly very interested in what Marlie had said, and he wouldn't let Emma hide.

He leaned in close to her ear and asked, "You talk about me all the time?"

"Emma, honey, I know you think you're in love with him." Marlie spoke as if she were talking to a kid who'd just been told there was no Santa Claus, and she sat down next to Emma.

In love with him? He hoped to Christ that was true. "You're in love with me?" George asked, hopefully.

Emma groaned. His heart was racing a mile a minute, and his palms were sweating. He took a moment to reflect on how a ghost could have sweaty palms, but he didn't care. He figured if his heart could race, his palms could sweat. And now his mind was racing, too.

How could she possibly be in love with him? He wasn't someone anyone loved. And besides, he was seventeen years older than she was. "I'm old enough to be your father," he stated, at the exact same moment Marlie pointed out, "He's old enough to be your grandfather."

"Hey! That is a gross over-exaggeration!" George exclaimed, then he reached over and lightly poked Marlie in the shoulder. She jumped slightly and looked startled. He hated to admit it, but he felt a satisfied moment of retribution.

The woman had tried to fix up Emma with someone else, for the love of God! On the other hand, she had also let him know—however inadvertently—that Emma was in love with him. He decided he could probably forgive the woman just about anything for that.

Apparently Emma had finally had enough of the both of them, and shouted, "Please. Just. Stop!"

Everyone stopped.

Bill must have decided that it was time to clear the room because he said, "Okay, kids, time for bed! The sooner you get to sleep, the sooner Santa can come."

There was a mad dash by all the kids out of the room and up the stairs. Apparently they didn't need to be coaxed into going to bed early on Christmas Eve.

Dave, in what appeared to be an awkward attempt to shift the mood, said to Hillary, "Hey, did you hear the one about the dyslexic devil worshiper?" He paused for a brief second of showmanship, then gave the punchline: "He sold his soul to Santa!"

Dave laughed heartily at his own joke, and Hillary, who must have been used to her husband's lame jokes, humored him with an eye-roll as they left the room.

* * * * * * *

Marlie spoke quietly to Emma, "Honey, I'm sorry… Can I blame the hormones?" Emma managed to snort a laugh, so Marlie continued, "I just want you to be happy."

"I know you do, Mar," Emma replied with a sigh, "and I love you, too."

Emma realized there was no way to take back what Marlie had just revealed, and she resigned herself to the humiliation as she watched George pace the living room. When he lifted his hands to run his fingers through his hair, she knew the whole situation was beyond repair, and she just wanted it to go away.

"Does he know how you feel?" Marlie asked, tentatively.

"Well, if he didn't before, he does now," Emma replied in defeat.

She looked up and watched George as he stopped pacing and looked directly at her. He didn't look happy, that was for sure. He looked confused and desperate. And she had no idea what to do.

"I don't understand you sometimes," Marlie replied with a confused expression on her face.

"Don't worry about it," Emma responded, trying to reassure her sister without actually being able to explain it. She sighed heavily, got up from the couch, gathered her things together, and said, "I'll see you in the morning."

She wanted so badly to be able to tell Marlie what she had been going through the last several days with George, but she knew that was impossible. Marlie would try to believe her, because that was who she was. She was supportive. But she would think Emma's over-active imagination had run away with her. Again. And given the fact that she already thought Emma's "infatuation" with George was nuts in the extreme, she'd never believe he was haunting her in the most literal sense of the word.

Marlie followed Emma to the front door, which George had already passed through. He was no doubt on the other side of it, waiting to pounce on her to demand an explanation.

She sighed sadly as she hugged Marlie, and said, "Merry Christmas, Marlie."

"Merry Christmas, Em. See you in the morning," Marlie responded with what sounded like genuine concern in her voice.

Emma went outside and quietly closed the door behind her.

Yep, she'd been right. George was pacing on the front porch.

"Just to clarify, you don't know anyone else who's in a coma right now, do you, Emma?" he asked.

She adjusted Bill's hat and looked at George with a bone-deep tiredness. She had to admit, there was something to be said for the feeling of catharsis, now that her secret was out. It was going to come out eventually.

"Look, George, I know you want to talk about this," she replied, "but I've had a really lovely night—well, apart from the whole yelling at myself in the bathroom bit. Can we wait until after Christmas is over?"

Meaning: could she please have the rest of the night to sleep peacefully in the delusion? Tomorrow was soon enough to have to face the brutality of his rejection. He wouldn't be brutal in the way he let her down—he could be hard, but he was never brutal—but it would hurt like hell just the same.

"After Christmas is over, I'll be dead!" he said.

Okay, so she had been wrong. That was brutal. It might be true, but it was still brutal, and her heart couldn't take it.

"Don't say that!" she shouted back at him.

He looked contrite as he said, "But we need to—"

"You said we wouldn't talk about this," she interrupted. She really couldn't do this right now. She just wanted Christmas Eve to stay happy.

"No, I said we wouldn't talk about—"

"Dttt-dtt-dtt," she stuttered in nonsense to get him to stop talking, and put her hand up to silence him. "We aren't talking about it."

"Wait… Which aren't we talking about?"

But she was suddenly too tired to work it out herself, so she headed to her car, got in, and settled into the driver's seat. She pointedly avoided looking at George, as she waited for him to materialize in the passenger seat.

"Buckle up," she ordered softly.

He just looked at her with an indulgent smile on his face, probably waiting for her brain to catch up with her.

Crap! She'd done it again. What was wrong with her? Dumbfounded, she shook her head and muttered, "Sorry," as she started the car and drove away from her sister's house.

"You'd better not be giving me the silent treatment again, Emma, because I really can't stand that."

She glanced nervously at him, and almost laughed. She loved him so much, it broke her heart completely.

"I swear I'll come back to haunt you for real," he continued, "and I'll be dressed as Santa."

She did laugh at that, and she gave him a tentative smile.

But he still looked grumpy.

It was going to be a long night.

CHAPTER NINETEEN

Still wide awake, and hung over from crying, Emma punched her pillow, then rolled over and was startled to see George lying next to her in the bed, staring up at her ceiling.

"How long have you been there?" she gasped, her heart racing a mile a minute.

"She was talking about me, right? Your sister, and what she said about you loving the guy in the coma. That was me, right?"

He seemed relaxed, stretched out with his legs crossed at his ankles and his hands stacked behind his head. But he sounded as if her answer mattered more than he wanted to admit. She felt as if she had the potential to completely destroy his world if she said the wrong thing.

"Yes. She was talking about you." She held her breath and waited for him to respond. Would he be angry?

"So, you're in love with me?" he asked, after a moment that had lasted for several years.

"Yes, George. I'm in love with you." She sighed. It felt like such a relief to finally get it out there. "I've pretty much been in love with you since the day I interviewed to work at Landon Literary."

He continued to stare at her ceiling, so she couldn't tell what his reaction was, but what he said next wasn't what she had expected.

"My father had a second family."

She blinked at him in confusion, not sure she had heard him correctly. A second family? What did that even mean? And why was he telling her this now?

"That's why I hate Christmas," he continued, as if that explained everything.

"Oh," she answered, because he seemed to be waiting for her, for something. But she was still very confused. She had no idea what he was talking about, and hoped he would finally explain it to her instead of giving her the short, cryptic version he'd kept giving her all along.

She so desperately needed to know what was going on in his head. Had her declaration meant the end of whatever precarious friendship she had managed to build up with him?

He rolled over until they were face to face on the bed. Technically, he was way beyond violating her boundaries rule, but she sure wasn't going to mention it. It was too nice having him here with her, especially considering she'd thought he'd already left her.

"His life with us was all duty, and completely sterile," he said, continuing his explanation. "I followed him one night after Christmas Eve dinner when I was ten, to find out why he always left the minute the dessert dishes were cleared, and where the hell he went each year."

He stopped for a moment, and she thought that was all he would say. But then he continued, "I found out he had a whole other, happy life, with a family he loved, who were obviously much more deserving of all his love than his real family. He didn't love us enough to want to spend Christmas with us." He finished his story in a rush, as if the whole thing had been waiting to come out of him for the past thirty-seven years.

She reached out to touch his face and stopped, knowing her hand would just go right through him. "Crap," she said in frustration. She really needed to touch him, and it was killing her that she couldn't. Part of the reason she couldn't was definitely because he was a ghost, and she literally couldn't touch him. But the other part was because she didn't know if he would even want her to touch him.

"That's four hugs now that you owe me," he said. Then he grinned and gave a small, shaky chuckle as he held up his hand and showed her four fingers. Then he asked, "Why?"

"Why what?" Was he going to start teasing her again about hugging so often?

"Why do you love me?"

"Oh, uh…well…because I do." She hadn't expected that. How was she supposed to explain her feelings for him?

"How?" he asked, continuing to push her for an answer. "How can you love a man his own father found so inadequate that he had to start another family, and whose mother didn't love enough to crawl out of a bottle and fight for him?"

He looked at her with forty-some years of insecurity in his eyes and she knew that she would somehow have to figure out a way to put words to what she had in her heart—it was that important to the ten-year-old boy inside him. She wanted to tell him that her heart was bleeding for him, because his father was a complete asshole, but she didn't know how he would take that.

"I love you because of who you are. I love that you have a kind heart, in spite of wanting everyone to believe you don't have one at all. I love that you take such good care of your brother." And because she couldn't resist a tiny jab at Harry, she continued, "In spite of the fact that he's old enough to start doing that on his own."

He snorted, and she held up a hand in front of his face to stop him from interrupting her, because she knew he was going to argue.

"I am so sorry about your father." Her voice cracked on the sob that was stuck in her throat. "He didn't deserve you and Harry. I see now why you are so protective of him."

He didn't say anything, and she worried that she had said too much. "What happened to your mom?" She was worried that she was delving too far into his painful history, and that it would shut him down again, but she needed to know more about him and what had happened.

"I don't know if she ever knew about my father's other life, but it was hard for her to feel so rejected," he responded. "She finally drank herself to an early death."

A family without love was beyond the realm of understanding to Emma, and she gasped at the pain in his voice. How could anyone—let alone a father—treat anyone like that? His wife. His kids. She couldn't even begin to fathom it.

"Oh, my God, George. I'm so sorry," she responded with heartfelt sympathy. "Did you ever confront your father, or at least tell him that you knew?"

"No."

She waited for him to continue, but he was silent. Just when she was sure she had gotten everything out of him that he was willing to give, he started again. "As a kid, I was too afraid of him. When I got older, and found out the truth, I figured it would only do more harm than good. I knew how angry and miserable I felt about it, and I didn't want Harry going through that. Sure, it would feel great to get back at my father, but at what cost to everyone else?"

Her heart broke for the boy he had been. No child should have to live with the kind of betrayal and deceit he had taken on. Yet that child had grown into, and shaped, the man she now loved. Would he be a different man today, had he not lived through what he had then? Would she still love him?

"What about your father's second family? Did you ever try to get in touch with them?"

"Only on paper. Harry and I have a friend who's a private investigator. I asked him to look into the family for me—names, addresses, stuff like that. But I never intended to meet them. I wanted to keep tabs on them to be sure they never got anywhere near Harry or my mother, or our money. They had our father, they sure as hell weren't getting anything else from us."

"Do you think they knew about you and Harry? Maybe your father lied to them, just like he lied to you."

"It doesn't matter. It's old history, and I've stopped keeping track of them. You can see now why I'm not a big fan of Christmas?" He grinned at her with a sheepish expression.

"I'm sorry I was so mean to you about that," she replied, no small amount of guilt in her voice. "To me, Christmas is all about family, and I can't imagine what you went through. But you still have Harry," she added hopefully. "And family isn't always about biology either, George. Family can be—"

He interrupted her by reaching out to touch her. She gasped and slowly closed her eyes. His touch was both soothing and electrifying at the same time. She felt utterly and blissfully content.

"I know, Em, I get it," he said softly in her ear. "I really like your family. I understand now why Christmas means so much to you. Thank you for sharing them with me. It was a very nice Christmas."

Every muscle in her body relaxed from his touch, and she yawned sleepily, before she said, "Tomorrow, we'll go back to Marlie's house for Christmas Day. We have traditional Anderson food for dinner this time."

"I can't wait to smell it, and not eat it," he responded, with a chuckle.

"Roast beef, twice-baked potatoes, sautéed green beans…"

"Will we get to throw potato on the ceiling?" he asked, with a hint of humor in his voice.

She smiled without opening her eyes as she felt herself getting sleepier, but she didn't want their night to end. "Chocolate Kentucky bourbon pecan pie for dessert."

"Shh, honey, you're rambling now. About food. Go to sleep, or Santa won't come."

A second later, she heard him add, "Don't worry, I'll protect you."

She felt his touch as he soothed her to sleep, using his hand to delicately trace her head and face, and she sighed. She felt a tingling on her lips, but she wasn't absolutely sure. She thought she heard him whisper in her ear, "I love you, too, Emma Anderson."

But that might have been her dream.

* * * * * * *

He stood over his body in the hospital bed at Rose Medical Center, challenging it—he dared it not to take him back. There was too much at stake now for it not to. He had never wanted anything as much in his life. And that was saying something, considering his life.

He floated over the bed and blended down on top of his comatose body, compelling it to take him back inside. After a few minutes, his spirit sat back up, and he groaned. "Shit."

He rubbed his fingers through his hair and sat there, utterly dejected, and more frightened than he had ever been before in his life.

He finally had something—someone—to live for, and he was going to die.

CHAPTER TWENTY

Emma was glad to see that the morning of Christmas Day was sunny and bright. The air was crisp, and there was a light snow falling. It was the kind of day she had always considered perfect for Christmas.

The only downside, of course, was George's impending doom, but she had to believe it wouldn't come to that. He was a healthy, vibrant man, never mind that he was in a coma. He would pull through before they disconnected his life support.

Everything would work out. It had to. The universe would never be so cruel as to give her something so wonderful only to take it away from her because of a stupid technicality.

He had told her about his late night trip to the hospital, and how it had been unsuccessful, but even he was now feeling more positive about the outcome.

Besides, George had made her promise that they would continue on with her family traditions until the last possible moment, and then they would face everything together. Those were his exact words—"Whatever happens, we will face it together"—and she had loved hearing him say it. She was feeling better about their future, because George was finally seeing a future—together.

She and George sneaked into Marlie's house and headed back to the kitchen, where Marlie and Bill were talking in hushed tones over their morning coffee. She kissed Bill on the cheek, then gave Marlie a hug and a kiss, silently telling her in her own way that all was forgiven.

"You really are into this hugging thing. You just saw each other last night!" George said.

She smiled and quietly wished Marlie and Bill merry Christmas, then asked for a status update.

"No sign of life upstairs yet?" she asked.

Bill cocked his head to listen, then declared, "I think I just heard Spencer hit the floor. Could be any minute now…"

They heard scuffling and bumping upstairs, followed immediately by stampeding noises down the stairs, and Emma knew that the excitement had just begun.

"Santa came! Santa came!" Jessica's excited voice cried out, alerting the adults that Christmas Day had officially been kicked off.

"Showtime!" Marlie said and smiled, as she refilled her coffee cup. She and Bill headed off to the living room.

"Wow, how can two small kids make so much noise?" George asked.

She smiled at him, and was overcome by how much he had changed in the last few days. She hadn't thought she could possibly love him more than she had before all this started with them, but she was wrong. He was her whole life, and she would do anything she could to give him the love and happiness he deserved.

Now she was scared, but she wouldn't show it, and she wouldn't give in to it.

She didn't know what to do. She had been convinced that his opening up to her last night and letting go of his story would undoubtedly return him to his body, and wake him from his coma. But it hadn't, and she was out of ideas.

In the living room, sitting under the tree, she saw that Spencer and Jessica were already going crazy over their stockings. Emma joined Marlie on the couch as the kids were frantically opening presents.

She saw George standing with Bill as they watched together from the sidelines, both looking excited for the kids with equal amounts of anticipation.

And it broke her heart.

CHAPTER TWENTY-ONE

Emma could see that Harry was red-eyed and distraught, as he stood at the foot of George's hospital bed signing forms with the doctor. The nurse who had been taking care of monitoring George's vitals was also in the room waiting to do her job.

Emma heard the doctor as he spoke encouragingly to Harry, "You're doing the right thing, Mr. Landon. He isn't there anymore, and this is how he wanted it."

"Maybe it's how he wanted it," Harry responded, and she could hear the anger from his grief, "but that doesn't help me to go on without him."

Emma stood with George outside the hospital room, watching as the doctor and nurse gathered around Harry at George's bed. She was in a complete panic because time had finally run out—he was still a ghost, and he still hadn't come out of his coma.

"I can't believe this is happening," she kept saying to herself.

"I'm sorry about the will, Em. If I could go back in time and change it all, I would," he replied.

His words made her finally lose it completely and she burst into tears. She felt like she was in a nightmare, and she couldn't wake up.

"I don't understand," she said again, hoping that someone would explain it to her. "I was positive that if you got into the Christmas spirit—if you worked out your past—you would come back. It's all my fault. You trusted me, and I let you down. I let everyone down."

He moved closer to her, and he seemed to want to put his arms around her, but couldn't. "You're so wrong, Emma," he said soothingly to her, "Christmas has entirely new memories for me, now. No matter what happens, I have my memories with you, and I will always remember them. Thank you for giving me the best Christmas I have ever had."

She frantically wiped at her tears and tried to be brave. She would not dissolve into a puddle when they only had a few minutes left together.

"I don't want to leave you, Emma. I would stay with you if I could. There are so many things I would change, now that I know."

She started crying again, then reached out to him, but he was fading.

"I love you." She was frantic that she wouldn't be able to tell him before he was gone, and blurted the words out without thinking.

Then he very carefully leaned in and lightly kissed her on the lips. She closed her eyes, savoring the moment, and the tingling sensation from the kiss, and she smiled through her sadness.

In the hospital room, she could hear the nurse as she shut off all the beeping machines, and the room went eerily silent.

She abruptly opened her eyes and saw George's ghost, smiling lovingly at her, but it had faded to a vague shadow. "Merry Christmas, Emma..."

Then he disappeared completely.

She fought back her tears, knowing that she couldn't let Harry see them, and she turned to go into the hospital room. She took several deep breaths to collect herself, wiped her eyes, and went into the room to stand with a very distraught Harry.

"Thanks for being here, Emma. I couldn't have done this alone," Harry said, his voice cracking with the grief he was obviously trying to contain.

The nurse removed George's breathing tube as the doctor officially asked, "Call it."

The nurse responded quietly, "Time of death, December 25th, 10:48 p.m."

Emma took Harry's hand in hers, needing the comfort of another person, while she watched as the nurse continued to remove wires from George's body and disconnect the machines.

The doctor turned to Harry and said with compassion, "I'm very sorry for your loss, Mr. Landon." Then he quietly left the room as Harry finally broke and started to cry.

"Time to go, Emma," he insisted.

She resisted, needing to stay as long as possible, needing one last moment with George. "I just need…" she started, and then swallowed hard, fighting back the tears.

"Come on, Emma, this isn't the movies. George isn't going to take a deep breath and miraculously—"

But Harry was interrupted when George's body miraculously took a deep breath.

Emma gasped.

The nurse who had stayed to help them ran into the hall to call the doctor back.

George slowly opened his eyes.

Emma was stunned. Was this real? Was she dreaming? She and Harry moved closer to George, as the doctor came back into the room and checked on his patient.

"Can you speak?" the doctor asked George.

Visibly dazed but definitely awake, George nodded slowly, then cleared his throat and said in a raspy voice, "Think so."

"What's your name?" the doctor asked.

Emma held her breath and waited as George took a moment to swallow. Then he responded in his usual assertive manner, "George Landon."

"Do you know where you are?" the doctor continued.

George looked around the room, then cleared his throat again, and replied, "Hospital."

"Good, George, good," the doctor responded. "Now, do you remember what happened?"

He closed his eyes briefly, as if trying to remember, then groaned and responded, "Hit by a kid on a bike."

The doctor nodded his head as if satisfied by the answers he was receiving from his patient. Emma, still holding Harry's hand, moved closer to the bed. She could hardly contain herself. She couldn't believe he was real.

"Welcome back, George. I knew you could do it," she gushed, and managed to stop herself from kissing him just in time. That would look really strange to the rest of the group.

But George gave her a confused look and said, "Emma? What are you doing here?

"You're your own Christmas miracle," she responded. It was true, he was alive. She wasn't dreaming; he was awake in the bed, and scowling at her like nothing had happened. Wait. He was scowling at her? Why was he scowling? He should be happy.

George groaned and shifted in the bed with a wince. "Oh, you aren't starting in on me with that stuff again, are you?" he asked, grumpily.

Emma was confused. What did he mean? Then her heart plummeted, because he sounded so much like his anti-Christmas George from before. She couldn't understand what had happened. Was everything completely gone, as if time had reset itself?

"Don't you remember?" she asked, trying again, hoping to jog his memory. But he stared at her as if she had grown three heads.

"You were in a coma for a week, George. How are you feeling?" Harry asked.

"Like I got hit by a kid on a bike," George barked back at him.

"Do you remember anything else? Anything?" she asked again, willing him to remember. But he looked at her in frustration and shook his head. Distraught, she prodded him again. "Nothing?"

The doctor patted George's arm and smiled encouragingly at all of them. He must have sensed that George was getting upset, because he said, "You're doing great, George. You rest now, and I'll be in to see you again in a little while." He gestured for Harry and Emma to follow him out of the room.

Emma numbly followed the doctor, and a buoyantly happy Harry, out of the room. She was thrilled that George was alive, but she was also shell-shocked that he didn't remember having been a ghost or anything of their time together. What had happened?

"I've never seen anything like this before," the doctor said, as he directed them to follow him to the nurse's station. "He's an incredibly lucky man to be alive right now. We'll keep an eye on him. But he won't be able to go home for a while."

How could he not remember? He'd told her he loved her. She wanted to curl up into a ball and die.

"But he's going to be okay, right?" Harry asked the doctor.

"He will need constant care when he does go home, and won't be up and around for a couple of weeks after that," the doctor instructed encouragingly.

"We'll take care of it," Harry responded with enthusiasm, as if he were the one who would actually be taking care of his brother. "I'll get round-the-clock nursing for him, and we will check on him regularly. Won't we, Emma?"

She was still numb, but she realized that she was being selfish. George was alive, and that was the most important thing right now. He would remember everything as he got better. He had to. He had told her he loved her. And she loved him, so she would do anything he needed. He was alive, and that was all that mattered.

She nodded and replied automatically, "Of course, anything."

"Good, good. I'll give you some references for nursing care," the doctor said as he led Harry to the nursing station.

She looked hopefully back again at George, but he was already sleeping.

Harry called back to her, "Emma, are you coming?"

She snapped out of it by shaking her head to clear it, then followed Harry to the nursing station. She would get George back on his feet again, and he would remember it all eventually. It was only a matter of time, and it would all come back to him.

CHAPTER TWENTY-TWO

She was officially depressed. George had come back from his coma three days ago, and she should be ecstatic. But he still hadn't recovered his memories of their time together when he was a ghost, and that was not a good thing.

She still didn't really know how he felt about her. Had he loved her before he'd lost his memory of it? He hadn't actually come right out and said so before he faded, but she felt certain that he must have.

Then again, maybe he was grateful to her for helping him come to terms with his childhood and his father's detachment, and that was the extent of his feelings for her.

She was so confused. And she was so…very…incredibly…sad. She was trying to stay positive, because after all, George was alive. But all of her hopes for a relationship with the man she loved were locked up inside his memory somewhere, and she didn't know how to get them out.

There was too much grief to try to hold inside, and the tears started to stream down her face on their own. She didn't know if she was back to square one in trying to get him to fall in love with her, or if it was already a lost cause. Would he have told her he loved her if their time hadn't been cut short? Or had she misinterpreted the emotion she had seen in his eyes before he faded completely?

She was making herself crazy. It didn't help that, while putting away all of her decorations, she stopped almost every ten seconds to look at the empty place where George's tree had used to be.

"Yep. Much easier to clean up," she muttered sarcastically to herself, remembering George's comment about it. She let out a quick chuckle that turned into a sob. Then she took a deep breath, and cleared her thoughts.

Determined to remain strong and to keep moving forward with a positive attitude, she wiped her tears away and added firmly, "I'd rather have a living George than an imaginary tree."

There was always the possibility that he would regain his memory eventually. He had loved her. She hadn't made the whole thing up. But it wasn't as if there were anyone who could corroborate the experience. Other than George. And that wasn't working out so well for her right now.

Maybe George's subconscious would not allow him to remember their experience together. Maybe he regretted telling her about his past so much that he'd blocked the entire experience from his memory.

No. She wouldn't believe it. He never would have shared any of that with her in the first place if he hadn't trusted her. That had to mean that he loved her. He would regain his memory. He had to. She would come up with a plan. She was good at plans and goals.

Look at how well her plan to get him to admit he loved her had turned out. It was brief, but it was real, even if he hadn't actually come out and admitted that he loved her. And, okay, so it hadn't exactly been her plan—she never would have thought of turning him into a ghost who was dependent solely on her—but the end result was the same.

He had loved her. And that had to still be inside him. Somewhere. She just had to find it again.

Her doorbell rang, and she was immensely grateful for the interruption of her thoughts. She opened the door to find a beaming Harry standing on her doorstep.

"I have great news, Emma!" He looked like he did whenever he started a new relationship—as if he had just met "the One" and couldn't wait to tell the world about her. It had yet to last longer than three weeks (and he always seemed to feel genuinely sorry for being the one to break so many hearts), but for the first few hours of the experience he was forever hopeful.

"Come on in, Harry, I could use some good news right about now. I hope your news is that the investigator you hired has been successful getting the pictures back from Crystal?" She stepped back from the door and gestured Harry inside.

"Alas, no, not yet. But I'm not worried. I spoke with him again yesterday, and he assures me he can do the job. He's the best, Em, don't worry about it."

He whipped his phone out from behind his back and waggled it in front of her face. "This is my great news. Look at this." How did he expect her to look at it when he kept waving it at her? She grabbed his hand to hold it steady in order to get a look at the book design he had up on the screen.

"Dean Erickson, *Fight or Flight*," she read aloud.

"We finished the cover design, and I think it looks fantastic."

It did look fantastic. The artwork was dark and mysterious, and gave the impression of danger. It made her want to pick up the book in a bookstore and at least read the story description on the back. He had said this would be a success, and it was beyond anything in her wildest imagination. It looked like Harry truly was on his way to making a success of himself in George's absence. George would be thrilled, and Harry would finally feel like a part of the company. Maybe he would start taking a more active role from now on.

She swiped to the next photo on the phone expecting it to be the book description, but instead found the acknowledgement at the beginning of the book.

Thanks, Harry, for taking a chance on me. Looking forward to getting to know you better outside the office. —Dean

How nice.

"This is wonderful. Good for you, Harry!" She was proud of him, and knew that George would be, too.

"I was hoping you and I could take this to George together to tell him about it. He didn't want to publish it in the first place, but I figure he won't be able to hit me if you're there." He grinned at her to let her know he was only kidding about the hitting part, which was silly because she knew that George would never hit his own brother.

Well, except for that one time…but Harry was drunk and had asked for it…and George had been a ghost…and Harry had no idea it had happened… so that didn't exactly count. Right?

"Let's wait until he gets out of the hospital to give him the good news. We should probably be sure he's completely out of the woods before throwing work stuff at him. Even if it is good work stuff. Don't you think?"

She wasn't sure why she had such a sense of foreboding about this book. George had been adamant about not touching this manuscript, and she still didn't understand that. Had he already been approached by the author, and didn't like the storyline? Had he read something in the manuscript that he hadn't liked? His instincts were usually so accurate with manuscripts.

Either way, she would wait to approach him with it until after he was out of the hospital at least.

Besides, she had her own work to do.

CHAPTER TWENTY-THREE

Emma was hoping that her wardrobe reenactment from the dinner would help jog his memory, so she had taken special care to be sure she looked exactly the same as she had on Christmas Eve—same little black dress with the lace inset, same French twist in her hair pulled up on top of her head, and her favorite black Adrianna Papells that she'd gotten for a killer deal at Nordstrom's last year when she was feeling particularly down about George and Crystal spending New Year's Eve together.

Here it was, New Year's Eve again, but this time George wasn't spending it with Crystal. Unfortunately, he was spending in the hospital, but he was making great progress and the doctor was planning to release him in a few days if he continued to show improvement. She was so happy that George was alive, and out of danger, that she wouldn't allow herself to feel too upset that he had lost his memory. And she hated the thought that he was stuck in the hospital for the New Year.

"I'm his fiancée. Of course I'm allowed in there. It's New Year's Eve, where the hell else would I be but at his side. You've made a mistake."

Emma recognized that voice. And not in a good way. Crystal was at the nurse's station, and from the looks of things, she was plaguing them. Or she might have been casting a curse on them, if the black cloud hovering over her head was any indication.

"You are listed—specifically—on the 'Do Not Admit' list. As a matter of fact, you are the only name on that list, so I'm fairly certain I haven't made a mistake."

Crystal didn't seem to be getting anywhere with the nurses, because they were all but ignoring her, and there was a security guard standing next to her. Good, let her get thrown out of the hospital. She was dressed for a formal ball, which Emma thought looked entirely out of place in a hospital, but apparently Crystal had been planning her own version of a celebration with George and hadn't expected to be refused entry to his room.

Emma walked past her and pretended she had never met the woman, which felt so wonderful, she stopped briefly to wish the nurses a happy New Year, and received exuberant responses in return.

"Happy New Year, Emma."

"Oh, don't you look beautiful."

"Harry was just wondering where you were. Go on in, honey."

She smiled at all of them, then waved and turned to go head down the hall to George's room. She was stopped, abruptly, by a cold hand on her arm.

"Just where do you think you're going?" Crystal said into her ear.

"I'm going to go celebrate New Year's Eve with George and Harry. But don't let me keep you from wherever it was you were going? You're obviously way too dressed up for a hospital visit."

Emma tried to brush off Crystal's hand but she dug her fingernails in and wouldn't let go.

"Don't think for one minute that I'll allow you to get away with this," Crystal hissed. "I have pictures, remember, and I'm not afraid to go that route if you push me."

Emma couldn't believe the audacity of the woman, making a scene as if she had the right to be here. Fine, so, maybe in Crystal's mind she did, but still.

"Is this woman bothering you, Emma?" Earl, the security guard, asked. He and Emma had spent a significant amount of time together over the last couple of days because he had to keep throwing out journalists and photographers who were constantly trying to get pictures of the "newly risen George Landon."

Apparently, George had caught the public eye from all of his fund-raising events, and now he had been elevated to some kind of Denver celebrity status. It made Emma laugh (she knew it would die down when some other person took the spotlight for something bigger than a man coming back from the dead on Christmas Eve), but it made George want to blow a gasket, and it was Emma's job to see that he stayed calm.

"No, but thanks, Earl. Crystal was just leaving."

Earl stepped in closer and placed his hand on the butt of his gun in his holster. Crystal must have understood his meaning, because she finally released Emma's arm, and backed away.

"Just remember the pictures," she snapped, then turned and stomped away.

Remember the pictures? How could she forget them. They still made her sick to her stomach every time she thought about them, which was pretty much constantly. But she was going to trust Harry, and his miracle-working investigator, and not let this hang over her New Year's Eve celebrating. She had other things on her mind—things in her own control—that she had to work on. Like getting George to remember her, for one.

Emma gave an apologetic smile to the nurses, then hurried down the hallway to George's room. She knocked on the door, and Harry's muffled voice told her to come in.

"Emma! Wow, don't you look good enough to eat." Harry gave her a hug, then a quick kiss on the cheek, and she was sure she heard a growl coming from the direction of the bed. "We were wondering when you would make it. I'm having a horrible time trying to get George to snap out of his dark mood, and celebrate the incoming year with me. We have a lot to celebrate, after all."

George was dressed in hospital scrubs, and was sitting on the bed, holding a deck of cards, and glaring at both of them. She was so glad to see him looking better, she could have cried—literally. The last (and only) time he had been in scrubs was when she had first seen him as a ghost, and her heart gave a little squeeze at the memory.

He's alive. That's the most important thing.

"I'm sorry if I interrupted a hot game of poker. Who's winning?"

"Your timing is perfect. George was winning." Harry winked at her, then pulled a chair over next to the bed for her to sit down. "Isn't our girl beautiful tonight?"

"When did she become 'our girl,' Harry? Last time I checked, she was my assistant, and not related to you in any way."

Ouch. Still his assistant, then.

Her dress hadn't triggered any memories, and that was a big let-down. He also hadn't complimented her, like he had the last time he'd seen her wearing it. But then, the "old George" would have been too worried about a sexual harassment lawsuit to have said anything like that to her before, so she really shouldn't be surprised. Or disappointed. (Even though she was both.)

He's alive. That's the most important thing.

"I can't stay. I promised Harry I would stop by and see how you're doing. I'm heading to my sister's house for a New Year's Eve party. She always does Christmas Eve dinner, too." She watched George closely to see if he had any reaction to that. Nothing. Not even an eye twitch.

He's alive. That's the most important thing.

"Okay, then, I'll just say 'Happy New Year' to both of you... And... uhh...I guess I'll see you next year, then." She hoped she was the only one who'd noticed the crack in her voice.

"I was hoping you'd at least stay until midnight, so that I could get a New Year's kiss—"

"Harry!" George barked. "We've discussed this. Repeatedly."

She smiled, then gave Harry a quick kiss on the cheek. "Happy New Year, Harry."

"Happy New Year, Emma. Although, that wasn't exactly the kind of kiss I was hoping for."

"We don't want to keep you from your sister's party. Thanks for stopping by." George started shuffling the deck of cards, and she knew that was her cue to exit. "Take a few days off, and then we can start work again next week."

"Happy New Year, George."

She hurried to the door, and heard Harry say, "Ha! You didn't get a New Year's kiss, because you are way too scary."

He's alive. That's the most important thing.

She hurried to her Jeep, as quickly as she could go in her four-inch heels. She sat inside and took deep, cleansing breaths to calm herself before she turned the ignition, and drove to her sister's house. She would have a glass of champagne...or two...or three...or several, and make merry with all of her family and friends. And she would celebrate the coming of a new year. Who knew what the next year would bring?

He's alive. And that's the most important thing.

* * * * * * *

Emma walked to the office, relieved to be finally doing something again. Ever since New Year's Eve, she had basically been on a paid vacation. What she was really doing was making herself crazy trying to get him to remember.

She walked toward the entrance of her office building, trying to stay warm inside her coat as the snow came down all around her. She held on to Bill's hat, which may have been lopsided but was amazingly warm. She had walked the whole way from the parking garage with her head down to avoid the snow hitting her in the face.

So far her attempts at getting him to remember weren't working. She had stopped by the hospital every day to check in with him, see if he needed anything, and help him begin getting back into the work flow again. But she had also taken the opportunity to drop subtle hints about his time as a ghost.

Nothing. Not a damn thing came out of it, other than making her look like an idiot (she once made the mistake of nonchalantly asking him if he had ever dressed up as Santa, and he looked at her like she had sprouted three heads and grown antlers).

So, it was time for Plan B—or C, or D; she couldn't remember which one she was on. He was going home tomorrow, and he wanted to start working again, so she would have more time to dedicate to her next strategy. In the meantime, she needed to get him distracted with work so that she could have the time she needed for herself.

She stepped off the elevator and into Landon Literary. Holiday Mood had taken down the office decorations, and she was again hit with a wave of melancholy over the end of the season that had once filled her with such optimism.

Focus. Just stay focused and positive, and everything will be fine.

"Hey, Emma! How was your New Year's?" Sandy asked from her usual post in reception.

"Hi, Sandy. Got anything for me today?" she asked distracted by the thoughts still through her mind.

"I hear George is finally getting out of the hospital tomorrow. That's great news."

"Yes, it's great news." Focus. She needed to be better focused for these types of questions. People would, of course, want to know how George was doing, and she was his assistant, so she should have all the answers.

News flash. She didn't have any answers.

"After so much time in a hospital, he was more than ready to go home," she told Sandy. "He asked for a few things from his office, so I'm going to take them over to him."

"I'm glad to hear he's doing so well. It will be nice to have him back again," Sandy said, in her usual upbeat way.

"He won't be ready to come back to the office for a few weeks more though. Not until the doctor clears him. But he's definitely much better." She nodded at Sandy to assure her of his progress, then turned and headed to George's office, deciding she was in no shape to be having a coherent conversation with anyone.

She approached the door to his office and stopped abruptly. She was suddenly swamped with emotion, and the memory of when George had found the mistletoe.

He came out of his office wearing an expression that told her someone had just peed in his morning coffee—either that or he had come across another romance.

"I want Harry to take a crack at this new author's manuscript." George handed it to Emma. Yep, another romance novel.

She groaned and rolled her eyes, knowing that she was the one who was going to have to review it. Harry seemed to hate romance as much as George did, which was surprising considering the number of women Harry had dated.

She gasped in surprise when she noticed mistletoe hanging over George's head. He followed the direction of her gaze and saw it, too. Then he stepped back as if he'd been burned. She tried hiding her laugh with a cough at the last minute, but was apparently unsuccessful if his response was any indication.

"Emma, that isn't funny, not to mention entirely inappropriate for the office."

"I certainly didn't put it there!" she cried, defensively. She was determined, not stupid. She would never even have considered trapping him like that.

But George kept on scowling at her, and said, "Get it down immediately."

Shaking her head in an effort to wipe away the memory, she continued into George's office to his desk and picked up a stack of manuscripts. Then she looked around absently, trying to remember what else it was that she needed to bring to him.

She opened a drawer, closed it, then opened another drawer, and saw the mistletoe inside. It was still in his desk.

She slumped into George's chair as tears came to her eyes. She was a wreck. How was she going to get through this—working for George as if nothing had happened—without having a complete mental and emotional breakdown?

She would just have to, that was all there was to it.

She shut the drawer with renewed determination, wiped her eyes and left George's office. She didn't have time to dwell on memories. She needed to hurry because she was meeting Harry at George's house to give him the good news about the success of the Dean Erickson book.

* * * * * * *

She pulled up in her Jeep outside of George's large Victorian home, where he lived in Cherry Hills Village. She carried the manuscripts and her bag up to the front door and rang the doorbell.

Crystal answered the door.

What.

The.

Holy.

Hell.

She was utterly speechless. The monster was still alive. This was what happened when you turned your back on the bad guy. They always sneaked up behind you in the end and stabbed you through the heart.

Life truly sucked. The Powers That Be were just plain mean.

Obviously, Harry's investigator friend wasn't all he'd been advertised to be, and this lying, cheating, conniving, manipulating, deceitful, lying—wait, she'd already said that one—lizard had moved in.

"Oh, hello, Ella. He's in the study," Crystal said haughtily, as she stepped back to let Emma inside. "Nice hat," she snickered sarcastically when she noticed Bill's present on Emma's head.

Emma removed Bill's hat and self-consciously stuffed it into her coat pocket. She was positive the "Ella" was meant to prove some point on Crystal's part, although she couldn't be sure, and certainly wasn't going to ask her.

"Thanks, Crys," Emma responded, inflecting her voice with as much sweetness as possible, as if she were speaking to her bestest friend on the planet. "It was a Christmas present, but I could get the name of the store where they bought it if you'd like to get one of your own. You know, they say that imitation is the sincerest form of flattery."

Crystal looked confused, then she glared at Emma.

"Just don't forget about the little chat we had the last time we met," Crystal hissed, all pretense of civility gone from her demeanor.

"I told you then, and I'll tell you again now, Crystal, he won't hear about it from me." Emma was getting awfully tired of being threatened by this woman. "Is Harry here yet?"

"Do I look like the butler? I'm not the one who's the hired help. Go back and find out for yourself." Apparently Crystal didn't enjoy answering the door for George's visitors, and she certainly didn't have the polish of a butler, so maybe George was using her to keep out the unwelcome solicitors.

Kind of like a gargoyle. Only less cuddly.

"Aren't you afraid of leaving Harry alone with George? Or did you have one of your 'Crystal bathroom talks' with him as well?" If looks could kill, Emma was sure she would have been the one making the next ghost appearance.

Luckily mere looks, however potent, don't have that kind of an impact, and Crystal was far too skinny not to snap like the brittle twig she was if it ever came to a cat fight, so Emma chose to ignore her and began her search for George's study.

Emma had never been to George's house before, and was more than curious to see the inside. She headed off in the direction where Crystal had vaguely pointed, and decided this would be an opportune time to snoop, just a little bit.

She poked her head inside the first door on her right, which turned out to be a closet filled with nice-looking men's coats. She took a deep breath and smelled the wonderful sent that was George before closing the door and moving further down the hall.

She could hear voices—first George's, then Harry's in response—and followed their sound until she reached the open double doors of what had to be his study, because that was where she found them. George was reclining on a leather couch with pillows behind his back and a blanket tucked around his legs, and Harry was sitting in a large recliner next to George's head.

The study was pretty much what she would have expected from George. It was rich, and imposing—lots of chocolate-colored leather and floor-to-ceiling bookshelves filled with limited editions. But it was also comforting—with its overstuffed armchairs positioned in front of the fireplace, holding soft chenille blankets and matching throw pillows, just begging to be napped in—and she knew it would probably have surprised him to know that she also expected that from him.

She felt like she had come home. There was a crackling fire, and a huge bay window, complete with a padded seat and large pillows, that looked out over a massive expanse of snow and mountains. She imagined this was also a spectacular sight in the spring when the wild flowers were in bloom. Or in the fall when the aspens were turning to gold.

Then she wondered if she would ever get the chance to see either of those sights in the future. She could imagine sitting in the window seat writing while George sat at his desk and reviewed manuscripts.

George had looked up when she came into the room, and he smiled at her as if he was genuinely glad to see her. He was probably wondering why she hadn't said anything yet, and she knew she had to bring her mind back to reality and stop letting it wander off without her.

"Hi, Emma," he said, greeting her enthusiastically. "Thanks for bringing those by, I really appreciate it."

"I don't mind," she replied, smiling warmly back at George. "I'm just really glad you're awake, and doing so much better. Hi, Harry."

She handed George the stack of manuscripts, and he took a few minutes to look through them.

"I was surprised to see Crystal answering the door." She looked pointedly at Harry, and he shrugged. Apparently she had been a surprise to him as well.

"Has Harry already reviewed these?" George asked, pointing to the notes in the margins. Then he added, "Wait. These notes are in your handwriting."

"Oh, uh, yeah. I, um…I did." She had forgotten that he would be back to not knowing that she did the manuscripts he assigned to Harry. She glanced at Harry for help, but he had gone completely pale, and she knew she wouldn't get any assistance from him. What was wrong with him?

She sat down in the chair at George's feet, directly opposite from Harry, and took a moment to arrange her things in an effort to buy herself some time. She had heard somewhere that it was best to stick to the truth as much as possible, so she said, "I reviewed those. For Harry. Some of them. Before he started doing them. Er…when he's not available."

Brilliant. That sounded absolutely terrible. But she knew that it was only the beginning of the small white lies she was going to be required to tell. At least for now.

George put down the manuscripts and looked at her in confusion. "Are you okay?" he asked with concern in his voice. "You don't seem your normal exuberant self lately."

"Has Harry told you about his big success yet?" She didn't know if now was the right time to blurt that out, but she was anxious to deflect his attention before he realized she was lying to him. Because he would realize it.

"No, what success?" He looked between the two of them, expecting someone to say something, but she still wasn't sure who was running this show.

"Yes, it's been a huge success, you'll be surprised. Emma, tell him about the great new author and the huge success." Harry was obviously nervous; he was repeating himself.

"No, Harry, this is your success, you should tell him the good news." Great. Now she was repeating herself. She really wanted Harry to be the one to get all the glory for this one, because he had worked so hard on it, and was so proud of it.

"Well, okay…sure…right…" Harry shifted his chair slightly so that he was a little further away from George, but still facing him. "While you were… uh…out, I discovered a brilliant new author, and we are have a contract with him to publish his book. He had originally planned to self-publish, but on a whim—that's how he said it—he decided to send it to us at the last minute. His manuscript was the cleanest one we've ever seen, so we were able to get started on it immediately. We plan to publish months earlier than expected—both e-book and paperback. Based on some advance reviews, we expect it to hit the bestseller list in record time."

"That's fantastic, Harry. I always knew you had it in you, it's in your Landon blood. You just needed to find the right author to give you your first big win."

George beamed proudly at Harry, who let out a long sigh of relief, and Emma was thrilled that it had all gone so well. She had worried over nothing.

"Who's the author?" George asked, still smiling.

"His name is Dean Erickson, and the book is—"

"Who did you say?" George's eyes turned glacial as they looked at Harry. She felt sorry that they were focused on Harry, but she felt even better that they weren't looking in her direction instead.

"Look, George, I know you didn't originally want to publish this one, but the work is really good. Did you read it?" Harry was rubbing his hands together in a nervous gesture, but he was standing up to George, and Emma was glad to see it. Maybe all he had needed was something to believe in, and he believed in this book.

"I didn't have to read it. I was never going to publish it. Ever."

"Well, I am. And it's already a done deal." Harry stood up from his chair and loomed over George. "It's going to be a huge financial success for

Landon Literary. And you can thank your incompetent little brother—who you obviously thought would never amount to anything—for all the money we've made from it."

"Oh, Harry, he didn't—" Emma started to say, but she was cut off when Harry yanked his coat from the back of his chair and stormed out of the room. She turned back toward George. She was so angry with him, she was shaking. She loved him, but he was way out of line.

"What is the matter with you? What is so wrong about this book that you felt justified in being so cruel to Harry over it? He has pulled off something amazing, in a very short amount of time, just to prove himself to you, and you eviscerated him."

"Don't start with me, it has nothing to do with you. He blatantly defied me on this. And I'm supposed to commend him for it? He has no idea who this kid really is!" He sighed, and all the anger seemed to just fall right off of him. He leaned his head back on the pillow and closed his eyes as if he was suddenly too tired to continue.

"It's not Harry's fault," he continued, without opening his eyes. He sounded as if he were speaking to himself. "How could he have known. I never told him about any of it."

"Any of what? What haven't you told him?" What was so wrong about Dean's manuscript that George would hate it so much? They had published controversial manuscripts before. What was so different about this one?

Unless it wasn't the manuscript that had him so upset. He had never read the manuscript—he'd immediately tossed it into her garbage can when it had arrived—and said he would never publish anything from the author. It wasn't the manuscript at all. He didn't like Dean Erickson. Did Dean have anything to do with George's father running out on their family, and all their Christmas Eve dinners?

She felt like she had just been punched in the stomach, and she gasped her next breath. Had she just helped Harry publish a book by his half-brother? The same half-brother George believed had all but stolen his father from him? No wonder George was so angry about it.

"Never mind. Let it go," George said, breaking into her thoughts.

Let it go? How was she supposed to do that? He had poured his heart out to her as a ghost. Maybe she could somehow find a way of letting him know that she understood him—that she knew about his secret—without actually saying it.

"George, I—"

"Thanks for bringing my work by, Emma."

That came out sounding an awful lot like he was dismissing her. And he hadn't even opened his eyes to do it. Had he seriously just treated her like she was the hired help? Darn it, now she was starting to sound like Crystal. And that just made her cranky.

"Maybe you should stop being such a sanctimonious ass, and just tell him." She hadn't meant to blurt that out—and she didn't even mean it... much—but he was really pissing her off, and she couldn't stop herself.

Following Harry's lead of a suave exit, she yanked her coat off the back of her chair. Unfortunately, one of the buttons got stuck between the armrest and the seat cushion, and she had to yank on the coat to dislodge it, which almost landed her on her keister when it came free. She grabbed the rest of her things and headed for the door to the study, hoping his eyes had still been closed.

Just as she was about to make her escape, Crystal breezed into the room as if she already lived there, and announced, "George, I'm feeling cooped up. I thought I'd go shopping."

"My assistant just called me an ass," she heard George say from the couch, and there was a definite note of humor in his voice.

"Did you hear me, George? I want to go shopping," Crystal whined in response.

"I don't care, Crystal, do what you want." There was no more humor left in his voice.

As she cleared the doorway, Emma glanced a quick look back at George and saw that he was already back at his work. She was still mad at him, and even though she tried not to, she couldn't help but feel smug that he had barely acknowledged Crystal's presence, let alone her demand to spend his money.

* * * * * * *

She was typing feverishly on her home computer, completely engrossed in her writing. She had been working on the basic outline of this manuscript for months, and hadn't been able to get anywhere with it. But suddenly, she knew exactly how the story would go.

She had awakened this morning with the cold, sad realization that she had all but wasted the last two years of her life pining for a man who was never going to notice her under normal circumstances. It took him getting hit on the head, literally, to need her enough to finally notice her.

And now that he was back in his normal life again, she was setting herself up to waste another two years of her life with that same man if she didn't do something about it. She needed to do something to get back the man who had been a ghost.

There had been no indication, not even a small glimmer, that he would ever get back his memories when he had been a ghost. So it was time for her to take control over her destiny. Again.

George had read her stories when he was a ghost, and he'd told her they were good. Logically (because that was how she would be approaching everything from now on), if he had liked them once, he would like them again. Her manuscripts weren't ghosts. They were real, and that wouldn't change.

So she would write all of it. From the hit on the head to the moment he woke up from the coma. She would pour everything she had into the story, and maybe, just maybe, it would get him to remember it all. Sure, it would be under the guise of fiction, but if he read the story—exactly how it had happened in real life—maybe it would get him to remember.

She had to try. She had nothing else left to lose. If this didn't work, she would have to quit her job and finally leave him. It was worse for her knowing that he had, for one brief shining moment, loved her. She couldn't continue this way any longer.

When her phone rang, she answered it absentmindedly, resenting the intrusion.

"Hello?"

"Emma?" Marlie's concerned voice asked through her phone. "Honey, are you okay?"

Emma was instantly sorry for her moment of resentment. She was still avoiding both of her sisters, because she didn't know what to say to them. She was a complete wreck—something that would never have escaped her sisters—and she hadn't had the energy to make up a plausible excuse. (Huh. That probably didn't bode well for her creative writing abilities?)

After all, her New Year's deadline had come and gone, and she was still working at Landon Literary, without a declaration of love from her boss.

She cradled the phone on her shoulder and continued writing, hoping this wouldn't take long.

"Yeah, sure. What's up?" she responded, belatedly realizing that she sounded snippy, and hoped Marlie wouldn't take offense.

"How's George doing?" Marlie asked as an obligatory opener, thankfully either not noticing or choosing to ignore Emma's curt tone.

"He's good. He's home now, and he's getting better every day," she responded. *Did I mention that I think he may have said he loved me? Except that I'm not sure about that part, and he doesn't remember it now anyway, and oh, yeah, that I'm a wreck?*

She wished she could tell her big sister everything.

"And how are you doing, now that he's back among the living?" Marlie asked, with genuine concern in her voice.

What was she doing? Marlie loved her, and here she was, acting like a brat toward her. She stopped writing, and sat back in her chair in order to pay more attention to the conversation.

"Marlie, I'm fine, really," she said, although she sounded only marginally convincing, even to herself.

"You seem worse now that he's out of his coma," Marlie responded, apparently not believing her either. "Honey, I'm really worried about you."

Emma wasn't sure what to say. She wanted to spill everything, if only just to unburden herself and to have someone to share what she was going through.

But she knew this wasn't an option for her, even if she could explain the craziness to her in any form of understanding. Marlie simply wouldn't believe any of it. She would try, but it would be completely beyond her realm of possibility. And without any way to prove it to her, the whole thing was hopeless.

She needed to get off the phone before she lost her hard-earned hold on her emotions, because her sister would see right through her. Yes, she had a new direction, and she was going to stick to it. But it was still fragile, and she could feel the foundation of it beginning to shake underneath her.

"Marlie, it isn't that I don't appreciate your concern, and you know I love you, but I'm on a roll here with my manuscript, and I'm almost finished. Can we talk about this later? Maybe celebrate when I've completed it?" she asked, hopefully. *Or, maybe you can help me pack my office up if it doesn't work?*

"Yeah. I don't mean to get in the way of your writing frenzy," Marlie responded. "Just call me when you come up for air, will you?"

She leaned forward and could feel the lump forming in her throat over the concern she heard in her sister's voice.

"Yes. Yes, I will," she whispered through the lump in her throat. "As soon as I'm finished. Promise."

"Okay, honey. Love you."

"Love you, too. Bye," she said, and hung up the phone as quickly as she could. Then she laid her head down on her desk, and sobbed.

CHAPTER TWENTY-FOUR

Emma sat in an armchair in front of George's desk in his home study, using her new tablet to take notes as he went through the numerous company receipts that had piled up during his convalescence. He looked much better, and was finally able to spend time sitting up in a chair again, instead of on his couch.

He was beginning to look like himself again, and she was very happy to see it. She knew he was looking forward to being able to go back to the office to work again.

"What's this receipt for a new tablet?" he asked, holding up the invoice for her to see.

"You gave—" she started to say. Then she remembered that the George in front of her hadn't been with her when George as a ghost had told her she could give hers to Laura, and she froze. "Uh…well…that is…I mean…I somehow lost my other one, so you needed to give me a new one," she stammered, trying to come up with a cover story on the spot.

"You lost it? That's not like you." He looked at her as though he didn't believe she could possibly be telling the truth, which she wasn't, of course. God, she really hated lying, even out of necessity.

"No, it isn't, George. I'm sorry," she replied, trying to look contrite, even though she was pretty sure he wasn't going to buy it.

He didn't.

And he looked very angry.

"Emma, I don't care about a lost tablet. Get yourself fifty of them for all I care," he said, almost shouting at her.

She looked up, startled by his outburst. Oh, boy. Yep, he was pissed. She had never lost anything in the whole time she had worked for him. She hated to tarnish her perfect record, but what else was she supposed to tell him? *Yeah, you see, when you were a ghost…*

"I just want to know what's wrong with you lately," he continued, but in a much calmer voice. "Is this about the fight I had with Harry over that author?"

"I—"

"Because I've looked at the financials, and I know that he was right. It will be a blockbuster. I'm not happy that he went behind my back, but considering I was in a coma, I thought I would cut him some slack on that one. I hope you don't truly believe that I'm such a sanctimonious ass that I can't admit when I'm wrong."

"I'm sorry I said that. I was upset, but I shouldn't have called you that."

"You were right, I was being an ass. I'm not sure about the sanctimonious part, but the ass part was true enough." He flashed her a self-deprecating smile, and she wanted to throw her arms around him and tell him how much she loved him. She also wanted to tell him that he had a very nice ass part, but that was probably inappropriate, considering. "I've already apologized to Harry. We've kissed and made up. So you can stop moping. I really hate it when you mope. Please, stop moping?"

"I guess I just have the post-Christmas blues is all." Her insides melted at the thought that he was worried about her. He looked so concerned that she desperately wanted to reach into his brain and pull out his memories. They must be in there, somewhere, waiting for someone to knock them loose.

"It's my fault, isn't it?" he sighed.

Hope flared in her heart. Had he remembered something?

But he burst her happy moment by saying, "I've got you working here, and at the office, and helping Harry."

He stood up, and came around to her side of the desk, which he leaned against in order to stand next to her. He was so handsome, and he'd started wearing his work clothes again. She wanted to cry, he looked so good to her. And all that concern in his eyes was focused on her as though, by some miracle, he really did remember that he loved her.

"What is it, Emma? Am I over-extending you?" he asked.

Okay, so he did, miraculously, care about her, which was definitely a new improvement over the old pre-coma George model. But was it an I'm-concerned-that-I-might-have-to-train-another-new-assistant-because-this-one-is-acting-like-such-a-ninny-hammer-that-she-can't-handle-the-workload kind of concern? Or was he actually developing feelings for her?

Flustered by all the thoughts in her head, not to mention his nearness to her—God, he smelled so good, she had missed that while he was a ghost—she tried to cover it by reaching into her bag and pulling out her finished manuscript. She clutched it in her lap like a shield, then took a deep breath and said, "I realize this is asking a lot, and probably taking advantage of my position, but I was hoping you would read a manuscript for me."

"Of course. Who's the author?" he asked, looking confused by her abrupt change in subject. "It'd better not be another Dean Erickson."

He smiled at her to let her know he was teasing, but she could see he wasn't completely over the whole situation.

"No. I am. I'm the author." Then she handed him her manuscript before she could change her mind. "I was told by someone once that my stuff was good enough to publish, and that I should bring it to you when I finished it. So I was hoping you would read it and consider it."

She held her breath as she watched him read the title page.

"Christmas Spirit," he read aloud, and chuckled. He chuckled? That was new. Why didn't he groan and remind her—emphatically—about how much he hated Christmas? "That is so like you already. Okay, give me the weekend to read it and I'll give you my honest opinion on it."

She let out a huge sigh of relief that he hadn't turned her down flat. She had been certain she was going to have a battle with him over a Christmas manuscript. This had to be a positive sign.

"I would really appreciate that, George, thank you." She smiled nervously as she stood up to leave.

"I got good news from the doctor today," he said quickly, as if trying to keep a conversation going with her so that she wouldn't leave yet. "He cleared me to return to the office, so I can start back again on Monday.

We can get back into our normal routine again. I hope that'll snap you out of your post-Christmas blues?"

"Sure, yep, that's great." She wasn't sure how much longer she could stay here with him without breaking down, and was already making a beeline for the door. "See you in the office on Monday then."

Her first hurdle was cleared. She had gotten him to commit to reading the story, and that was a really good step. She had so much riding on that story. Now she just had to wait and see what he thought of it. And even more importantly, if he remembered it.

"Have a good weekend. I'm sure I'll like the manuscript." He smiled at her and she almost melted into the floor. God, she loved his smile. She smiled back and their eyes held for a moment.

Then Crystal came barging in, with her usual practiced bad timing, as if she had nothing better to do than stand outside and wait for this precise moment each time Emma came to visit.

Crystal was wearing her winter coat, and carrying George's coat in her hands, apparently anticipating an excursion. Somewhere to spend George's money, no doubt.

"Come on, George. You promised that today we could go shopping. You still haven't bought me my Christmas present, and I know just the thing," she said, then sneered at Emma.

Hearing Crystal refer to the engagement ring she had been planning to convince George to buy her hit Emma like a slap to the face. She was so devastated it made her sick, and she knew that their time had finally run out. The investigator hadn't come through, and there was nothing they could do about it.

She had to get away. Fast.

She hurried out of the room, and rushed through the front door to reach her car before the dam could burst, and her tears could start gushing.

* * * * * * *

George couldn't understand what had upset Emma so much that she felt the need to run out of the room, but he had to admit he hadn't wanted her in the same room with Crystal. Crystal was toxic, and it was time to get her the hell out of his life.

What she had done to Harry and Emma was unforgivable, and he only had himself to blame for it. Their relationship had gone on far too long, and he should have called it quits long before he even went into the coma.

"George? Did you hear me? You still owe me a Christmas present."

"We're done. Pack whatever you have here that belongs to you, and get out. I've already made an appointment with a locksmith to have the locks changed."

He flinched slightly at his own words. Had he spoken too harshly in his desperation to get away from her? No—if anything, they weren't harsh enough, considering who she was, and what she had tried to do.

"This is so sudden. You can't possibly mean what you're saying." She stepped toward him, and he moved around so that his desk was between them. The thought of her touching him made his flesh feel like it was covered in maggots.

"I mean it. I don't ever want to see you again. We're over."

"Oh, I don't think so, George. You see, I have pictures that you might be interested in seeing that—"

"You mean these pictures?" He pulled a handful of pictures from his drawer and tossed them across his desk as if they were too revolting to touch. It made him sick to know that she had done that to herself in order to control him through Harry. How had he ever allowed himself to be so manipulated by her? Harry had been right about her the whole time.

Emma was right, he was a sanctimonious ass. He almost smiled, remembering her indignation on Harry's behalf. Emma was the kind of woman a man wanted at his side, not this bitch in designer clothes standing in front of him.

"Silly George. Those are just copies. I have—"

"A flash drive? As in this flash drive?" He produced the flash drive Harry had given him and showed it to her. Then he tossed it to the floor, and crushed it with the heel of his shoe.

It was incredibly gratifying to watch her blanch.

He was sure it would be even more gratifying to watch her car drive away from his home. Forever.

"It's time for you to go. If you think for one minute that you can pull your shit with me again, you will regret it." He took her by the elbow and propelled her out of his office, down the hall, and out the front door. "And if you ever come so much as within a hundred miles of Emma, I'll bring you up on so many charges you will be looking through the bars of a prison cell for your next three lives."

He had no idea what prompted him to say that last part, but he knew he meant it. And it had felt so good to say it. He decided that even more gratifying than seeing her car drive away would be slamming the door in her face.

CHAPTER TWENTY-FIVE

George was sitting behind his desk on Monday morning, and he was feeling wonderful. It was so good to be back in the office working again. He'd been there almost an hour when Emma came in.

She was still wearing her coat, which he thought was unusual, but he smiled at her, and was genuinely glad to see her.

He appreciated all of her help in getting him back on his feet again, but he'd somehow missed their office routine together. He'd missed her banter, and her spunk, and he'd even missed her arguing with him. She hadn't argued with him in a long time. What was wrong with her lately?

He hoped his news about her manuscript would cheer her up.

"There you are. Come in, I want to talk about your manuscript," he said by way of greeting, hoping she would take off her coat.

For some reason, the fact that she was still wearing it gave him an uneasy feeling, as if she wasn't planning to stay. That thought gave him a moment of panic, and his heart stuttered in his chest.

She came into his office and sat down nervously, as if she was uncertain about being there. Something was very wrong, and he didn't like it at all.

"It needs some editing," he continued, hoping that talking about the manuscript would help. "But I think it's really good, Emma. I hope I don't sound egotistical if I ask…" he stopped for a second, wondering if he should ask. "Did you get this idea from my being in a coma?"

She nodded her head, but still hadn't said a word, which was starting to worry him.

"Well, thanks for not using my name then. I think this is certainly something we would want to publish here," he said. He looked thoughtfully at the manuscript for a moment, then asked, "I just have one question. Why the tragic ending?"

"It's a tragic story," she replied, sadly.

He had never seen her like this before. It was starting to worry him.

"No, it isn't," he said. "At least not until the end. Come on, Emma, I've always taken you for the hopeless romantic. What happened here?"

He started to panic, and he didn't know why. He was tense waiting for her response.

He had loved the story, which was significant, because it was a romantic story, and he hated those. Plus it was around Christmas, and he hated that. But he had loved every moment of this one. She had pulled him along, every step of the way. Right up until the very end, which he hated.

She would need to change it before they published it. He would never agree to it being published the way it currently ended. He rationalized the angst he felt under the belief that it wouldn't sell with the ending she had given it.

She shrugged sadly, and he saw her swallow hard. Was she trying not to cry? What the hell was going on with her? Had someone died? She had family here, didn't she? A couple of sisters or something? He hoped nothing had happened to them, but he wasn't sure if he should ask.

"I can't explain it," she croaked, "that's just how the story ends."

"But it makes him seem so shallow and—"

"He isn't shallow!" she interrupted vehemently. "It's just the way it turns out."

Frustrated, he tossed the manuscript onto his desk in a huff, and asked, "But why—"

"I can't do this," she said abruptly, and shot out of her chair. "I thought I could, but I can't."

Panic started to take hold of him, and he stopped short. What the hell was happening? What did she mean? He tried to calm her down, to appease her, to keep her from leaving him.

"I'm sorry," he said, as calmly as he could manage considering his insides were in a knot. "I didn't mean to offend you. I'm just trying to understand—"

"I quit, George. I can't work for you anymore," she said, interrupting him again. And she rushed out of the room.

She left him.

Fear like he had never experienced before in his life sliced through his entire body, and he stood immobile for several seconds.

"Emma!" he called after her. Panic kicked in, and it finally got him moving again.

When he reached Emma's office area, he saw that she was talking with a woman and a little girl.

"You haven't returned any of my calls," the woman was saying, and she was looking at Emma with concern. "So Jessica and I thought we'd stop by to see how you're doing, and take you to lunch."

"Uh, sure, okay..." Emma replied, but he could see there was definitely something wrong, and tears had started falling down her cheeks.

Jesus Christ, what happened? Someone had to have died. Why hadn't she told him? He would give her time off. But she wasn't quitting on him. That was for damned sure.

He watched, frozen to the spot where he stood, as she went to her desk to hastily gather her things, and his heart sank.

"Emma, what the hell—" he asked. He would get answers from her, goddamn it, and he would get them now.

"Hello again," the little girl said in a happy voice, and she smiled up at him.

Confused, he looked down at her, wondering who she was, and how she knew him. Then his mind reeled, and he saw her in a completely different place and time.

"Hello again," came a quiet voice from behind him.

He could feel the increasing thump, thump, thump of his heartbeat, and knew this little girl was somehow significant to him.

"Uh, hello?" he asked, trying not to scare her away. "Do you know who I am?"

"You were with Aunt Emma at the zoo, and then when we went to see Santa," she replied, apparently not scared of ghosts.

She had seen him before. He had known her before. How could that be possible? He had only just met her.

"Are you Aunt Emma's George?"

Yes! Yes, he was! He wanted to call out to her, to tell her that, yes, he was Emma's George. Tell her! Tell her, he was Emma's George!

He shook his head to clear it, and wondered what the hell had just happened. Dazed and confused, he looked over at the woman standing with the little girl—Jessica, the little girl's name was Jessica.

How did he know that?

"Have we met?" he asked the woman. She looked so familiar. But he was confused.

"I'm Marlie, Emma's sister," she replied, extending her hand for him to shake. "You must be George. My daughter, Jessica, and I stopped by to see if we could steal Emma away for a bit to have lunch together."

He was right. The little girl was Jessica. He knew that. And he'd know the woman's name, too, before she'd even said it. Marlie.

"Uh, yeah, sure," he replied absently. His head was starting to ache, and he still had unfinished business with his Emma—his assistant, he meant. "Emma, may I have a minute with you before you go?" he asked as politely as possible, but was still making it abundantly clear that he wouldn't take no for an answer.

He wasn't about to let her leave, even for lunch with her sister—hell, especially for lunch with her sister—without making sure she wasn't leaving him permanently.

"I don't think so, George," she replied, and he could see that she was shaking.

He felt a sharp stab of pain in his chest; was he having a heart attack?

"What's going on, Emma?" he asked as calmly as he could, but he couldn't keep the shake out of his voice. "You have been acting so strangely lately. I don't understand."

"I'll give you two weeks' notice, but I can't work for you anymore," she replied, and he heard Marlie gasp behind him.

"Okay, honey," Marlie said, almost in a whisper. "Jess and I will just go, and wait for you in the lobby or..."

George heard scuffling behind him, which he figured must mean they were leaving. He didn't care what the hell they did, as long as they didn't take Emma away from him.

But she looked like she was going to bolt at any minute. Over his dead body. She wasn't going anywhere until they cleared up whatever this was. He couldn't let her leave him. He needed her, goddamn it. Didn't he?

He glanced up at the hideously ugly hat that she was nervously fiddling with on the top of her head, and he gasped in recognition.

"Oh, my God, that hat…" he whispered.

His world spun, as he flashed back to a memory he hadn't known even existed.

"Oh, I got Bill's! I got Bill's!"

What an ugly hat. But she was so beautiful, and she was all he could see.

"On you, Emma, it's a classic."

She preened in the deformed hat, smiled at him…

And his brain exploded.

He came abruptly back to the present in the office, and staggered under the weight of the pain in his head. He stepped back, and swayed. He watched from a daze as Emma reached out and took hold of his arm to steady him.

"George?" she asked with genuine fear in her voice.

He heard her calling his name as if from the other end of a tunnel.

His world tilted again, as he looked at her hand on his arm, and was immediately catapulted into another phantom memory—in the hospital, Emma touching his arm…

He remembered it all.

"George? Are you all right?" she asked, every word still laced with fear. "You're scaring me. Are you okay? Do you need to sit down?"

Was he having a brain seizure? Was he going to end up back in a coma? Sweet Jesus, his head hurt so much. He was going to die.

"Jessica, and Marlie…" he whispered, barely able to get the words out through the pain in his head. "And that Bill's hat…oh, Christ, Emma."

He remembered everything. He looked at her, searching for confirmation, to be sure he wasn't imagining it all. "That's Bill's hat, isn't it?" he asked, needing to know, frantic to hear her confirm it. "And that was Marlie, and your niece Jessica who were here. I met your whole family. Didn't I?"

She nodded carefully through her tears, and he could see she was just as scared as he was.

"Oh, Emma," he said, his voice breaking on a sob.

Then he took her face in his hands and he kissed her. He held on to her, all but crushing her against him, worried that she would leave him, and not willing, or even able, to let her go. If he was going to die, he wanted it to happen while he was with Emma. She would get him through it, just like she did everything.

He would never let her go.

It felt so good to finally kiss her. He was actually kissing his Emma. Lips to real flesh-on-flesh lips. She felt so damned good.

The pain in his head subsided to a dull ache—something that could undoubtedly be cured by a mild painkiller. He wasn't going to die. He refused to die. Not now that he finally had Emma in his arms.

He kissed her eyes, and tasted the salt from her tears. He kissed her nose, then her cheek, and then the other cheek, before returning again to her lips.

"Oh, God, Emma, it was all right there in your manuscript, and I didn't remember it," he moaned. How could he have forgotten the best thing that had ever happened to him? "Then I saw Jessica, and Bill's hat, and you touched me, and it all came rushing back to me."

He was overwhelmed by his emotions, especially fear that he had almost gone the rest of his now-corporeal life without her. He held her in his arms and rocked her as she cried into his chest.

"Jesus Christ, I was a ghost. How was that even possible?" He held her face in his hands and looked into those amazing green-gray eyes that he knew had to hold the secret of life and death. "You made it possible. It had to have been you. I was there for you."

"You said you would always remember, and then you forgot," she said on a sob.

"Oh, Emma," he whispered gently into her ear. Sweet Jesus, her words nearly broke his heart. He had almost lost her. He didn't know how he would ever make it up to her, but he would spend he rest of his life trying. "Jesus, I'm so sorry…I didn't know… How could I be such an idiot?"

She continued to cry into his shoulder, soaking his shirt with her tears, but he didn't care. She could stay there, soaking his shirt until the end of time for all he cared. Just so long as she stayed with him. And she was holding on to him as if he were a lifeline.

"And then you went shopping for engagement rings with that—that—" she started to say, and she punched him in the arm.

"Nooo. I most definitely did not." Christ, he loved this woman. She had punched him in the arm, and he loved that about her. She would always keep him humble, and she would always keep him guessing. There would never be a dull moment in his life with her.

And he knew she would never, ever abandon him. Not when he was a ghost, not when he was acting like a sanctimonious ass, and not even when he had temporarily forgotten her.

He tugged her back from him to be sure she was looking into his eyes. He wanted there to be no misunderstandings when it came to Crystal. He articulated his words very slowly, and very succinctly, to be sure his point was made, "I. Did. Not. It never would have happened. Do you hear me? Never."

He didn't have to admit to her that he'd been a complete shithead about Crystal, because she knew everything about his past, and she still loved him.

"She came back into my life and my house like she owned both. She showed up on my doorstep the minute I was released from the hospital, and told me she was there to take care of me. In the beginning, I was too tired, and too drugged up, to really know she was there. Then when it became clear that she was only there to gain access to my money, I simply ignored her, like I always had before, believing she would eventually go away when I stopped spending money on her. It is what people do around me, after all."

"That's not true—" Emma sat up and looked like she was ready to punch him again.

"Shh, Emma, I was joking. Mostly." He smiled to let her know he was still making a joke, then continued with his story. "Harry eventually told me the whole story. I got confirmation from the detective Harry hired that the pictures had all been destroyed, and Crystal is now, finally, out of all of our lives."

"How can you be so sure? She's like a cockroach—cut off her tail and another one grows back."

"I think you're talking about a lizard."

"Either way, if you cut off her tail, you end up so distracted by it thrashing around, you don't notice her sneaking up and biting you in the butt. And I happen to like your butt."

He was so stunned by a comment like that coming from her—however complimentary, and however glad he was to hear it—that he just stared at her, having no idea how to respond for several seconds.

"Well, let's just say," he started to say, then had to clear his throat. "She and I no longer run in the same circles. Not if she knows what's good for her."

"'Bout time," she muttered.

"Even before Harry came to me, I had already decided I didn't want her in my life. I think, even then, I was trying to remember us. For some reason, I just knew that my original reasons for keeping her around were no longer good for me. I was so angry that day you were there, and she implied that I was taking her ring shopping, that I physically walked her out of the house. I called the locksmith and had them come change the locks within thirty minutes after she was gone."

She settled back into his arms, and she felt absolutely amazing. Solid. There. His arms didn't mist through her.

"And one more thing. Harry told me what Crystal said to you—that she could influence my decisions. I need you to know that she never had that kind of power with me. She flat out lied to you. My previous assistant, Kelly, wasn't pregnant. Kelly left to marry her high-school sweetheart. She and Harry never had anything going on."

"Thanks for telling me that, but I hope I'm not such a dope as to believe Harry would ever get some poor woman pregnant and leave her hanging like Crystal said. And never in a million lifetimes would I ever believe you could treat a woman so badly as to fire her because of it if he had."

He had no idea what he had ever done to instill such trust in her, but he was damned if he would ever risk betraying it.

"I almost lost everything…" he said, softly. "And the whole time, I could feel something was not right—I wasn't right, you definitely weren't right.

But I just couldn't figure out what was wrong." He pulled her away from him again and looked into her eyes. "But I remember now. I love you, Emma Anderson."

She burst into tears, and he worried he had said too much. Then she was kissing him. First one eye, then the other. Then one cheek, then the other. Then his nose, and finally, finally, his mouth, and it was so good. She tasted like promise and hope.

She tasted like love.

When they eventually came up for air, he said, "Hey. I remember this, too. I've stored up at least four hugs that you owe me."

She laughed, then hugged him. And he kissed her again, as if his life depended on it.

Because, to him, it did.

EPILOGUE — ONE YEAR LATER

Emma carried her usual bowl of fruit compote with her to Marlie's front door. But this year, she was followed by a very corporeal George, who carried a load of presents in his arms. The house was decorated in the same decorations as the year before, except this time an inflatable Santa stood on the other side of the yard from the snowman.

She shivered when she saw it, but it was mostly for George's benefit, and he laughed. She had a whole new appreciation for Santa now. He still gave her the willies, but now she had George, and he would always protect her from scary costumed characters.

They went inside after a brief knock on the door, and continued on through the hallway into the Fulton kitchen. They were greeted by loud cheering from all of the family members who had collected there in various stages of cooking and merriment.

She began her rounds of hugs and kisses to each family member, and she noticed that George was smiling indulgently at her. When she had finished with her rounds of greetings, she turned to see him embracing each of her family members, one by one. She was emotionally overcome by the moment as she realized how much he had changed in only a year.

She watched as he finished his rounds hugging, kissing, and wishing every person in the room a merry Christmas.

He looked inordinately pleased with himself as he wrapped Emma in his arms and kissed her.

"See that?" he asked, with no small amount of pride in his voice. "I've really got the hang of the whole 'Yes, we just saw each other this afternoon at the Zoo Lights, but it's been more than three hours, so it's time for another hug' routine of your family."

She hugged him—of course—pouring all the love she had for him into it. "I do see that, and you're wonderful. You even made sure not to leave out Anita, our housekeeper." She nodded at their cleaning lady, who stood at the kitchen sink, eying George with suspicion.

He didn't look too thrilled to hear that he had, for all intents and purposes, made a pass at a complete stranger, and he asked, "I don't suppose she's related?"

"Well, no," she replied, with a chuckle. "But she has been with Marlie for so long, she's practically a member of the family. Does that help?"

He waved sheepishly at Anita, and she looked like she wasn't sure if she should hit him or hug him again.

They were saved from having to decide when the doorbell rang, and they both bolted from the kitchen to answer it. Emma opened the door to a smiling Harry, who held the biggest poinsettia she had ever seen.

"Hi, George. Merry Christmas, Emma," Harry exclaimed from behind the plant.

"Merry Christmas, Harry. I'm so glad you could come," she replied with excitement. She was thrilled to see Harry had taken her up on her invitation to join them this year. George took the plant from Harry so that he could come into the house, and Emma gave him a hug before he could even step over the threshold.

"Thank you for inviting me. George told me this would be the best adventure I've ever had, so I'm really looking forward to it," Harry said, gushing with as much, if not more, excitement as Emma had seen from the kids.

"You can let go of my fiancée now, Harry," George threatened, but Emma could tell there wasn't any heat behind his words. Then she saw him smile, and he gave Harry a hug.

She saw that Harry was momentarily surprised by the demonstrative gesture from his older brother, but then he smiled and hugged him back.

She watched as the two brothers held each other for a long moment, and she felt her eyes water. These were two amazing men. And they loved each other in spite of the crappy childhood their parents had given them.

Harry was lucky he'd had George through all those years, giving him the best Christmases he knew how. He had protected his younger brother through all the heartache and pain.

* * * * * * *

Later that night, after the kutia had been thrown, and another magnificent dinner had been served, Emma helped Marlie, Bill, and a very pregnant Laura—accompanied for the first time in several years by Jack—herd all the kids into the living room.

She pulled George over to the couch where they could sit together, and watched as all the others took places around the room to get ready for the story. She held George's hand, blissfully happy to be able to physically have him with her this year.

She noticed that Harry, beaming from his first year's experience at a Fulton Christmas Eve dinner, had chosen to stand by Bill's sister Mary. And, big surprise, he was flirting with her.

But Mary was no dope. She could handle anything he threw at her, and might even give him a run for his money. That would be fun to watch.

"You know, George told me that there would be food throwing, but I didn't believe him," Harry said. She was pretty sure he'd really been expecting a food fight.

As the kids all helped pass out the "Marlie and Bill" presents, she watched Harry in anticipation to see how he would react to getting a present as well. He looked surprised when Jessica handed him one, and Emma felt a moment of sadness that this small gesture was so foreign to him.

"I get one, too?" he asked, and there was a definite sparkle of excitement in his eye.

"Of course, Harry. No one is left out on Christmas," Marlie told him, as if giving presents to her sister's future brother-in-law was an everyday occurrence in her home.

She loved her family so much.

Harry beamed like a ten-year-old as he looked over at George and exclaimed, "This has been quite the adventure, George."

George grinned at Harry, then turned and smiled lovingly at her.

Laura reached across George to grab her hand. Or, at least, she tried to grab her hand, but her massive baby-belly got in the way. She was absolutely convinced that Laura was going to have twins. No one could possibly be that large—and only in the belly—and not be having multiples.

"Oh, let me see that ring again," Laura said, and examined the sparkling two-carat emerald-cut diamond ring on her ring finger. "George, you have mighty excellent taste. Or did Emma pick it out?"

"George picked it out. It was a complete surprise to me!" Emma replied, somewhat indignantly. She did not want her sister, or anyone else, believing she would be anything like that gold-digging Crystal who would haul her man into the jewelry shop and force him to buy her the most expensive ring in the shop.

She held up her own hand, which was still wrapped through George's, and admired the ring too. Then she sighed, just as Laura had, and said, "And I love it."

"And he's taking you to Disney World over New Year's. That's so cute!" Laura remarked, teary-eyed over the gesture, obviously hormonal from the pregnancy.

Emma exchanged a secret look with George, as Jessica came up to him and, without a single hesitation, climbed into his lap as if she had been doing it for years. He didn't look surprised. He looked pleased, and Emma gave him a questioning look.

"You and Jessica apparently have a lot in common," was all he said, as he wrapped his arms around Jessica, kissed her on the top of her head, and settled more comfortably with her onto the couch.

She went all soft and gooey inside as she watched her once emotionally distant fiancé shower her niece with affection as if he'd been doing it for years. Yes, he had come a long way, and she was more in love with him than ever.

"Uncle George?" Jessica asked, and Emma could hear the beginnings of a manipulation coming in the tone.

"I really like the sound of that," he said.

Oh, yeah, he was putty. He was so screwed. *Just wait until you hear the rest of it and then decide*, she thought.

George might not suspect Jessica's intentions, but Emma had known her a lot longer, and she knew Jessica was going to hit him up for something big.

"Can I go to Disney with you?" Jessica pleaded.

And there it was.

She knew exactly how easy it was for Jessica to get "Uncle George" to cave to her every demand—he seemed to have developed a soft spot when it came to her youngest niece—so she rushed to respond before he ended up agreeing to take all of the kids along on their honeymoon. "Not this time, honey," she said, breaking it gently but firmly. "This is a special trip just for me and George."

"But I tell you what," George put in, obviously caving to Jessica's sad pout, and probably all the disappointed sounds coming from the other kids. "Next time, we'll take all of you guys."

The kids were all thrilled, and Spencer even gave a quick high-five to Jessica, who jumped off of George's lap and did a victory dance, complete with fist pumps in the air, and a Charleston-esque dance with her knees, as only a gloating five-year-old could do.

But Emma was not entirely pleased by the prospect. It wasn't that she didn't love all the conniving little buggers dearly, but seriously. Was he out of his mind? "We will?" she asked. He had finally lost it. That was the only explanation for it.

"Don't worry," George whispered back to her, "we'll take their parents, too."

"And will Charlie be allowed to go with us?" Jessica asked.

Emma looked back at George for an explanation.

"Who's Charlie, honey?" he asked Jessica with such patience and kindness that Emma knew he would make a wonderful father.

"The boy in Aunt Emma's tummy. Will he get to go to Disney World with us next time?"

Emma gasped. How did Jessica know that? Emma had found out only yesterday herself from her doctor, who had confirmed that she was three weeks pregnant, but she hadn't told anyone yet. She had planned to tell George tonight when they were alone together, and was going to tell her sisters tomorrow after she had talked to him, so Jessica couldn't possibly have known.

George looked at Jessica as if she were some kind of wise woman instead of a five-year-old girl. He took it for granted that she was telling the truth—he believed her without question.

"How did you know?" She wasn't entirely sure if she was asking Jessica or George the question, but since they were the only other two people involved in this strange conversation, she decided to wait and see who replied first.

Before either of them could answer, however, Marlie clapped her hands, to draw everyone's attention back to the presents, "Okay, on three, everyone. One…two…three!"

They all ripped open their presents, and each person pulled out different knitted socks. They all made lots of noise thanking Marlie and Bill, and of course there were hugs all around.

Emma watched in anticipation as George opened his present and pulled out one normal-looking sock, and one incredibly long sock. He smiled broadly as everyone laughed and cheered.

"A Bill sock!" he exclaimed. And he looked genuinely happy. "This is, without a doubt, the second-best Christmas present I've ever had in my life."

"Second!?" Bill asked. "Sheesh, I'm offended. What was your first?"

George put down his socks, and took Emma's face in his hands.

"Emma, of course," he replied. And he kissed her.

Emma heard sounds of "Aww" from the grown-ups, and sounds of "Eeeeooowww" from all the kids, but she was too happy and lost in the kiss to really care either way.

Her heart was beating rapidly in her chest, and she could feel the heat creeping into her cheeks when she eventually, and reluctantly, pulled away from George's kiss. She honestly didn't know if the flush was the result of embarrassment due to the attention they were receiving, or from the heated desire she always felt whenever George kissed her.

Or touched her.

Or got within ten feet of her.

She glanced sideways at George, and saw the heat in his face as well, and realized that, since he never got embarrassed, he wasn't asking himself the same questions that she was asking in her own head.

"Okay, so, I know this isn't our usual tradition," she said, then cleared her throat, and rushed to continue, "but George and I have a present we want to give all of you."

As if they had practiced their act several times, right on cue George handed out presents, all the same size, and all wrapped in the same paper, to the adults. When she saw that they all had a package, she imitated Marlie's earlier countdown, then said, "Go!"

She waited with nervous excitement and anticipation as she watched all the adults eagerly rip off the paper on each of their packages.

"Oh, Emma, your book!" Marlie said in admiration.

"Emma Anderson, *Christmas Spirit*," Laura read from the cover.

Harry came up to her and pulled her aside from the group that was now completely distracted by asking George questions about the book.

"Will you do me a favor and let George know that I have to get going? I'm meeting up with Dean and Anna Erickson for drinks. I want to see what Dean has in mind for his next book."

"Really?" she asked, knowing that there had to be some other reason behind meeting up with an author about a book—specifically, that he was less interested in what Dean had to say than he was in seeing Anna again. She was also worried that Harry still didn't know exactly who Dean Erickson was to the Landon family. She was still against George keeping it a secret, but it wasn't her place to tell it. She also had no idea what Dean knew—if anything—and that was a nerve-wracking unknown.

"Yes, really," he replied, and she waited for him to continue. "Okay, fine. His sister is hot, and I really like her. Happy now?"

He winked as if to show that it was no big deal, but she knew better. The sister was female, so he would undoubtedly fall in love with her, at least for a few days. Maybe he already had.

"I'll let George know you left." She gave him what she thought of as her best grown-up concerned look, then gave him a hug to soften the look. "Be careful though, Harry. I don't want to see you get your heart broken."

He smiled at her, as if to say, "Who, me?" Then he gave her a brief kiss on the cheek, and left the room in a hurry, as if he were worried she would ground him for the night.

She found George in the middle of the group, and pulled him aside to talk privately.

"You need to talk to Harry," she said, trying to keep her voice down so that they weren't overheard.

"Okay. What did he do this time?" He smiled at her, and she felt herself instinctively smile back. His smiles were so warm and loving now, and she hated to say what she knew would make it fade.

"You have to tell him the truth, before he stupidly falls in love with his own half-sister."

ABOUT THE AUTHOR

Julie Cameron is a screenwriter and book author of humorous women's fiction and romantic comedy.

Although a long-time Colorado resident, she finds downhill skiing an utterly frightening endeavor, and is therefore, much happier hanging out at the base of the slopes reading, or diligently working on her latest storyline, while drinking Chai tea lattes (coconut milk, no whipped cream).

When she isn't writing, she's spending time with her family and friends or thinking up excuses to take her nieces and nephews out in search of a chocolate fix.

She invites her readers to check in with her on her website:

www.juliecameron.net

If you enjoyed reading *Christmas Spirit*, please post a review on Amazon or Goodreads.

Made in the USA
Middletown, DE
05 November 2015